Elizabeth studied the handsome man next to her.

When had she lost her touch? Most men jumped at the chance to have twenty-five beautiful women fawning over them.

"You owe it to America to be on the show."

"Somehow I think you're exaggerating." Rick chuckled.

She was losing him. He wasn't interested in money, love or fame. What else could he want? She changed gears. "If this is about reliving history, we'll do a better job this time. You won't end up humiliated and alone."

"It must be nice to control the universe."

She reached over and put a hand on his arm, and tried to ignore the skitter in her stomach when she felt his muscles underneath the denim jacket. "Tell me what you want, and I'll guarantee it."

If only she could have what *she* truly wanted.

Dear Reader,

One of my favorite television shows is *The Bachelor*, and I love the idea that you can meet the love of your life on a reality show. Of course, the reality is it doesn't always work out that way, and I wondered what would happen if a bachelor was rejected on live television in front of an audience of millions? How could he come back from that and find a second chance at love? And what if it turned out to be with the wrong woman?

With those questions in mind, I started the story. I named my bachelor after my dad and gave him a lot of my dad's qualities. I discovered that I wasn't only writing a romance, but a story that would honor my dad's memory in a small way.

I hope you enjoy the story as much as I did. And I'd love to hear from you at www.facebook.com/syndipowellauthor.

Syndi Powell

Syndi Powell

The Reluctant Bachelor

First published in Great Britain 2013
by Mills & Boon, an imprint of Harlequin (UK) Limited,
Eton House, 18-24 Paradise Road, Richmond, Surrey TW9 1SR

© Cynthia Powell 2013

ISBN: 978 0 263 91116 9

33-0913

Harlequin (UK) policy is to use papers that are natural, renewable and recyclable products and made from wood grown in sustainable forests. The logging and manufacturing processes conform to the legal environmental regulations of the country of origin.

Printed and bound in Spain
by Blackprint CPI, Barcelona

SYNDI POWELL
started writing stories when she was young, eager to find out what happened after the happily-ever-after in her favorite books, and has made it a lifelong pursuit. She's been reading romance novels since she was in her teens and is thrilled to join the Mills & Boon® team. She lives near Detroit with her husband, stepson and a cat and dog who believe they run the household. She loves to connect with readers on Twitter, @syndipowell, or on her Facebook author page, www.facebook.com/syndipowell author.

Dedicated to my dad, who I hope can read this book from heaven. I love and miss you. And to my mom, who introduced me to reading romance books in the first place and started the love affair. Thank you both for your love and support.

PROLOGUE

RICK ALLYN TUGGED at the sky-blue tie that had been looped around his neck by one of the production assistants of *True Love,* a dating reality show. Only moments away from proposing to the one woman he'd never believed he'd find, he should feel anxious, right? The butterflies running bases in his stomach only proved his human nature.

After all, Brandy could say no.

But she wouldn't. Not to him. At twenty-five, he was the entire package—looks, smarts and, after his agent worked out the details of his contract, a major-league baseball player.

Lizzie Maier walked toward him. Serious, as always. She was wearing a purple power suit; her long brown hair was tied up in some ridiculous style that only emphasized the sharpness of her cheekbones. And the grass-green of her eyes.

He held up his hands in surrender. "What did I do now?"

Lizzie shook her head and reached up to

straighten his tie. "She's almost ready for you." She didn't look him in the eyes, but kept her focus on his suit and the fit of it. "Are you sure about this?"

Finally she looked up at him. "Brandy's an amazing woman. Beautiful. Smart. What man wouldn't want to be married to her?"

"Right." Lizzie nodded, then tapped her earpiece and shook her head. "They're still not ready. Rick, I should tell you—"

"Lizzie, relax."

"It's Elizabeth."

"Not to me." He winked at her. "I'm going to propose. She'll say yes. Then you're going to throw us the biggest, most romantic wedding that has ever aired on television." Rick rolled his head around his neck to get out the tension. "Now, let's get this show on the road. The rock in my pocket is weighing me down."

"What if she doesn't pick you?"

Rick laughed and shook his head. "She's going to pick Wade? Give me a break. It's not like all of us didn't warn her about him. Brandy's a smart girl. She knows."

"Rick—"

"It's fine. Really, Lizzie." He straightened his shoulders and touched his tie. "I'm getting the girl. I'm winning her heart. And you can print that in the tabloids."

Lizzie tapped her earpiece again. "Okay, they're ready for you." She studied him, then sighed. "You've been a good friend to me during this show. Thanks."

He winked. "Let's go propose on live television."

CHAPTER ONE

FIVE YEARS SHOULD be enough time for people to forget. In a world of thirty-second sound bites and high-speed internet, one person's fifteen minutes of fame should be a distant memory in a few months at most.

But Rick didn't live in a world of shoulds. If he did, he'd be happily married to Brandy. And Lizzie wouldn't be sitting in the stands at the annual Pickle Play-Off game.

Get your head in the game, Allyn. This is for the championship.

He clapped his hands and crouched into a running stance at second base. His line drive had been good enough to get him there, but he needed one more solid hit to get him and the guy on third home to win the game. The young man with Down syndrome up to bat might dampen anyone else's enthusiasm. But not Rick's. Because tonight was his night. He could feel it down to his cleats.

Rick cupped his hands around his mouth. "C'mon, Jeffy. Hit me in, buddy."

Jeffy looked up at him and nodded. He bit his tongue as he got into position in front of the catcher.

The first pitch. "Ball."

Rick stood and clapped his hands once more. "Good eye, Jeffy."

Jeffy swung at the next ball. Missed. "Strike one."

"Wait for your pitch, buddy." Rick put his hands on his knees, rubbing the left one to ease the ache—a remnant of a car accident five years before—then returned to his running stance, ready to make a dash for third if the opportunity arose.

The next ball floated across the plate. "Strike two."

The crowd got to their feet. They could be one pitch away from winning it all. Or losing. They stomped. Shouted. Cheered. Jeffy's mom hid her head in her hands and turned to the well-dressed brunette in a purple power suit beside her.

Why was she here?

Rick shook his head. *Stay focused.* "C'mon, Jeffy. Hit her out of here!"

He held his breath as the next ball pinged off Jeffy's bat and rolled toward first base.

"Foul ball!"

At third base, Tom saw his opportunity and

sprinted toward home before the opposing team could react. He slid safely into home plate and tied the game as Rick reached third base.

One hit was all they needed. One solid hit to get Rick home.

He held his hands up. "Time-out." He started walking toward Jeffy. Time for a pep talk.

THE OLDER WOMAN sitting beside Elizabeth on the bleachers covered her eyes. "I can't look."

Elizabeth looked from the woman to the young man talking with Rick at home plate. "Is that your son?"

The woman turned and smiled at Elizabeth. "You're not from around here, are you?"

"Afraid not." She gripped the handles of her Kate Spade bag tighter. "I'm here on business."

And business was exactly what she should be doing rather than sitting on a hard wooden bleacher, waiting for a chance to talk to Rick. He looked good. Better than good. But five years hadn't changed him. Same brown hair that looked as if he'd run a comb through it sometime that week. Same warm grin that could make a girl's toes curl. And if she could get close enough to see his brown eyes, she knew she'd see the familiar twinkle that played with his good-guy image. Five years and he still didn't see his potential beyond this hick town. Good thing she was there to change all that.

The woman next to her held out her hand. "I'm Martha. Otherwise known in town as Jeffy's mom."

Elizabeth turned her attention back to Martha and shook her hand. "Elizabeth."

"Jeffy loves the game, but because he's slow, coaches won't let him play." She turned adoring eyes back to the two men standing at home plate. "Except for Rick, bless him."

Rick walked back to third base as Jeffy returned to the batter's box. Swung the bat a few times. Hunkered down, ready for his pitch.

Martha squeezed her eyes shut. "Oh, I can't watch."

Elizabeth took the woman's hand in hers. "I'll watch for you." You could get through anything with someone holding your hand.

The pitch. "Ball two."

The crowd let out their breath and clapped. "Jeffy! Jeffy! Jeffy!"

The pitcher glanced at third base, then threw the ball at the baseman. Rick shook his head. "Just pitch the ball, Stu." He turned back to Jeffy. "Nice and easy, now. Just like practice."

Jeffy nodded and tightened his grip on the bat.

The coach from the other team laughed. "No worries, folks. We've got the game. That trophy is as good as ours."

Stu shook off the catcher's first two calls. He nodded and threw the ball.

Crack.

Martha's eyes opened. "He hit it?"

Elizabeth grinned and helped her to her feet as Rick flew toward home and planted his feet on home base. He then stood to watch Jeffy charging toward first base before the ball could get there.

His feet touched the base.

The ball hit the baseman's glove.

"Safe!"

With a roar, fans rushed the field, carrying Jeffy away in their excitement. Elizabeth helped Martha down from the stands, but even his own mother couldn't get to Jeffy through the crowd. Everyone was hugging him. Shouting and crying. All trying to get the chance to put their hands on the young man the other team said couldn't play.

Elizabeth couldn't help but smile. This was better than anything on television.

MARTHA WALKED UP to Rick and hugged him. "Thank you for believing in Jeffy."

"Thanks for letting him play." He patted her back. "You're bringing him to the diner after?"

"He wouldn't let us miss it." She wiped her eyes and turned to find her son amid the crowd.

The opposing coach cleared his throat until Rick turned around and accepted the trophy. "Thanks."

The coach shrugged. "We underestimated you."

"The underdog has to win at least once." They shook hands briefly before the coach walked away.

"Still tilting at windmills?"

At Lizzie's voice, Rick turned to face the inevitable moment. It had been coming since he'd spotted her in the bleachers. She looked good. Too good. Despite the fact that she wore her power suit like armor.

"You've been avoiding my calls."

He started to walk around the bases, picking them up and slapping them together to get off the dirt. "Because they all say the same thing, Lizzie. And my answer hasn't changed."

"If you'd just listen—"

"I don't need to. *True Love* was a onetime shot. I don't need to relive that time of my life. I've moved on." He bent and stuffed the bases into the equipment bags, zipped them shut and hoisted them over his left shoulder. He waved with his free hand to some friends. "See you at the diner," he called after them when they honked their car horns.

"No offense, Rick, but it doesn't look like you've moved much from when I met you five years ago."

Rick turned to observe her. One of television's top reality-show producers stood on a dusty baseball field wearing designer clothes that cost more than what most of the people in this town made in a month. Her haircut, though attractive and stylish, probably cost enough to pay the grocery bills. She didn't have a clue about how his world operated. Yet here she was. Standing on his turf. Trying to convince him to make another mistake.

He opened his mouth, a smart retort on his tongue, but instead stalked off the field toward the parking lot, where two vehicles remained. He glanced at the rental that obviously belonged to Lizzie and shook his head.

"Something wrong with my car?" He could hear the smile in her voice.

He put the bags in the back of his truck but didn't look at her. "It's a convertible."

"I know."

He turned to face her. "In Michigan." She didn't get it. Probably never would, Rick was sure.

Lizzie's smile faded into a frown. "And?"

Rick shrugged and sighed as if to say it was her funeral. "The weather changes every five minutes here."

"But I look good in a convertible."

He sighed. Some things really didn't change. "Always going for style over substance."

"Are you judging me?" She took her sunglasses from the perch atop her head and slid them over her eyes. "I thought we'd gotten past that. I thought we were friends."

Rick swallowed and tried to fight the feeling that he'd messed up again. "Friends who haven't talked or seen each other since I got dumped on television." He took off his ball cap and hit his thigh with it once. Twice. "I apologize, Lizzie. It's still a sore spot."

"And it's still Elizabeth."

Rick grinned and wiggled his eyebrows. "Not to me."

She strode to her car and took a sleek leather briefcase from the front seat. With a few quick snaps, she opened it and retrieved a thin envelope. "Our offer has increased."

He glanced at the envelope, then at her. "You could offer me twice as much and my answer would still be no."

Lizzie fiddled with the contents of her briefcase before placing the envelope back inside. "Rick, this is a chance of a lifetime."

He swallowed. Yeah, like the chance that had made him a joke on every national newscast for a month. "I already had one of those, remember?"

Lizzie sighed and rubbed her forehead. "Could we at least discuss this over coffee?"

He chuckled. "At the diner we only have half-and-half, not that flavored creamer you like." He finished throwing the equipment bags into the bed of his pickup truck before slamming the tailgate closed. Turning, he nearly ran Lizzie over.

"How did you remember the creamer?"

Rick shrugged. "How do I remember that Frank gets pancakes with butter and no syrup every day except on Saturday when it's French toast? How do I know that Miss Maudie wants the crusts cut off her sandwiches and put into a doggie bag to take home to her Yorkie?" He flipped the keys in his hands over a few times. "It's my job."

"I'm not your job."

"But I'm yours?" He glanced at the empty ball field and then back at her. "Why are you here? Why not send one of your interns? Backwater Michigan is a long way from Hollywood for a business call."

"I needed to see you."

He raised one eyebrow. "Interesting."

ELIZABETH TRIED NOT to groan. This wasn't the way things were supposed to happen. She'd come in person to convince him to do the show, which should have impressed him. Instead it seemed to make him even more resistant to the idea. He was supposed to be desperate for her.

Desperate for the show. That was what she meant.

Rick opened the passenger door of his truck. "Convince me. We'll talk on the drive to the diner."

That was more like it. She looked back at the blue convertible. "And leave my car here?"

"It'll be fine." Rick glanced up at the sky. "But you might want to put up the top. It could rain."

Elizabeth looked up. Not a cloud could be seen in the sky. "I'll take my chances."

"Your rental agreement covers water damage?"

"There's no possibility of rain." Besides, when in all of her twenty-eight years had she done something just because some man told her to? She hopped up into the truck, clicked the seat belt into place and turned to Rick. "I don't understand why you won't do the show."

Rick sighed and shifted the truck into Drive. "You're relentless."

"That's why I'm the best." Because she knew which buttons to push to get what she wanted. She only needed to dig a little more. "It's a great opportunity. Aren't you interested in finding love? In meeting the woman you're destined to spend the rest of your life with?" She leaned closer, her voice softer, more intimate. "It can work this time. I know it."

"Why? It didn't back then." He drummed his fingers on the steering wheel to the beat of the Kenny Chesney song playing on the radio. "Call me crazy, but I don't relish the idea of going through that again."

"It will be different."

"How? I'll still be making a fool of myself on TV." He shifted his gaze to her. "Besides, I had more fun talking with you between takes than on any of those fantasy dates you sent me on."

She glanced at him before looking out the window again. "Everyone wants you back."

"Everyone?"

She could feel the heat in her cheeks. "You're the most popular contestant the show has ever had. We get hundreds of letters a week asking us to bring you back." She faced him again. "You owe it to America to be on the show."

"Somehow I think you're exaggerating things."

She was losing him. He wasn't interested in money, love or fame. What else could he want? She changed gears. "If this is about re-living history, we'll do a better job this time. You won't end up humiliated and alone."

"It must be nice to control the universe."

She reached over and put a hand on his arm. Ignored the skitter in her stomach at the feel of his muscles underneath the denim jacket. "Tell me what you want, and I'll guarantee it."

He turned into the parking lot of the diner and parked in the back. "Time's up."

She sighed. When had she lost her touch? Men jumped at the chance to have twenty-four beautiful women fawning over them. But then Rick had never been a typical man. "If you would just give me a chance…"

He scratched his head and replaced his ball cap. "Think that's what I just did." He got out of the truck, then poked his head back in. "See you inside."

Elizabeth watched him walk toward the diner. She could hear the loud shouts from those inside as he entered. She had to make him realize he needed to be on the show. Give him the thing he wanted most, whatever that was.

The perfect cheeseburger. That was what she wanted more than anything. Unfortunately, she didn't eat cheeseburgers anymore. And it didn't help that she sat outside a diner that she suspected must serve them to perfection.

Elizabeth slammed her hand on the dashboard, then tried to shake away the pain. This was crazy. She could have sent anyone else to come out here to talk to Rick, so why torture herself?

Her cell phone sang a Diana Ross tune, and a chill passed over her. "Hi, Mom."

"Bethie, I'm in an awful fix."

Elizabeth closed her eyes. How many times had she heard those same words? "Who was he this time?"

"I didn't know he was married. Honest." Her mom sighed. "And now he fired me."

Of course. They always did. "Mom, I can't talk right now. I'm working."

"I only need a couple of hundred this time." Her mom's voice became whiny, which was not a good sign. "My rent is overdue, and my cupboards are bare. Please, Bethie. You remember what this is like."

The goose bumps intensified on Elizabeth's arms, and she shivered. She couldn't forget, even in her nightmares. "Have you been looking for a job?"

"I've applied at a few restaurants, but you know how this economy is." Her mom started crying. "Who's gonna hire a washed-up waitress when they could hire any of a dozen half my age? What am I gonna do?"

Elizabeth swallowed and closed her eyes, massaging her forehead in circles as if the motion would turn back time. Give her a different mother. A different childhood. "Tell me where to send it. I'll have it there by tomorrow morning."

"You're the best daughter, Bethie."

"Thanks, Mom."

"I love you."

Her phone beeped, and she glanced at the incoming phone number. The head of development at the studio. "Mom, I've got another phone call coming in. Text me with the details later, okay?"

She switched to the other line. "Elizabeth Maier."

"Did he sign the contracts yet?"

She wasn't ready to deal with pressure from the studio. Couldn't he give her a few days at least? "You're always to the point, Devon."

"That's why they pay me the big bucks." He chuckled on the other end. "I don't need to remind you what's at stake. We want Rick."

That had been made abundantly clear. "Yes, sir."

"You got this job because you promised results. Don't let us down."

"I always deliver." Always had. Always would. She straightened her blouse and sat up straighter. "That's why you promoted me."

"Didn't hurt that your boss was having an inappropriate relationship with one of the bachelorettes, either." Devon paused. "The story's been leaked on the internet and hits the newsstands tomorrow."

Just what she didn't need. This could make her job even harder. "So much for sitting on the scandal."

"We need a home run for this show or the studio's pulling the plug, Elizabeth." He let that sink in. "And you promised that Rick would be ratings gold."

"He was last time."

"So get him to sign. Or..."

The threat hung unspoken between them. Elizabeth cleared her throat. "It's like I told you. I always deliver. He'll do it."

Devon hung up the phone on his end. Elizabeth stared at her cell before quietly turning it off and placing it in her bag. So it was Rick and her job or nothing.

A sudden chill made her shiver again, and she rubbed her arms. She couldn't go back to the ways of her childhood. To not knowing where she would live or what she would eat. She'd scratched and clawed her way out of poverty and would never return.

Never.

She needed a new plan. Because more than Rick's future was on the line.

WHEN RICK ENTERED the diner full of folks in bright green uniforms, applause broke out. He held up his hands to summon quiet for a moment. "This is definitely a night to celebrate. And luckily, we know exactly how to do that at the diner."

Cheers sounded around the dining room. Rick walked behind the counter, found an apron and put it on over his softball uniform. His employees looked as if they'd already been taking drink orders, so Rick started at one end of the diner and took food orders. The bell above the front door jingled. Lizzie nodded at him before taking a seat at a table with Jeffy and his mother.

Once everyone had given their orders and food was delivered, Rick drifted over to stand by Jeffy, who smiled around a big bite of his bacon double cheeseburger. Lizzie picked at her chef's salad, dressing on the side, but stared at Jeffy's burger. Some people and their dinner choices. "You doing okay here?"

Jeffy's mom finished her strawberry shake. "Couldn't be better. Could we, Jeffy?"

Jeffy nodded and gave him a thumbs-up. Rick grinned back. "You folks enjoy your dinner. It's on me tonight. Gotta keep my champ happy so he'll play for me next year."

He walked to each table, stopping to chat for a while with team members and their families. That was why the diner sponsored a team every year. Sure, the trophy this year would look great proudly displayed by the cash register. But it was about the friendships that survived off the field year after year. Rick's family was more than just his mom and brother. This team was as close to him as blood. Family forged by sweat.

By the time the last fry had been eaten and the last plate cleared from each table, Rick was ready to collapse on his sofa and call it a night. Unfortunately, an hour remained until closing, and the dirty dishes soaking in the sink called his name. He groaned and rolled his shoulders to loosen them. A clap of thunder caught his attention. His eyes fastened on Lizzie, whose own eyes opened wide in fear.

She rose on one knee and glanced out the window to watch torrents of rain. "My leather seats!"

Gotta love Michigan weather.

Not that he hadn't warned her. The problem was that she had no clue about how his life really worked. And maybe that was his solution to getting rid of her. He supposed if he couldn't get rid of her, maybe he could convince her to do the show his way, in his hometown. If he could gain some control that way, he might agree to it. He approached her table and watched the summer rain pound the parking lot. "That's why you have insurance."

She turned and shrugged at him, but her lower lip still jutted out farther than her top lip. Not that he should be looking at her mouth. Instead, he let his gaze settle on the unshed tears in her grass-green eyes. Man, he couldn't stand to see a woman cry. "Listen, I have an idea."

She brightened slightly. "You'll do the show."

He sighed. *Relentless.* "I can't leave my life for three months while you and the other execs mess with it."

Her eyes narrowed. "You're suggesting a compromise?"

He put one hand on the table and the other on the back of the booth. Leaned in close enough to catch a whiff of her perfume. "I'm suggesting that you spend a week getting to know me. The real me. How my life really works now. And not that Hollywood version you created." He sighed and shook his head. "How can I expect to find my true love if she doesn't meet me where I live?"

Lizzie shook her head and glanced around the diner. Sure, it could use a gallon of paint and even more of elbow grease, but this was home to him. When she turned to face him again, she was still shaking her head. "People want fantasy in their reality TV shows. Ironic but true."

"There is an appeal to small-town living. The pull to lead a simpler life." He leaned in even closer to her. "Give me the chance to prove it to you."

Her eyes sparked with interest. "I give you a week to convince me, and what do you give me?"

He sighed. *Definitely relentless.* "If I can prove to you that we could do the show here, then I'll do it. I'll be your guinea pig again."

"You really mean that?" A smile played around her mouth.

He held out his hand. "You give me a chance, and I'll give you one." They shook on it. Rick nodded. "Good. We'll start here at five tomorrow morning."

The panic in Lizzie's eyes made it all worthwhile.

CHAPTER TWO

ELIZABETH ARRIVED at the diner when the sky was still a dark grayish-blue with only a hint of pink in the direction of the unrisen sun. Even the roosters had enough sense to keep sleeping, but here she stood. Waiting for Rick to come down and let her in to the diner to start their...what had he called it? Small-town education?

She lightly tapped her cheeks in an effort to wake herself. This tired feeling was more than jet lag. She'd dealt with that often enough to be immune to its effects. Maybe it was the déjà vu being in a small town had brought out. She'd grown up in hick towns; her mother worked restaurant jobs with their low wages, meager tips and free food. And the chance that Elizabeth could sit in a booth for a few hours so her mom didn't have to pay a babysitter.

Before she could plumb her past any further, the door opened and Rick stood there smiling at her. He should look as tired as she felt, but instead he beamed at her as he ushered her inside. "Ready for your first look at my life?"

She stifled a yawn and nodded. "Does the first look have to come so early?"

"My day usually starts an hour before this, but I thought I'd give you a break." He leaned toward her, and for a brief moment she wondered if he was going to kiss her. He reached past to turn the sign on the door to Open.

He motioned for her to follow him, and she walked behind him into the kitchen. Savory smells of bacon and sausage assaulted her, making her stomach growl. What she wouldn't give for a sausage patty right now. He opened an oven door, peered in, then adjusted the temperature. When he turned back to face her, he frowned. "Why are you wearing that?"

She glanced down at the outfit she had painstakingly chosen for their day: one of her best power suits in cherry-red and teetering black heels. "I believe you mentioned I'd be meeting people from your town."

He nodded. "And they'll eat you alive wearing that. Don't you own a pair of jeans?"

Denim wasn't exactly a staple in her wardrobe, but glancing at what Rick was wearing told her it was a part of his. She wiped at an imaginary smudge on her skirt. "I'm sure your friends will appreciate good taste."

"The grease will ruin that fancy getup within the hour. Go back to your hotel and change." He turned his back to her and started whisking eggs with flour.

Grease? There'd been no mention of that when they'd made plans for today. What exactly was he planning? "You don't expect me to actually work here, do you?"

Rick turned back to her with a dazzling smile. It was easy to see why the cameras fell in love with him. "You wanted a glimpse into my life, right? Since Mom handed the diner over to me, I'm here twelve hours a day, six days a week. So that's where we're starting."

She crossed her arms across her chest. *Nope. Not happening.* "You don't have anyone to cover for you today?"

"It's the Lake Mildred Pickle Festival. Busiest weekend of the summer. I'm going to be swamped with orders in about ten minutes and won't get a break until after the Ladies' Book Club finishes their last cup of coffee." He continued to whisk and paused only to add more flour.

She glared, hoping that the effect would turn him into stone. "I thought you were the owner and manager here."

"I'm whatever they need me to be. Besides, it's fun."

Sigh. Not her idea of fun. "And I'm supposed to help you out?"

"That's the idea, Lizzie."

She grumbled on the drive back to the bed-and-breakfast to change into the outfit she'd least likely have a fit over if it got ruined. She fumed as she drove back to the diner and parked behind it, where the employees left their cars. And she moaned when Rick threw a clean apron at her and pointed to the stack of dishes that had accumulated in her absence. "Washing dishes? Really?"

Rick started to whistle as he placed slices of bread in a large toaster and pressed the lever. "It's where all good cooks start."

"But I'm not a cook," she muttered under her breath. She couldn't even make toast without setting off the smoke detectors in her apartment.

She wrinkled her nose at the dried gobs of egg and grease on the first plate. There had to be better ways to get Rick to do the show than this. She glanced behind her at the man in question, who cracked eggs onto the hot griddle. If she could just find out why he'd done the show the first time…

"Dishes don't wash themselves, Lizzie."

He threw the eggshells into the large trash can next to him as if they were basketballs and he were Kobe Bryant. He walked over and turned on the hot water, then squeezed a healthy dollop of dish soap into the sink. Pointed to the three sinks, the last full of clear liquid. "Wash. Rinse. Sanitize." He pulled the hose closer to her. "And don't be afraid to get a little wet."

She rolled her eyes and dropped the first dish into the sudsy water.

RICK SWALLOWED A LAUGH as Lizzie glared at him over her coffee cup. She looked like a drowned rat. Her long brown hair was plastered to the sides of her head; her clothes clung to her slight form. Her carefully applied makeup had run two hours ago, leaving her face streaked in brown and blue. "Good job, Lizzie."

She rolled her eyes and forked a bite of French toast into her mouth, pausing to moan after the first bite. "What do you put in these?"

He shrugged. "Little cinnamon. Lots of love."

Again with the rolled eyes. She'd be lucky to end the day without a massive headache if she kept that up.

"So are you done torturing me?"

Torture. Interesting word choice. She'd agreed to get a glimpse of his normal life, and now she considered it inhumane. If only she knew. "You'll probably want to freshen up before the lunch crowd gets here." Panic washed over her face, but he held up one hand. "Don't worry. You're done with the dishes. Jeffy should be here anytime."

Her shoulders relaxed. "Thank goodness."

"But I am short a waitress."

Lizzie stood up and threw her napkin on the table before storming out of the diner. Rick chuckled and took another sip of his coffee. Mission accomplished. Better that she leave now than wait until it was too late.

The bell above the door chimed again. "Ricky."

He glanced up and swallowed a groan at the sight of his older brother, Dan, wearing a suit and tie. If Mr. High and Mighty stooped to grace the diner with his presence, the news couldn't be good. Didn't matter that the diner belonged to the family empire along with the pickle-canning plant and brightly colored cans of pickles on store shelves. Rick knew that the diner didn't even register on Dan's radar.

"Need a cup of coffee?" Rick stood and

retrieved the coffee carafe from behind the counter, hooked a mug with one finger, then joined his brother in the back booth. He poured the coffee into the empty mug before topping off his own. "Still drink it black or should I find the creamer?"

"Black's fine."

Rick nodded and took the seat across from Dan. "What's wrong? Is it Mom again?"

Dan shook his head, then glanced behind him at the customers gathered at the diner. "We can talk here?"

Any news his brother had to share would be sure to make the gossip rounds in Lake Mildred before too long. "Sure."

Dan sighed, rubbing the space between his eyebrows. "I'll be glad when this whole economic downturn is over."

Downturn? Was that what people losing their jobs, homes and lives was? Rick took a sip of his coffee, mostly to keep from saying what he really wanted to say. "Just tell me what you came here for."

Dan leaned forward. "I heard that producer is in town."

Biting the inside of his cheek, Rick nodded. So that was what his visit was about? A pretty face? "Yeah, Lizzie's here. She might be back in about twenty minutes if you want to talk to her."

Dan frowned. "Why would I talk to her?"

"She's cute. All wrong for you, of course. But she does fit your type." Rick poured some creamer into his coffee and stirred it. "Smart. Pretty. No nonsense."

"I'm not looking for a date, Rick." He took a sip of his coffee, then placed the mug on the table. Rubbed his forehead and twitching eye. "She wants you to do that show again?"

He sighed. He couldn't escape the show, not even with his family. "Don't worry. I already told her to forget about it."

Dan frowned and shook his head as if Rick had said the worst thing in the world. "Why would you do a stupid thing like that?"

Wait. His brother wanted him to do the show? "If memory serves, you didn't want me to do the show the last time. Hated it when I left. Then resented me when I came back home."

"I was stupid, okay?" He glanced at his cell phone. "All of Dad's talk about what was good for the family? The company? I think I get it now."

Rick remembered the discussions he and his dad had had over the show. In the end, it had come down to Rick choosing to help save the family company. "You got it five years too late."

"I wasn't CEO then. I didn't realize what a boon that show could be." Dan adjusted the lapel of his suit coat. "Last time, our sales went up almost thirty percent. We got distributors in a dozen more states that sold our product. Business at the diner tripled after they aired your hometown visit." He leaned in closer. "We could use that kind of publicity again."

"No."

Dan shook his head. "What's changed? Dad told you to do the show then. I'm telling you now."

Telling him what to do yet again. Well, Rick wasn't the same little brother who went along with Dan's ideas. He had his own life. His own choices to make. "I'm smarter this time around. I won't do it."

"I get it." Dan jutted his jaw forward, the same way he had since they were kids and he thought he was not only right, but that Rick would be convinced of it, too. "You need to think about it. I'll call you in a few days."

"Call me next week. The answer will still be the same."

Dan stood and placed a hand on Rick's

shoulder. "You've got to think of the family, little brother."

Rick shook his head and bit back a laugh. "I am thinking of the family. You're focusing on the company's bottom line."

"You don't understand the hole we're in. And if we fail, this town will never be the same—" Dan broke off and shook his head. "Never mind. This was a mistake."

Rick got to his feet and leaned in toward Dan. "Why would we fail?"

"Maybe if you read those company reports I send you more than you read the sports pages, you might understand why I'm here." Dan took one last sip of coffee before slapping the mug on the table. "Thanks for the coffee."

Rick was getting pretty good at making people storm out of his diner.

ELIZABETH STARED INTO her suitcase as if a waitress uniform would magically appear. Thankfully, she'd never had to go the same route as her mother. She'd known someone who knew someone offering a job as a page on a studio lot when she turned sixteen, and she'd been into television ever since. It was all that she knew. All she wanted. That was why she had to use this week to convince

Rick to do the show. If that meant washing mountains of dishes and pouring rivers of coffee, she'd do it.

A pair of khakis peeked at her from the bottom of the suitcase, so she pulled them out and found a sleeveless green shell and matching short-sleeved top to go with it. It was better than nothing. Or at least better than the sopping oxford and slacks that hung over the shower curtain rod in the tiny bathroom of her room at the bed-and-breakfast.

She returned to the diner to find Rick barking orders to his cook through the window. He looked comfortable here. As if he knew that he'd be doing this for the rest of his life.

Unfortunately.

Didn't he see that he had so much more to offer? She'd watched the dailies again from the last show he'd done and knew that he was made for bigger things than running a small-town diner. Maybe he didn't want to work for the family company, but he wasn't being challenged here. That was where she came in. She needed to broaden his horizons. Provide him with a better life. Success on the show would mean opened doors for him, and he could write his own future. Be a celebrity chef if he wanted. Get his own cooking show and endorsement deals.

"I'm back." She did a Vanna White impression and turned around. "Will this suffice for a waitress?"

Rick looked her up and down, then grimaced. "You sure you want grease to touch that silk shirt?"

"It's either this or another suit." She put her hands on her hips. "I didn't exactly plan on working at the diner this entire week with you."

"The diner is my life now." He looked at her outfit again. "We'll go shopping after lunch."

She could handle shopping. That thought might get her through whatever he had in store for her. "Is that part of my small-town education?"

Rick grinned and handed her a clean apron to tie around her hips and a blank order pad. "I'll help you with the first three tables, and then you're on your own. Got it?"

She produced a popular television show and made it look easy. How hard could this be? "I think I can handle taking a few orders."

Again with the smile. Why did she get the feeling that there was more to this?

"I'll still help you with the first three. They can be tricky."

Rick chose the first table of two older

women, who chatted with each other more than glancing at their menus. Elizabeth approached them. "Good afternoon, ladies. What can I get you today?"

Talk ceased as they turned to look at her. Perused her outfit. Glanced at Rick. Then sighed collectively. The woman with salt-and-pepper hair spoke first. "Well, aren't you the cutest thing?" She turned to Rick. "Where did you find her?"

Rick stepped forward and clasped his hands behind his back. "She's just helping out a few days for the Pickle Festival. So be gentle with her."

The two women gave each other telling glances. The fading redhead turned to Elizabeth. "What soups do you have today?"

Elizabeth glanced at the back of her order pad, where she'd written them. "Chicken noodle. Clam chowder. And vegetable."

The women resumed looking at their menus. The salt-and-pepper looked up at Rick. "Char's coming in for the festival this weekend, you know."

Rick gave a tight smile. "You must be looking forward to seeing your daughter."

Elizabeth glanced at him. He tugged at the collar of his T-shirt and rolled his head on his shoulders. Clearly not a good topic.

"What she's looking forward to is seeing you again, Rick. Should I tell her to give you a call?"

Rick shifted on his feet until Elizabeth stepped in. "Actually, he'll be busy with me this weekend. Working the festival and all." She glanced at Rick. "Isn't that right?"

Rick sighed and nodded. "Yeah, that's right. It's gonna be pretty busy, Mrs. Stanfill." When the older woman wrinkled her nose, he quickly added, "But I'll be sure to say hello if I see her in town."

Red gave her friend a sideways glance, then offered a big smile to Rick. "Donna will be in town, as well. You be sure to say hello to her, too."

Rick nodded, but he looked as if he'd agreed to pour salt into old wounds. "Elizabeth, why don't you go ahead and take their orders? I've got to check on something in the kitchen."

Rick left her standing alone. She took a big breath. "So what can I get you?"

ELIZABETH WAS CONVINCED that he'd chosen the three most difficult tables to train her on. They all wanted specific orders rather than something off the menu. Maybe he'd put them up to it. Maybe he'd told them to be difficult.

She groaned and hoisted the tray of food for the second table onto her shoulder like Rick had shown her. It was heavier than it looked, and she almost sagged under its weight. A drop of oil dripped from the tray onto her blouse.

Great. She'd definitely need that trip to the clothing store. How did people not have to buy a wardrobe at the end of the day working in food service? If nothing else, she would appreciate how hard her server worked the next time she ate at a restaurant. She promised she'd tip better if she could get through this afternoon.

By the end of the lunch rush, she found herself again at the back booth, her feet up and resting on the seat across from her. She'd developed blisters. She must have the way her feet throbbed and ached. She needed better shoes. New clothes. What else would this glimpse into Rick's life cost her?

"Here." Rick set a plate laden with a BLT and fries in front of her. "My specialty, just for you."

She wrinkled her nose at the bacon but one whiff of the sandwich made her stomach grumble loud enough for Rick to hear. He chuckled.

"Thanks." She laid a napkin on her lap and took a tentative bite.

Mmmmmmmm.

Rick grinned and left, only to return momentarily with his own sandwich. "Mind if I join you?"

"Think the diner will survive without us?" She took another large bite and tried to chew faster to get to the next one.

"I think we have time to eat. You don't have to rush." He looked around the dining room, which held a few stragglers left from the rush. "Shirley's here, so she can take over."

Elizabeth took another bite of her sandwich and groaned again in delight. There was something different about the bacon. "What's your secret?"

"If I told you, then it wouldn't be a secret anymore." He smirked at her. "I bake the bacon rather than frying it. Sprinkle it with Cajun seasonings and brown sugar to give it a little something special."

She wiped her mouth with her napkin. "This is fantastic."

"Thank you."

They ate in silence until Elizabeth pushed her plate away. It held only a few of the fries and a stray piece of lettuce. She patted her very full belly. "I can't eat another bite. What are you trying to do to me?"

He looked her over. "You could use some fattening up."

"Now you sound like a grandmother." Not that she'd ever known one personally. Yet another part of childhood she'd missed.

Rick stuffed the rest of his sandwich in his mouth. They smiled at each other, not saying a word. Not needing to. When he was finished, he wiped his mouth and rubbed his flat stomach. "That really hit the spot."

It felt good to sit. To put her feet up and relax. She almost hated to ask, but she did. "So what's next on the agenda?"

"I show you around town. The Pickle Festival kicks off tonight, so what better way to see it than that? The rides. The food. The people." He winked at her. "You won't be able to resist."

If only that were true. "Even if we agree to tape here, you'll still have to come to L.A. for the live finale. That's a tradition we can't break."

"I'm not asking to break anything. Just change it a little."

Elizabeth nodded, then attempted to get

to her feet, which protested. She sat back down. "As long as we're not talking about long walks anywhere, I'm in."

CHAPTER THREE

SEEING THE NATURAL beauty of Michigan would woo Lizzie, who would in turn convince the suits, so Rick followed the scenic route along the lake. The sun glanced off the smooth dark green surface of the water while boats drifted in the distance. Picturesque cottages and run-down fishing shacks shared the shore, providing its tenants with lake living.

When it was safe to do so, he pulled the truck over to the side of the road and held out his hand to help her down. She groaned as her feet touched the ground, only reminding him that working in his diner had taken a lot out of her. But she was a trouper. Whether it was to convince him for the show or something else, it didn't matter. He admired her spunk.

"I was thinking that this would really look spectacular on film." Though he still had no desire to do the show, the idea of filming here was growing on him. It could be just the boost the Lake Mildred economy needed. He turned back to gauge her impression. "It's amazing here in the spring. Summer. Fall. Even winter with all the snow."

Her eyes widened. "Snow?"

She'd probably never seen a snowflake, much less a foot of the white stuff dumped overnight. "When were you looking to film the show?"

"A live Valentine's Day kickoff. Then live again for the finale in time for the May sweeps."

"So snow, then budding flowers. Nice." He looked out over the lake and took a deep breath. He'd tried the California atmosphere, but he'd been homesick for this the entire time. The clean air. The lap of the waves on the shore. Even the splash of fish, who were practically calling his name to catch them. "We could do a ski fantasy date. Or an ice-fishing expedition. Later in the spring, they could even try out for my softball team."

"You really want us to come here? Disturb the peace of your small town?" She looked around her. "I'll admit this would look good on television. Practically a postcard from Middle America. But we wouldn't leave this place the way we found it."

"Besides bringing your audience a taste of real America, you'd also be bringing local jobs for the time you're here. Jobs that people could really use." He stepped closer to her. "You'd need people to drive. To build. To cater. Sure, you could bring some of those people from L.A. out here, but think of what you could save by hiring locally. You could improve the town's economy."

She looked at him as if he'd suggested that they could cure cancer while they were at it. "We're a television show. Don't give us too much credit."

"Lizzie." He stepped closer. "My dad always told me that with our money came responsibility. I had to give back in any way I could. If I do the show, I want to be able to help the people who have supported me. Will you help me do that?"

She sighed. "You've given me some things to think about, but I'm going to need more than this. Where would I house twenty-four women? As well as a crew of two dozen more. The bed-and-breakfast I'm at is nice, but let's be realistic. We need something a lot bigger."

Rick nodded and considered the issue. "What about some of these abandoned homes? Couldn't you rent one of those?"

"And fix it up with what money? The studio owns a mansion specifically for this show. It works for a reason."

She always had to look on the bleak side,

didn't she? But he could see the wheels turning in her head behind the skeptical expression. She might be throwing up objections, but he could tell she saw the benefits. "What if you don't pay me for my time on the show? What if you instead use that check to do this?"

She turned and looked at him closely. "You'd do that?" She didn't seem convinced.

Rick knew it could work. Bring the show. Put people to work. Keep some kind of normal life while living it out in front of a national audience. It had to work. "To get the show here? Yeah."

She crossed her arms. "Keep talking."

"Consider the tax breaks the state would give you for filming here. The cost of living is less, so you'd be getting bargain prices on the things you take for granted in Hollywood."

"Let's say we could rent a house around here. Two dozen women sharing one, maybe two bathrooms? Even that's a little too real for television."

Rick grinned. "And a whole lot of fun."

Lizzie held up her hands. "Okay. Show me more."

BY THE TIME they got in the truck and headed back to the diner for dinner, Elizabeth was dog tired. She doubted she'd be awake long enough to eat, much less call Devon with an update. And she had to admit the idea of filming here had started to wiggle into her already clicking mind. It would be a change, something that could spark ratings for a show that was starting to show its age. Rick might be onto something.

Instead of going to the diner, however, Rick turned his truck into the driveway of a large Victorian house with a wraparound porch and pulled around back near the lakefront. Elizabeth looked at the manicured landscape outside and frowned. "We're having dinner here?"

Rick wiggled his eyebrows. "First we're going to catch it. Then we'll eat here."

Elizabeth groaned. "You're taking me fishing? Haven't you tortured me enough for one day?"

"Think of it as part of your Michigan experience." He got out of the truck and retrieved fishing poles and a tackle box from behind the front seat. "And you haven't really lived until you've eaten something you've caught."

Elizabeth rolled her eyes. This was not what she had signed up for. Still, she was hungry and she'd agreed to do what was necessary to get Rick for the show. "Fine. But I'm not cleaning any icky fish. You get that job."

"Sure, Lizzie."

"Elizabeth," she muttered under her breath as she followed him to the dinghy tied to the dock on the lake.

Rick held out one hand and helped her step into the boat. She spread her arms to catch her balance before taking a seat on the narrow wooden bench. Rick untied the boat from the dock and stepped inside, pushing off. He took a seat, then pulled the chain for the motor. They putted out to the center of the lake while Elizabeth watched the sun lower in the west behind a wall of magnificent trees. She closed her eyes.

"This place is getting to you."

She opened her eyes. "I'm tired."

"Mmm-hmm." Rick steered them out farther and cut the engine. He handed her a pole. "Have you ever fished before?"

"When I was a kid, my mom took me to the Santa Monica pier. Some guy let me hold his pole while he ran to get a hot dog." She shrugged. "All I did was stand there."

"So you're an expert."

He opened the tackle box and removed a small plastic container. It was full of black dirt and wriggling worms. Elizabeth wrinkled her nose and shook her head. "I'm not putting one of those on my hook."

"Relax. I'll bait it for you."

He removed one long worm and wound it around her hook while Elizabeth squelched a squeal. She wasn't naive. She understood the circle-of-life thing. Instead of allowing Rick to think she was squeamish, she accepted the pole. "Now what?"

"Cast it out toward the middle of the lake."

She looked at him and raised one eyebrow. "Cast is something I hire for a show."

"Ha-ha. Watch me." He swung the rod back slightly, then flicked it forward, sending his line out in a perfect arc that Elizabeth doubted she could repeat.

In fact, she couldn't repeat it. After three failed attempts, Rick cast the line for her. She sighed. "What's next?"

"We wait." He wound the reel in a bit and lifted his face to the sky, his eyes closed.

Elizabeth watched him. He had a boyish charm that the audience had loved. He was also funny and sensitive. Why he was still single after all this time was a mystery to her. He was the type of guy who should be a husband and father. "What happened after you came home last time?"

Rick opened one eye and groaned. "Do we have to talk about that?"

"I'm surprised that some woman didn't snap you up the moment you arrived home, single and willing." She wound the reel a couple of clicks like she had seen him do. "You still want to get married and have kids, right? So why didn't you make that happen?"

Rick rubbed his forehead with his free hand. "Were you not there when I got publicly humiliated?"

"It's been five years. People forget."

"You have hundreds of letters a week that say otherwise." He turned his gaze on her. "I guess no one wanted to date a loser."

"You're not a loser." Elizabeth pulled her pole back slightly, mirroring Rick's movements. "You are a catch. And any woman who doesn't realize that is not only blind, but also not worth your time."

"Then I live in a town full of the sightless." Rick reeled his line in and cast it farther out. "Do you know they had a viewing party at the diner for the night of the finale? All my family and friends were gathered together to watch me propose. Instead they saw me dumped and humiliated."

"I think you're the only one who's not over that already." She glanced at his eyes shadowed beneath his ball cap. "But I do have one question."

"Only one? You're slipping."

"Did you love Brandy?"

He swallowed and adjusted the ball cap again. Then he moved his fishing pole and wound the reel a couple of turns, clearly stalling for time. "Yes." His voice croaked. "And the crazy thing is I thought she loved me, too. Only, she was pretending for the cameras."

"You don't know that."

Rick looked up at her with troubled eyes. "She chose him over me. How else do you explain it?"

She reached out and touched his knee. Then she quickly removed her hand. "You knew she was dating you both. That there was a chance…"

"But it felt real." He shrugged. "That's why I'm conflicted about doing the show. How am I supposed to know what's real and what's for the sake of the cameras? How can I trust my heart to someone else who might be pretending?"

She longed to remove the hurt from his eyes. "That's why you have me. I'll protect you. Like I should have the last time." She glanced out toward the lakeshore. "We were friends. I should have…" She looked back at him. "I want to be friends again. And I'll help you get what you want."

"How do you know what I want?"

"Because it's my job to figure it out. With your help, of course."

He gazed into her eyes until she supposed he could see her soul. If they were any two other people, this would be the perfect moment to kiss. Her lips tingled at the thought.

Rick leaned forward. She closed her eyes. "I think you've got a bite."

Her eyes flew open, and she tugged on the line. Sure enough, something was resisting at the other end. She squealed and stood up. Rick reached out and put a hand on her calf. "Careful. You're going to capsize the boat."

She wound the reel and shouted as a long silvery-green fish appeared at the end of her line. "I caught a fish!"

Rick reached up to steady her, and she threw herself into his arms.

Later, as they sat dripping wet at the campfire, she could point out where she went wrong before the boat capsized. Thankfully, Rick never raised his voice. Unfortunately, he didn't say a word, either.

Elizabeth held out her hands toward the fire to absorb the heat. She looked over at

Rick, who pulled his hooded jacket closer around him. "I'm sorry. Again."

Nothing.

She looked into the fire, hoping to find the right words. "I know you warned me, but I was so excited. I've never caught a fish."

Still nothing.

She sighed. "I'm sorry it got away."

He cleared his throat.

She settled farther into the Adirondack chair. "And that we lost your fishing pole."

His eyes flickered to hers briefly, then concentrated on the campfire again. Elizabeth closed her eyes and rested her head on the back of the chair. Silence was good. They were both tired. And wet.

Her stomach growling broke the silence. Rick's answered in turn.

And they were both hungry.

"I want to make this up to you." She leaned forward. "I'll treat you to the best dinner. Anywhere you want."

"Lizzie…"

She sighed. "He speaks."

"Don't worry about it." He stood and smothered the fire, then walked toward the house.

Elizabeth watched him leave, then rose and ran after him. "We still need to eat dinner."

Rick stopped and looked at his wet clothes, then hers. "No one would serve us like this. And I'm too hungry to change." He turned back and continued walking.

"Where are you going?"

"Mom probably has enough food in her cupboards to feed your entire crew for three months." He grinned at her. "First one there gets dibs."

And with that, he sprinted toward the house. Elizabeth laughed and ran after him.

GREEN OLIVES. Sweet pickles. Crackers and cheese. Leftover pasta salad. It was a feast, and Rick enjoyed every bite.

They sat on stools at the kitchen island while they ate with their fingers. He stopped eating momentarily to find napkins. He handed one to Lizzie, who grinned around a mouthful of salad. He opened the refrigerator and pulled out two cans of soda and placed one at each plate. "You must be thirsty."

Lizzie nodded her thanks and opened her drink. She looked around the kitchen. "Where's your mom?"

Rick popped the top of his drink and took several long pulls. It burned going down, but it was that good kind of burn. "It's the first night of the Pickle Festival, which means

she's probably manning the fried-pickle tent."
At Lizzie's frown, he continued, "You haven't
tasted heaven until you've had a fried pickle.
Trust me."

"I heard you mention it before, but what
exactly is a pickle festival?"

"Last night's championship game was the
kickoff to a weekend full of pickles here.
Courtesy of Allyn Pickles, of course." He
fished out a sweet gherkin from the jar and
handed it to her. "It's a huge deal for the
town every year. Financially speaking. Lots
of tourists. Family reunions. Homecomings.
Everyone looks forward to it."

Lizzie looked down at her clothes. "Speaking of a huge deal, we didn't get any clothes
for me. I can't work in your diner dressed in
my regular clothes."

"Next town over also has a Meijer, which
is open twenty-four hours." Lizzie's mouth
gaped, and Rick laughed. "We may be backwater, but we do have some conveniences."
He nodded at her empty plate. "So eat some
more and then we'll shop."

She stifled a yawn. "I don't know how
much longer I'll be functioning. What time
are you planning on torturing me tomorrow?"

She did look exhausted. He'd put her
through the wringer and had plans for more.

"You did such a great job today, I'll let you sleep in. We can meet at seven."

"That's sleeping in?" she moaned.

He shook his head. "You've had early calls for the show. How is this different?"

"For all you know I complained then, too." She tried to laugh, but it didn't sound right.

Rick frowned. Something didn't add up. "I thought you were a producer. Shouldn't all this be part of your job?" Lizzie stuffed the pickle into her mouth, making talking impossible. His frown deepened. "What aren't you telling me?"

She chewed, then swallowed. "It's complicated."

"You are still on the show, right?"

She nodded. "I'm executive producer. For now."

"For now?" She was about to fill her mouth with crackers, but he stayed her arm. "Tell me."

She sighed. "It's no big deal."

"If you can't tell me, then yes, it is."

She looked down at the plate. Finally, she lifted her gaze to meet his. "If you don't do the show, we're canceled."

CHAPTER FOUR

ELIZABETH POURED the eightieth cup of coffee that morning before returning to the kitchen. Rick turned to beam at her from the dish sink, and her breath caught in her throat. Remind her why this man wasn't taken. She shook her head at the stupidity of the women in this town out in the sticks. Being small-town didn't mean being foolish, but these women needed to get a clue and snap Rick up before two dozen gorgeous contestants descended here.

She paused. Was she really considering moving the show? She shook her head. This place was getting to her.

A bell over the door signaled a new customer. Elizabeth took a deep breath and walked into the dining room, almost mowing down an older version of Rick. He glanced at her outfit. "You're the producer?"

Elizabeth held out her hand. "Dan, right? I'm Elizabeth." She marveled at the strength of his handshake. "And yes, I'm the producer.

But at the moment, I'm a waitress. Can I get you some coffee?"

"He likes it black and strong." Rick joined them and leaned on the counter. "Shouldn't you be checking the floats or bands or something?"

Dan accepted the cup she offered him and took a sip. "It's been done."

Elizabeth frowned. "Floats?"

Rick nodded toward the windows, where people had started gathering on the sides of Main Street. "The Pickle Parade starts at noon. And Dan the man is the grand marshal again."

"That's what I came to talk to Elizabeth about." Dan leaned against the counter. "Ever ridden in the back of a convertible and waved to a crowd?"

Rick stepped in between them. "Forget it. She's busy."

"Pouring coffee and slinging hash? I need her more." Dan sighed and ran his hand through his hair, reminding Elizabeth of his brother. "Miss Brown County can't make it now, and the people need to see someone new. Someone classy." He glanced at Elizabeth. "She'll have to do."

She was sure there was a compliment in there somewhere. "I can't possibly do it dressed like this." She glanced at her brand-spanking-new purple T-shirt and jeans.

Dan grabbed her hand. "Martha's across the street. I'm sure she'll have something that will fit you."

Rick grabbed her other hand. "Dan, Elizabeth never agreed to do it. When are you going to stop and realize that not everyone jumps when you tell them to?"

Dan pulled her closer to him. "She has to do this. It's her responsibility."

Rick tugged her back to his side. "It's your responsibility to make sure that people show up. Not hers."

"Gentlemen." Elizabeth removed her hands from theirs and held them out to separate the brothers. "First of all, I can choose for myself. Second—" she looked between them, then nodded "—I'll help out."

Rick stared at her. "Lizzie, you don't—"

"You wanted me to get to know the community, right?" She smiled wider. "What better way than from the back of a convertible?" She turned to Dan. "So where's Martha? Let's see what she has."

Dan grinned back at her, and she was struck by how good the Allyn boys looked. "I knew I liked you. Come with me."

Rick watched from the sidelines as Lizzie, dressed in a pink sparkly dress, passed by sitting on the back of a red convertible. She even blew a kiss to him. Or perhaps to the kid standing in front of him, but it landed in his general direction. He'd take what he could get.

When the parade ended, he locked up the diner and joined the crowd as they walked down the street to the park, where rides and booths had magically appeared over the past few nights. He found Lizzie still standing near the convertible, surrounded by a group of local men who were trying to get her attention. When she turned and smiled at him, he lost his breath.

Must be the gasoline fumes.

He moved through the crowd and parked himself closest to her. "Madam, I believe we have a date."

She raised one eyebrow. "We do?"

"With a deep-fried pickle. I believe I promised you one?" He put his hand at the small of her back. "I know where they sell the best."

She sighed deeply as they left the crowd. "Thanks for the rescue."

"Part of my service." He steered her in the direction of the large tent at the center of the park. "They're smitten with shiny new things."

She ran her hand down one hip. "Miss Martha does wonders with sequins and a short deadline."

"You look fabulous." He motioned to the open tent flaps. "Now, prepare yourself for a culinary treat that few can top."

He grabbed her hand and walked behind the counters. They skirted past several deep fryers and walked to the far end of the tent. Rick pulled a basket out of one of the fryers and tipped it onto a cloth-covered plate. He held out a golden disk to her lips. "Open."

Lizzie opened her mouth, and Rick placed the deep-fried pickle on her tongue. "Now, tell me that isn't the best thing you ever ate."

She chewed slowly. "It's good."

"Good? It's fabulous." Rick took one and popped it in his mouth. He closed his eyes and let the flavors play on his tongue.

She swallowed the pickle and looked around the tent. "Are you allowed to come back here and help yourself?"

"My question exactly." His mom walked around the tables and poked a finger at Rick's chest. "Who's watching the diner?"

Rick rubbed his chest. "It's closed until five for dinner, Ma. It's fine."

She shook her head, then glanced at Elizabeth. "Miss Brown County?"

"Not quite. Elizabeth Maier from—"

"*True Love.* Yep." Rick's mother glanced at Elizabeth's outstretched hand but didn't shake it. "Thought I recognized you. What are you doing here?"

"Ma…" He should have known his mother wouldn't be happy Lizzie was there. "She's in town on business."

"As long as she's not here to mess with you again." His mom looked back at Lizzie. "Are you?"

Rick put his hands on his mother's shoulders. "It's business, Ma."

"I asked her, not you." She moved around him and walked up to Lizzie.

"Ma…" Not that his mom would take the warning, but at least he could say he had tried. He braced himself for the confrontation.

Lizzie looked down at her feet, then up at his mother. "I assure you, Mrs. Allyn, I have the best intentions."

His mom stared her right in the eyes and gave her the look he'd dreaded as a kid. It meant she knew what he was up to and she wasn't having one bit of it. "And was it your best intention for my son to get dumped on television?"

"No, but it is my intention to find him a wife." Lizzie took a step closer so that she could tower slightly over his mom.

Rick watched as the two women squared off, neither one conceding. "Ma, I'm going to show Lizzie more of the festival. But we'll see you for dinner tomorrow?"

He leaned over and kissed his mom's cheek. Then he held out his hand to Lizzie. "Now that you've tried the fried pickles, you have to taste the dill-pickle soup."

Lizzie wrinkled her nose, but she followed him.

THIS SMALL TOWN could do things to a person. She'd only been in Lake Mildred two days, and part of her was wondering what living there would be like. People smiled and said hello. Acted as if she'd been one of them for years. She didn't feel rushed or anxious. She hadn't thought of her voice mail or email for hours. In fact, she hadn't glanced at her cell phone since the parade two hours before.

Rick turned toward her when she sighed. "It gets to you, right?"

She shrugged and pulled on the hem of her dress. She should have changed after the parade. Or at least after they'd sampled the fried dill pickles, the dill-pickle soup, the gherkin mousse. She should have passed on that last one. But the pickle pâté had been fabulous. The lure of the festival had kept them in the park, enjoying the booths and the people surrounding them. "I guess it is getting to me."

He stopped at the ticket booth and purchased two wristbands, then tied one to her wrist. "Which ride should we try first? The tilt-a-whirl or the scrambler?"

She put a hand over her stomach. "I'd like to keep my lunch down, thanks."

Rick laughed. "Where's your sense of adventure? Your joie de vivre?"

"It prefers not to spend life with my head in the toilet." She looked around at the rides. There had to be something tame. "Why not the Ferris wheel?"

Rick glanced up at it, then grabbed her hand and sprinted toward the line. "You won't believe the view up there. You'll be able to see the whole town."

"All square mile of it? Can't wait."

When they reached the beginning of the line, Rick let her take a seat first before joining her. They got locked into the seat, then took a deep breath as the operator gave a thumbs-up.

The view at the top took Elizabeth's breath away. Trees grew lush and green. The sunlight glinted off the lake and winked with the promise of fun times. Small homes were built around the town square and farther beyond. Cottages lined the lakeshore. Part of her suddenly yearned for a place in this community.

Rick nodded. "I told you it was spectacular."

"You weren't kidding." The camera would love it. She turned to him. "You understand that our coming here would forever change the peace and quiet. We couldn't leave this place as it is now. For months, it would be chaos with the contestants and crew. We'd clog your streets and your businesses, and leave the mess for you to clean up. And then the gawkers would descend."

"What I know is that it would bring jobs and money to people who need both more than you know." He pointed at a home with a tree house in the backyard. "It would mean Steve wouldn't lose his house." He pointed to another with a covered porch. "Or that Shelly could feed her kids this winter."

Elizabeth closed her eyes. She knew what it was like to be hungry. What it meant not to know if there would be dinner that night. "I can't guarantee Devon will go for this idea."

Rick settled back into the seat. "You tell him it's either you have me here or I don't do it at all."

"That's a pretty big threat."

He reached out and touched her hand. "I won't let you lose your job over me, but I won't lose myself in the process, either. I'm not going to lie, the idea of doing the show again is making me quake in my sneakers. But as long as we can establish some ground rules, if we can do it my way, then everyone will be happy."

Uh-oh. His way? She was the producer here, not him. "You ask for a lot."

Rick shrugged. "So do you."

She watched the emotions play over his face. He wanted to save this town, but at what cost to himself? He was a good man. Too good for this business. Elizabeth reached out and touched his face, then snapped her hand back as if he'd burned her. What was she doing?

"Lizzie." The hoarseness of his voice seemed to shock even him.

"Elizabeth."

He leaned back and looked out over the treetops. "Come to Sunday dinner tomorrow afternoon at my mom's."

After the confrontation in the food tent, that was a shock. "Why?"

He turned to her. "Because that's what I do every Sunday. Spend it with my family. And maybe if we talk some more, we can figure this out. Give my mom a second chance. Isn't that what you're offering me here?"

Was it? Elizabeth wasn't sure anymore.

ELIZABETH ADJUSTED her black skirt and straightened her pink linen jacket while wondering for the eighty-ninth time why she had agreed to do this. She'd gone to great lengths to secure contestants in the past, but this topped them all.

She exhaled as she saw Rick come down the back stairs from his apartment to where she waited by her convertible.

"Good morning." He leaned over and kissed her cheek.

She glanced at her watch. "It's technically afternoon."

Rick grinned and shrugged. "Close enough." He moved next to her to lean against the car. "Ready for this?"

Elizabeth's insides vibrated with tension, and she clutched her stomach. "I'm not hungry."

"We'll eat. Talk. Maybe watch a ball game. And have a great afternoon." He bumped her shoulder with his. "My family wants to get to know you."

Why? She was about to change Rick's life again. Maybe coming here hadn't been a good idea. If she hadn't been so worried about her job... Instead of asking, she smiled. "Then I'd love to."

Rick's shoulders sagged in what looked like relief. "Thanks. You'll be saving us from a week of leftovers—roast-beef sandwiches, roast-beef salad, beef pâté."

Elizabeth wiped the sweat off the back of her neck. "Your mother made a roast in this heat?"

Rick shrugged. "She likes to cook."

What would it have been like to have grown up with a mom like that? Elizabeth couldn't even begin to imagine. "Is that where you learned it?"

He nodded. "She taught me everything I know. She's the best."

"Which you obviously use in your job." She turned and looked at him. "Did you know the diner would be your life the last time I saw you?"

He took so long in answering her, she thought at first he hadn't heard what she'd said. At last, he sighed. "No, it's not where I pictured my life passing. I imagined ball fields and team buses. But things changed after the car accident. And the diner stepped in and took the place of that dream. I spend most of my days there because it's easier than looking at my life and wondering what the future holds."

"So what do you want?"

He patted his stomach. "To go to lunch. I'm starving."

She unlocked her car door and stood in the opening while she looked at him. "Should I follow you out to your mom's?"

Rick peered past her to the inside of her car. "Actually, I'll ride with you. Can we put the top down?"

She shook her head. "You're worse than a kid."

He grinned at her, and a punch landed in her stomach. *Wow.*

With his help, they put the soft top down on the convertible and she settled into the driver's seat. He bounced slightly in the seat and tried all the knobs on the dashboard. She playfully swatted his hand, then turned the key in the ignition. "It's a car, not a toy."

He chuckled and settled back in the passenger seat, eyes closed and sun streaming onto his face. "I love Sundays."

"I can tell."

He opened one eye and looked at her. She turned her gaze back to the road. "You don't?"

She shrugged. "In my world, it's just another day. Another day of phone calls, meetings and… Why are you staring at me like that?"

"You really need to find a hobby." He turned his focus back to the road. "Turn left up here, and we'll follow the lake to the house."

RICK HELPED LIZZIE out of the car, then walked around the house to the back door.

He opened the door and popped his head inside. "Mom?" The smell of roasting beef tickled his nose, so he knew she was around somewhere. He turned back to Lizzie. "She's probably changing from her church clothes."

Lizzie looked down at her suit. "Do I look okay?"

He smiled. Always worried about how she looked. He wore his Detroit Tigers T-shirt and favorite jeans. He didn't have to worry. "You're not meeting my family as a girlfriend, so stop worrying. They'll love you."

"Until they find out I'm bringing you back to the show again." She shut the door behind her. "We really need to talk."

He held up a hand. "I know. Later." It was definitely a conversation that could wait.

His mom entered the kitchen and walked over to him. She kissed him on the cheek. "My handsome boy." She turned to Lizzie. Her expression changed from affection to distrust. "I've agreed to be civil, for Rick's sake." Lizzie fidgeted until his mom looked her over and sighed. "Rick's right. You need some fattening up. I hope you're hungry."

Rick took a step between Lizzie and his mom. Better to keep them at a distance for now. "Is Danny here yet? I'm starving to death." He patted his empty stomach again.

His mom rolled her eyes. "Never mind him, Lizzie. He's always hungry."

"Elizabeth."

His mom checked on the roast in the oven, then turned to them. "Rick, you're on table duty. Lizzie, if you'd help me make a salad, then we'll be able to eat once Dan arrives. Now, why don't you tell me more about what's going on with you two."

Lizzie colored as pink as her suit. Rick cleared his throat. "I've agreed to do the show again, Ma."

She stopped pulling vegetables from the crisper and turned to face him. He swallowed and felt exactly like he used to when wait-

ing for his father to come home and discipline him for goofing off in school. He hadn't
wanted to blurt it out like that, but it was better to say it now rather than waiting for Dan
to start spinning this to his advantage. He
watched for his mother's reaction.

She nodded and took a seat at the kitchen
island. Rick helped to put the vegetables
on the counter and shut the refrigerator. He
chuckled, trying to keep it light. "I didn't
expect you to be overjoyed, but speechless?
Wow."

"Why do you want to put yourself through
that, honey?" She put her hands on either side
of his face. "Do you think you could handle
it again?"

He glanced at Lizzie, who started to peel
the plastic wrap from the head of lettuce.
His producer wasn't being any help, so he
shrugged. "I'm still single. Still haven't found
the right woman. Why not open the odds up
a little in my favor?"

"It didn't work the last time." She shook
her head and buried her face in her hands. "I
begged your father to let you off the hook.
We didn't need that ridiculous show to survive."

"Mrs. Allyn, the chances of Rick finding

a wife are better this time. He'll be the focus of our show. The one doing the choosing."

His mom turned to her. "I can't believe you're torturing him again with this. You don't know what it was like when he came back. The pain—"

"Ma." She turned back to him. He'd do anything to ease the worry in her eyes. "I know you're trying to protect me. But this time will be different."

"How can you be so sure?"

He winked at Lizzie. "Because we're doing it my way this time."

Lizzie paled but gave a weak nod to Ma when she looked at her. "Rick wants more control this time. We still have to work out the details, but he wants to film here in town."

Rick crossed his arms. "I more than want it. I'm going to have it or there will be no show."

Lizzie accepted the knife from his mom. She started to chop the tomato. "I understand that you want to avoid what happened last time, but there are certain requirements, restrictions, that the show places not only on the contestants, but—"

He held up one hand. "Don't try to produce me right now, Lizzie." He turned back to his mom. "When are you going to stop worrying about me?"

She tried to give him a smile, but he could see what it cost her. "You'll always be my baby."

He hugged her and rubbed her back. "Someday you'll have to trust me to make big-boy decisions."

"What's wrong?"

Rick turned to Dan, who had entered the kitchen, shrugged out of his suit coat and hung it on the back of a stool. "Mom's worried about me doing the show again."

Dan rolled his eyes and crossed his arms over his chest. "So you're really going to do it."

"Yes, Dan. I think so." He glanced at Lizzie, who watched his reaction closely. "I'm almost positive." He turned back to his mom. "I don't want to make the same mistakes, so that's why we're doing the show here. You'll get to know all the women throughout the whole process. And give me advice." He turned to face Dan. "When I ask for it."

"Taping here means that we can showcase Allyn Pickles even more. Make a national audience aware of what we offer." His mercenary brother's eyes glazed over with the possibilities, and Rick sighed and patted his mom's arm.

"I'll set the table, and we can discuss this over dinner. Okay?"

She nodded, but he could tell she wasn't really there. He walked to the cupboard and pulled out dishes and glasses, then disappeared into the dining room. It was mindless work, but that was what he needed to clear his mind.

"What happened after the show last time?"

Rick glanced up from a dinner plate and frowned at Lizzie, who stood in the doorway watching him. "You're supposed to be making a salad."

"Your mom took over, so I came in here to talk to you."

He finished placing the plates on the table and turned to the sideboard drawer where his mom kept the cloth napkins. He folded four and walked around the table, placing them where they belonged next to each plate. "I don't need to talk."

"What happened that's got your mom so scared for you to do this show?"

She stepped in front of him so that he had to look at her or push her out of his way. He chose to look at her. "It's complicated."

"That's my response. Get your own."

He sighed and moved around her to retrieve the silverware from the sideboard. He pulled out four forks, four spoons and four knives, then slammed the drawer shut and braced his hands on either side of him. "It wasn't good."

She placed a hand on his shoulder. "I want you to do this show, but not if it's going to hurt you."

He looked down at her soft mouth. "You want your job. Dan wants his publicity. The town needs the money. Do I really have a choice?"

"You always have a choice, Rick." She dropped her hand but kept her gaze on his. "Tell me what happened last time."

He closed his eyes. "Some people run when trouble comes. Others throw themselves into work." He opened his eyes and saw her watching him, a frown marring her brow. He might as well tell her the whole story, because his family would if he didn't. "I retreated to my family's cottage. Didn't go out. Didn't work. Cut myself off from everybody and everything. I couldn't sleep, wouldn't eat. I became disoriented and got behind the wheel of my car to drive back home. I didn't wake up until I hit a tree. After crushing my knee in the accident, I lost even my dream of playing with the pros." He straightened his shoulders and cleared his throat. "But I won't let it happen again. And you're going to help me make sure of that."

CHAPTER FIVE

By February, Lake Mildred was ready, poised on the brink of either publicity or infamy. Rick poured another round of coffee for his regulars and tried to maintain his good mood despite their incessant questions.

Would the production crew hire local people to help out as they had agreed in the contract? Rick knew they would and had signed papers to make it so. Lizzie had promised, and he knew he could trust her.

Would the show bring more tourists in? Probably, depending on the ratings. If it was popular, they'd want to come experience the place for themselves. If it ended as it had before, they'd want to come gawk at the man destined to be alone.

Would he find a wife? He prayed that he would. There was no other option on this. Either he met the woman meant to be his wife or he'd choose someone who was close enough to his list of expectations and hope that love would grow between them. He wearied of going to bed alone, waking up alone. He didn't want to keep living with only his thoughts.

He replaced the coffee carafe in the machine and leaned on the counter. Ernesto, the cook, came out from the kitchen and joined him. "You ready to give this all up?"

Rick snorted and glanced around the dining room. "It's only for a couple of months. Don't get used to not having me here."

"You're the lifeblood here at the diner. In the community." Ernesto put a hand on his shoulder. "What you're doing for us now is…" His voice broke, and he shook his head.

"I'm not a savior, Ern." Rick pushed himself off the counter and went to stand at the front window, watching as road crews filled in potholes that had cropped up after each thaw. There had been talk of repaving, but it wasn't sound fiscal judgment in the winter.

But it was more than the potholes being filled. Rick had added fancy coffee drinks to his menu, and a bright copper espresso machine had arrived that he'd had to learn and teach his staff to use. Lizzie said it would draw the crew and contestants in like mosquitoes to a bug zapper. Outside the diner, the community task force had repainted benches, shored up docks and ordered more road salt for the snow that hadn't stopped since New Year's Day.

All so he could find a wife and Lizzie could keep her job.

Rick turned away from the window and walked back into the kitchen. Freshly baked cakes lined the stainless-steel counters, cooling and waiting for frosting.

The phone rang, but Rick let Ernesto answer it by the cash register. Probably another take-out order. Or one more reservation for the viewing party on Valentine's Day. While Rick met the future Mrs. Allyn, and twenty-three other beautiful women, at a huge catered party at the Veterans of Foreign Wars hall, the town would gather at the diner to watch it unfold on live television.

Ernesto opened the swinging door and handed him the phone. He stared at it, then put it up to his ear. "Rick Allyn."

"Do you always answer your phone so formally?"

He grinned at the familiar voice. "Lizzie."

"You're never going to call me Elizabeth, are you?" She sighed over the line, making his smile wider. "Do you have plans tonight?"

"If you're here and available for dinner, my schedule is free."

She chuckled. "I'll take you up on dinner.

The plane just landed, and my stomach is demanding real food. We need to go over some things before my crew arrives tomorrow."

His skin warmed, and he held the phone tighter. "You're really here? I won't have to settle for talking on the phone and picturing you hanging on my every word on the other side of the country?"

"We can even sit side by side if you want." She muttered to someone on her end of the phone, then sighed. "They didn't save my convertible for me. Can you believe it?"

"It's winter, Lizzie. Get the four-wheel-drive SUV with heated seats. Trust me." He glanced through the cutout window into the diner, where people tried to catch a peek of him. "You won't believe the changes in town since you were here last."

They hung up with plans to meet at the diner once she had checked in at the hotel where she and some of the crew would stay.

TO KILL TIME, Rick buzzed through his apartment, making sure it looked presentable. He'd been raised to keep a tidy room, but it had never been easy for him. He liked his things out and around him. He knew Lizzie wouldn't want to be surrounded by stacks of newspaper with sports stats. His baseball mitt sat on the kitchen table though it hadn't been used in months. The comforter of his bed was dragging half on the floor.

A tapping on the apartment floor brought Rick's attention back to the present. Ernesto's signal that Lizzie had arrived at the diner. He double-checked the tiny space, then took the stairs to the kitchen two at a time. Ernesto motioned with his head to the dining room. Rick took a deep breath and pushed open the swinging door.

Lizzie wasn't alone.

A man stood next to her with a large bag over one shoulder and a camera in the other hand. They didn't hear Rick approach over their discussion about where to set the camera up for the first interview.

Cameras and interviews already? His stomach started to ache. "What happened to dinner with real food?"

Lizzie turned and smiled. "Talk first, eat later. We need to get these one-on-one discussions finished before the live premiere."

He nodded, but the ball in the pit of his stomach grew rather than shrunk. "One-on-ones. I remember those."

"Good." She pointed to the back booth. "We could set up there, make it look intimate. Charlie?"

The guy with the camera looked at the fluorescent lighting in the diner and shook his head. "Intimacy? Not with this lighting. Is there somewhere else we could do this?"

Rick thought of all the cleaning he had done and gave a short nod. "My apartment's upstairs. It's not big, but it would give that intimate feeling you want." He motioned to follow him through the kitchen and up the stairs. He paused only once, when Ernesto bobbed his head to the pie that was cooling on the counter.

Once upstairs, Rick watched Lizzie survey his domain, wondering about her thoughts. It was small but tidy. Exactly what he needed. A worn-out sleeper sofa that had graced the family room growing up. A big-screen television. The place wouldn't win any design awards, but he liked it. This was home.

Charlie set up in the living area so that Rick could sit in the recliner while Lizzie lobbed questions from the sofa. When he left to retrieve more lights from the SUV, Rick turned to Lizzie. "I never liked these."

"I remember." She nodded and started ticking items off on her fingers. "We have a lot to do and less than a week to do it. We've had a crew refurbishing the two houses you found for the women to stay in. As it is, they'll finish them up only hours before the contestants arrive. I have a laundry list of items to locate or buy, interviews to schedule and film, your family to prep." She closed her hand in a fist. "We need to multitask, which means interviews and dinner tonight."

"Didn't you plan on prepping me for this interview?" He shook his head at the edge in his voice. He was disappointed. He'd admit it. Tonight was supposed to be about two friends catching up on the past few months. Not a Q&A in front of a third party. "I was hoping we could relax tonight before the real work starts."

"It's been nothing but work since I landed in L.A. last August." She consulted her clipboard, then set it aside. Fully looked at him for the first time. "Are you okay?"

He shrugged, pretending that it was no big deal. "Honestly? No. I've been nervous since Christmas. Might have to stock up on the pink stuff to calm my stomach." He chuckled. "Other than that, I'm great."

"You'll be fine. Remember—you're the one in charge this time." She picked up her clipboard again and glanced at it. "Except for one tiny thing."

He frowned. "How tiny?"

She looked up at him. "I'm the executive

producer. So I'm really the one who calls the shots." She stood up when Charlie entered the room. "Let's get set up and knock off some of these interviews. Then dinner. And I'll be spending the rest of the evening in the editing bay." She consulted her notes. "I thought we'd tape the segments about your initial impressions of what you're looking for in a true love. Then also discuss what went wrong last time."

"Nothing like ripping off that bandage." He pinched the bridge of his nose. "Fine. Let's get it over with."

ELIZABETH THUMBED THROUGH her cards while Charlie checked the light levels on Rick. She wouldn't show up on camera, so she was worried less about what she looked like. However, this was the audience's first look at Rick since his humiliation five years ago. He needed to look good. Confident. Ready to find love again.

Her schedule had the crew arriving tomorrow afternoon, then a short preproduction meeting followed by a tour of the town and facilities. Party plans needed to be finalized. The female contestants arrived two days after that, which meant making sure the houses were ready. Devon would turn up the day after the contestants for the final walk-throughs and rehearsals, and before she could sneeze they'd be airing live.

She rested her head on the back of the sofa and closed her eyes. She thrived on the adrenaline of getting a show off the ground, but sometimes she wondered what it would be like to have a job that began at nine and finished at five. What would it be like to live a normal life?

"We're ready, E."

She lifted her head, opened her eyes and prayed that this interview would start things off right.

Charlie handed Rick a clapboard with the identifying information on it: take number, scene number, location and producer. It might seem like a cliché to the viewing audience, but it was vital to the editors who pieced the show together from interviews like this. She read off the information, then said, "Roll cameras." She adjusted her note cards one more time. She glanced at Rick. "Ready?"

He couldn't even look at her; he focused on something beyond her against the wall. "Doesn't really matter, does it?"

She held a finger up to Charlie and leaned toward Rick. "Close your eyes." He did after a long moment, but he looked as if he didn't want to. She closed her eyes, as well. "Now, picture the woman you want to spend your life with. Not her physical features, but what she could add to your life. To enrich it. Make it sweeter. What would she be like?"

She opened her eyes and looked at the man before her. She swallowed hard. Those weren't questions she was ready to answer herself. "Okay. Now open your eyes." She caught her breath. "Rick, what are you looking for in a true love?"

"My true love is a woman who believes in me." He smiled. "Even when I'm doing something she thinks is absolutely crazy. A woman who sees me as I am and loves me anyway. Someone who can turn my life upside down, yet make it better. I want a partner. An equal, but someone who's more than me, like a complement to what I'm not. I want us to be a team. An unbeatable one."

Elizabeth nodded and made notes. Ideas for other questions that would further probe his answers. "Have you ever met anyone like that?"

He stared down at his hands, then back at her. "I thought I had, but maybe I was wrong."

"Maybe? Do you mean Brandy?"

He shrugged. "She wanted someone else."

Charlie grunted and kept filming. Elizabeth turned to the next card. "Why do you think that things didn't work out last time? And have you learned from your mistakes?"

"Things didn't work because I was too immature. I didn't know what I really wanted, but I grabbed on to something that looked awfully close." He settled farther into his chair and rested his ankle on his other knee. "I've learned about myself in the past five years. I know what I want. And I also know that I'm willing to work on finding it."

She nodded and made more notes, not really paying attention. Was she setting him up for disappointment? Sure, the show was based on the belief in love at first sight (or at least by the sixth week), and as producer of that show, she believed it. Almost. But she'd seen all the relationships forged on her show end in separation. What did that say for true love?

She turned to Charlie. "Cut." She stood up and moved to the front door. "Let's take a quick break, Charlie. Get something to eat. Rick, you're doing great. Just keep concentrating on the mental picture of your true love." She opened the door. "I'll be right back."

She walked down the stairs and found the cook in the kitchen. He flipped burgers and checked orders without a second thought. He was as attuned to his job as she was to hers. She gave the cook a smile. "Hi, Ernesto."

He nodded at her. "Everything okay?"

"Couldn't be better." She looked around for one of the plastic tumblers and filled it with cold water from the tap. Rick didn't stock his diner with designer bottled water. Or he hadn't until she'd told him he should for the crew and contestants. She strode to the walk-in and found five cases of bottled water cooling on the shelves.

Just another reminder of how she was turning his normal life inside out. But was it for the better?

She turned back and found Ernesto watching her. "Rick get the espresso machine I sent?"

He turned back to his grill. "More buttons on that thing than you need to launch the space shuttle."

"He'll get good use out of it. Especially for the next couple of weeks." She leaned against the counter. Tried to ignore the stomach grumblings that the aroma of the burgers on the grill caused.

"And after that, what happens?"

Elizabeth shrugged. "It's his to keep."

Ernesto and shook his head at her. He

pointed to the aprons hanging up. "Dishes need washing if you got time."

She held up her hands. "They've finally recovered since the last time, but I appreciate the invitation." Maybe she'd offer to buy an industrial dishwasher for the diner, too. "We've got more work to do upstairs."

"Work."

She nodded. "Interviews. Plotting how the show will go once the women arrive. Making plans."

He pointed to a cloth-covered pie. "I made dessert. You take it to him?"

She nodded. "Sure." She started to walk back up the stairs but turned back. "You don't like me."

"I don't know you, but Rick does." He looked up at her. "He likes you."

She thought of Rick and felt her cheeks warm. "I know. He's become a good friend."

"But I don't like people who hurt my friends."

"I wouldn't, either." She took her glass of water and the pie up the stairs so they could finish filming and she could call it a night and return to her room to work. That was what she needed to get through these doubts. More work.

And less thinking.

RICK ADJUSTED HIS SHIRT and glanced at Charlie, who adjusted the lights one more time even though they'd been perfect a moment ago. "So you like the snow?"

The cameraman shrugged. "I grew up in Florida. Never saw much of it."

"That's gonna change." Rick chuckled and thought of how most of the crew would be experiencing firsts here, too. "It's all part of the Michigan experience."

Charlie grunted. Obviously not much for conversation. Rick tapped his fingers on his knee while he waited for Lizzie to return. What was taking her so long anyway? The sooner they finished these interviews, the better as far as he was concerned. "How was your trip here?"

"Fine."

Okay. Thankfully, Lizzie returned with Ernesto's pie in one hand. "I brought some dessert."

Rick stood and took the pie from her. "Dessert before dinner? Perfect. I'll serve."

He found three plates and cut generous pieces, then handed them out. "I could use a break. You guys?"

Charlie accepted his plate of pie and a fork. Took a bite and closed his eyes. "You made this?"

"I wish. I don't have the pie gene." He handed Lizzie her plate and fork. "Ernesto is the genius here."

They ate silently for a moment, reveling in the caramel and apples. Rick stood. "I could make us coffee?"

Charlie held up one hand. "Just water for me."

"I'll take a cup." Lizzie paused in eating. "I'm going to need new clothes if I eat like this every day while we're here."

"You know what my mom would say about that." He chuckled and walked into his kitchen area to fill the coffee carafe. "I only have milk up here."

Charlie looked between the two of them. "Am I missing something?"

"Rick has the bad habit of remembering what everyone likes to eat and drink." Lizzie shook her head. "It may work for the diner, but how am I going to use that to find you a wife?"

"Does everything have to be about that?" Rick scooped coffee into the filter basket, then swung it shut and started the machine. "I'm more than the diner. More than finding a wife."

"Not for the next couple of months." Lizzie balanced her plate of pie on her knee and used her fork to point at Rick. "You need to live, eat and breathe the show. Nothing is more important."

And make his life just like hers? Rick joined them in the living room area. "I'm not saying it's not important. It's just not everything."

"It should be."

Rick crossed his arms over his chest. "Well, I'm not you." He handed the cameraman a glass of water. Okay, so he let the diner consume his life. It was better than being alone. Right?

Charlie cleared his throat as he accepted the drink. "Do I need to be here for this fight?"

Lizzie whipped her head around at him. "We're not fighting. We're discussing."

"Right." Charlie held his hands up in surrender. "My bad." He stayed silent and continued to eat his pie.

Rick chuckled and returned to the kitchen counter. He'd missed this bantering. Missed Lizzie more than he'd realized.

He shook his head and prepared two cups of coffee before turning back to the two, who watched him. "No more discussing. Let's finish these interviews."

Lizzie smiled in response. "Now, that's what I'm talking about."

RICK'S MOM GREETED Rick and the crew when they arrived at the house. He held the door open as they unloaded the van of the lights, cameras and other equipment. He joined them in the family room, where his mom had laid a fire. It looked cozy. Homey. And the audience would want to join the family who lived here.

He adjusted the pictures on the mantel and glanced over his shoulder to find his mom watching him. She turned in a circle. The hem of her dress swished around her legs. "How do I look?"

He walked to her and kissed her cheek. "Fabulous. Like always." He turned in a circle. "And me?"

She patted his cheek and walked into the adjoining kitchen. Took a plate of cookies from the counter. "I made these for the crew."

"They're gonna love you for this." He grabbed one before she could slap his hand. "Are you ready for this? Because I'm not sure I am."

She knit her eyebrows together and let out a big sigh. "Not exactly the time to be having doubts." She put her arm around his waist. "But we can get through this together. We'll find you the perfect wife. And the perfect mother of my grandchildren."

Rick groaned. "Let's get to the wedding before we start discussing kids, okay?" Talk about jumping ahead. Though the thought of a couple of rug rats running around the old house made him smile. He could imagine future holidays surrounded by his wife and kids. "Okay, I'm ready for this."

Lizzie joined them in the kitchen. "Good. Because we're ready, too." She glanced at the plate of cookies. "Peanut butter?"

His mom held out the plate. "Help yourself, dear."

"I really shouldn't." But she took one and bit into it. "These are too good to resist, though. Thank you. The crew will love you."

"That's what I said." Rick took another cookie, but this time his mom did slap his hand. "What? I was going to share."

Lizzie looked between them. "Are you two always like this? Close? Affectionate?"

His mom examined his producer for a long moment. "You wanted natural. That's what you're getting. What is your family like?"

Lizzie shoved the rest of the cookie in her mouth. Rick knew her family life was hardly idyllic, but the avoidance spoke more than actual words might. He put his arm around his mom. "Why don't we give the cookies to the crew and get set up in the family room? Once we finish the interviews, we can have the salads and wraps I brought for lunch."

"And you blame me for trying to fatten everyone up." His mom took the cookie plate into the family room, where she was cheered by the crew.

Rick glanced at Lizzie. "You okay?"

She nodded, but her cheeks burned and the rest of her face paled. "Family is one of those touchy topics."

He placed a hand on her shoulder. "I know." He might not know the details, but he knew her reaction when families were brought up. So he changed the subject. "Dan's been upstairs all morning, trying to decide on what to wear. Suddenly he's nervous about being on camera."

"He's something else."

Dan appeared in the doorway of the kitchen. "Did I hear my name?" He walked forward and turned around. "Did I choose the right suit?"

Rick choked back his laughter as Lizzie stared at his older brother. Dan wore a red blazer, white shirt and navy pants with an American flag tie. He looked as if he was running for office rather than supporting his brother on a reality show. Rick knew he wouldn't wear that on-screen, just like he knew Dan had brought another suit. Lizzie, on the other hand, opened and closed her mouth. Probably trying to figure out the right words to say and the right way to say them. Rick's mom walked into the kitchen and shook her head. "Go change, Dan. We don't have all day."

Rick burst into laughter as Dan winked at Lizzie and left the room. She whirled and glared at Rick. "He wasn't serious?"

Rick shook his head and wiped his eyes. "You should have seen your face."

His mom thrust out a tray with coffee cups, sugar and creamer on it. "Stop torturing the girl and make yourself useful."

He obeyed, taking the coffee to the crew before returning to the kitchen to find Lizzie and his mom chatting about the filming schedule. Dan came into the kitchen wearing a navy suit but no tie. He held the flag tie in one hand, a yellow one in the other. "Tie or no tie?"

Lizzie turned and nodded at him. "Much better. No tie. Let's keep it casual."

Dan glanced at Rick, who wore a light blue sweater and khakis. "Or too casual."

"I've done these before. You're going to

want casual after hours of filming." Rick leaned on the counter. "But the suit looks good on you."

Lizzie sighed. "Why don't we get started? The sooner we do, the sooner we finish." She grabbed the clipboard she'd left on the kitchen counter. "And the sooner we can find you your wife." She walked toward the family room, then turned. "Just think. You'll be meeting your wife in two days."

Rick tried to smile despite the growing knot of dread in his stomach.

CHAPTER SIX

RICK ADJUSTED HIS TIE and winced when Lizzie walked up to him, slapping his hands away. "You're going to ruin all my work."

"I didn't realize being producer meant dressing your star." He tipped his head back so she could get closer to straighten the tie.

"My job is to make sure this all goes the way it's supposed to." She smoothed it down his chest and patted it softly. "There. Perfect."

Rick took her hand in his and let them rest against his chest. "Do you think Mrs. Allyn could be here?"

"Your mother's out there somewhere." When he opened his mouth to protest, she winked and squeezed his hand. "Your future wife is definitely here. What do you think?"

"I hope so." He had twenty-four women waiting in the VFW hall, there for the sole purpose of meeting him. Trying to win his affection. His future wife could be out in that room while he stayed in the kitchen waiting for his cue. He was ready.

Wasn't he?

One of the production assistants entered the kitchen. "They're ready for you in five minutes."

Rick dropped Lizzie's hand and peered into her face. Was that concern looming behind those green eyes? "Showtime already?"

She nodded and grabbed her clipboard from the counter behind them. "We've aired your interview about what you're looking for, and they're finishing each of the women's bios. We'll come back from commercial break, and then you're on."

Rick adjusted the tie once more. "It's hard to breathe with this thing on."

"The tie is fine. It's you that's having problems." She reached up and laid it smooth again. "Your idea about a Valentine's dance with the seniors from the nursing home was inspired. I couldn't have planned it better myself."

Rick felt his cheeks warm. He looked down at his feet, which were covered in uncomfortable leather dress shoes. "I remember how pleased as punch my grandpa was when a young thing paid him some attention after Grandma died."

"Seeing the women in this light is going to really help the audience perception. Maybe give us less drama than the catfights they might expect. But why not show off a better side of humanity, right?" She took a deep breath. "We needed to change the focus of the show after the last producer left, and I think you might be what we need."

"Don't give me all the credit, Ms. Executive Producer." He glanced over her shoulder at the line of studio personnel watching them. "I don't remember all the suits the last time I did this."

She leaned in closer and dropped the volume of her voice. "They want to make sure I do my new job right, I guess. Don't let it worry you. I got this." She winked at him, and the previous nervousness fled from her demeanor. He could tell that she was now in the zone.

He nodded. So was he.

ELIZABETH ADJUSTED RICK'S microphone and checked the levels to make sure it was picking up sound. One of her assistants had already done it, but her job meant that she double- and triple-checked anything and everything. "Talk clearly, but don't shout. The mike is strong enough to pick up even a whisper." She picked up an earpiece from the counter behind her and handed it to him. "Take this.

If you get lost or tongue-tied, I can guide you through."

He shook his head and tried to hand it back. "And I thought we were having a nice moment. No."

She sighed, knowing that she could lose this battle, and she never lost. "Just in case. I'll be your Cyrano."

Again, he handed it back to her. "We're doing this my way. And we're keeping it real."

She groaned and wanted to stamp her heels. Unfortunately, she didn't think that would serve her cause. "Real isn't selling on TV."

"We have an agreement." He closed her hand on the earpiece, and this time she accepted it. "I don't need you, but thanks."

She smiled up into his eyes. "But you do need me. Otherwise we wouldn't both be here again."

"Funny." He took a few deep breaths. "Okay, let's do this. I'm ready."

Charlie walked by them with his handheld camera. "Network says we're back from commercial in ten."

Rick's bravado paled slightly. Elizabeth adjusted his tie again. She wasn't about to lose her star now. "Remember. They're here because of you. They want your attention. They want your love. You don't have to be anything but who you really are." She turned him around, then pushed him through the swinging doors into the hall. "Knock 'em out."

RICK BLINKED at the bright lights and couldn't see one face in the crowd that he knew was gathered in front of them. He held up a hand to shield his eyes from the glare. "I know they talk about the bright lights of fame, but this is a bit much."

He heard a few chuckles. *Score.* "Happy Valentine's Day, everyone. And welcome to Lake Mildred." He'd had a speech all prepared, but the words failed to come to mind. Instead he rubbed his hands together. "Let's get this party going with an oldie but goody."

He turned and nodded toward the director, who started the band playing a slow tune popular when his parents had been young and dating. Good choice. He walked into the crowd and found a woman who had to be eighty years young. "Care for this dance?"

She tittered and blushed as he helped her walk out onto the dance floor and started to sway slowly while she hung on to her walker. "You taught ninth-grade English, right?"

The older woman nodded. "You always were the charmer, Ricky."

A young woman with more hair than dress

approached them. She beamed widely at them. "Mind if I join you both?"

And so the group dance began. Some of the women gathered the seniors to do a slow-moving train around the room, while others rounded them up in groups of two and three to dance. Rick looked around the room. He turned back to his dancing partners. "I think this is the beginning of something special, don't you?"

They swayed until the end of the song, then clapped politely to the band. Lizzie walked out into the hall and called, "Cut. Great job, everyone. We'll be back from commercial in two. In the meantime, enjoy the refreshments and another song from Jimmy's band."

She walked toward Rick and gave him a soft clap of her hands. "Good work. Keep it up." She looked around the room. "Find your wife yet?"

"You should have been a comedian."

She wrinkled her nose. "Not enough money in it. I'd much rather be the lowly producer." She leaned in to him. "Your mom called and said the crowd at the diner loves it so far."

Rick nodded. "Good." He adjusted his tie and tried to swallow.

"Relax." She smoothed his tie. "We're back

in thirty." She started to walk away, then turned and winked at him. "Just act natural."

Natural. Right. He could do that.

As they returned from commercial, everyone started to dance to a faster tune. One of the seniors pulled a young woman onto the dance floor and taught her how to do the hustle. Elizabeth wilted in relief in the kitchen, where they'd set up the production hub. She watched the playback screen as her show sparked to life. Inspired idea, really.

Devon approached her, snagging a canapé from a tray meant for the guests. "So far, so good."

Elizabeth kept her eyes on the monitor. "I promised you ratings gold. And I deliver on my promises."

"So you keep saying." He swallowed the appetizer, then stepped between her and the monitor. "But this Goody Two-shoes act can't last. Not if we want to keep our viewers. They're expecting catfights. Backstabbing. And gossip galore about what's really going on behind the cameras." He glanced back at the monitor. "That's what sells."

"Romance sells. Not smut. But somehow we've forgotten that." She nudged him aside as she watched Rick talking to a few of the women at the edge of the room. They looked young. Happy. Their whole lives ahead of them. "Bob liked keeping it dirty, and the show suffered. We're trying something new."

"We'll see how long the audience buys the Osmond-family vibe before turning on you." He snatched a couple more appetizers. "I'm going back to the hotel."

"You can depend on me, Devon." She turned back to the monitor. "They're going to love Rick. And everything he is."

He grunted in response and left the room, followed by a handful of his assistants who told him what he wanted to hear.

That was fine. She was going to make great television by giving America a bachelor who could run for president if he wanted. A man of character. Integrity. And she'd do it without stooping to the dirty tricks her predecessor had tried. Good television didn't have to mean playing to the lowest common denominator. It could mean showing the best of what the human race had to offer.

While she dreamed quixotically of a better future for pop culture, Rick entered the room. "I think we have a problem. Mr. Jackson's heart stopped."

RICK RAN BACK into the hall with Lizzie close behind him. One of the young women kneeled on the floor next to Mr. Jackson. "Harry, can you hear me?" She checked his vitals and glanced up at them. "He's unresponsive."

Rick marveled at her quick response to help. "You're a doctor?"

"Labor and delivery nurse." The blonde in the navy evening gown began compressions. "Never thought my medical training would come in handy here. Told myself that doing the show would be a nice break." She paused and started to blow into Mr. Jackson's mouth.

Rick kneeled beside her and watched for his chest to move. "What can I do?"

"Time my compressions." She glanced behind them at the wall of people and turned to Lizzie. "Think you can get them to give us some room?"

Lizzie nodded and started crowd control while Rick watched this amazing woman will the old man back to life. She closed her mouth around his and blew air into his lungs. Paused. Blew again. And sighed when the man started breathing on his own.

Mr. Jackson looked up at her. "Are you an angel?"

The young woman shook her head, but Rick had to disagree. He found himself grinning at her.

She moved slightly out of the way as paramedics entered the room with a gurney. Rick stood and held his hand out to her and helped her to her feet.

Here's a woman any man could fall for without hesitation.

"I'm Rick."

"I know. I'm Melissa."

He leaned in closer. "Are you sure it's not Missy?"

She blushed and looked down at the floor. It only made her look more lovely. "Only my dad calls me that."

Rick held out his hand to her again. "Well, Missy, it's an absolute pleasure to meet you."

The moment broke when the paramedics moved them so they could take Mr. Jackson out to the waiting ambulance. Rick watched, debating whether he should go with them. He turned back to Melissa. "I think I should..." He motioned to the door.

She nodded. "You'll let me know how he is."

Rick leaned over and kissed her cheek. "You betcha."

ELIZABETH NURSED a coffee that had long grown cold as she waited in the emergency room lobby for word on Mr. Jackson. A slight dip in the Naugahyde sofa told her Rick had joined her. He sighed. "Some night, huh?"

She nodded and kept her focus on the television tuned to the late show. "We made the eleven o'clock broadcast."

"Already? But it just happened."

Elizabeth shrugged and took a sip of coffee. Shivered at the bitterness. "It happened on live television." Her phone buzzed on the sofa between them. "That's been going off the hook ever since."

Rick picked up the phone and glanced at the caller ID. "It's a local number."

"You could answer it and give them a quote." She turned and finally looked at him. His tie was loosened and askew. His hair looked as if he'd run his hands through it more than once. He looked rumpled. Exactly the way she felt. "They're going to want to know why it took us eleven minutes to get an ambulance. Why we continued to film as a man fought for his life."

Rick groaned and ran his hands through his hair. "I didn't think of the cameras. I was focused on helping Harry."

"That's a great sound bite, but you should be prepared for some backlash." Elizabeth rose to her feet and walked to the trash can to toss her coffee cup inside. She turned back to Rick. "I couldn't have planned what happened. I couldn't have known…"

Rick approached her and placed a hand on her shoulder. "No one could have."

"But I should have. It's my job to prepare for the unknown." She wrapped her arms around her middle. "Tonight I failed."

Rick leaned down to look directly into her eyes. "Mr. Jackson is going to live. That's what's important here. He's going to get another chance."

"Through no fault of my own." She walked back to the sofa and collapsed on it. She rested her neck on the back and shook her head from side to side. "I should have known. I should have—"

"Don't get stuck on the should haves, Lizzie. Stop beating up on yourself." Rick took a seat next to her and held her hand in his. "You did good."

"By casting a nurse?" She shivered again. "My job is not to just produce this show. It's to protect it. At all costs. When you mentioned the nursing home, I should have planned all contingencies. Instead I got caught up on…" She glanced at him. "I wanted to find the perfect wife for you."

Rick gave her a tiny shrug. "Maybe you did."

Already? Elizabeth raised one eyebrow. He certainly hadn't wasted any time. "The nurse?"

"Missy."

She nodded. "She's cute. Sweet. Obviously good at her job." Elizabeth peered at him. "So I'm guessing she'll get the first immunity charm?"

"What can I say? I'm a sucker for a woman who can bring men back to life." He shrugged and leaned back on the sofa. "I'm only sorry we missed the first elimination tonight. Seemed kind of anticlimactic after the medical drama."

"We'll film it tomorrow and air it on our episode next week." She glanced over at the discarded clipboard. "Of course, it makes chaos out of my schedule, but…"

"You going to be okay now?"

She nodded slowly. "Mr. Jackson will be okay. You've found a possible wife already. And my job just got more interesting. What more could I want?"

AFTER THE PREVIOUS night's excitement, the dinner preceding the elimination ceremony seemed tame. Rick mingled among the women, looking into each one's eyes and asking himself if they should stay or go.

The cameras were everywhere, but he tried to ignore them. Better that he concentrate on other things. Like what the petite brunette was saying. "You were really great the last time you were on the show, right? And so I told my mom, 'I gotta meet this hunk.' And here I am."

Rick raised his eyebrows at that. "Hunk?"

The woman blushed and looked down at her hands. "Well, how else would you describe yourself?"

"You're very kind. Thanks." Give her a point for flattery. "So what is it you do in the real world, Becky?"

"I was a teacher before the layoffs."

Rick listened to her talk about how hard it had been. He'd seen enough of that in his town. He'd been fortunate to be born into a family that had become the largest employer in the county. Blessed enough to have inherited his job even after losing his baseball dreams. "It's hard out there."

"Things happen for a reason, though." She shrugged. "Maybe I had to lose my job so I could be free to come here."

Rick felt a shiver of unease. Blame the economy. Or loss of education funding. But don't use him as an excuse. Too much pressure.

A second woman joined them, followed by

a third. Soon he found himself surrounded by a group of beautiful women, only half of whose names he could remember. He glanced across the room and saw Missy watching them. He winked at her and smiled as she blushed. Maybe being the bachelor in charge of this game wasn't so bad.

"BEING THE BACHELOR is hard." Rick frowned at Elizabeth, who scratched another name off her clipboard. "I don't want to hurt any of these women. They're beautiful. Smart. Funny. But they're going to think something is wrong with them if I send them home."

"You're doing fine." She consulted the list. "You've got two more to reject."

Rick groaned and winced. "Exactly. They'll think I'm rejecting them. Think of what I'm doing to their psyches."

"You need to dial back on some of this melodrama, Mr. Allyn. They just met you." She glanced at the crew gathered in the garage of the home where they filmed. She'd spent days converting it into a production room but had failed to consider it wasn't insulated. She shivered and drew her parka tighter around her. "You click with some people and not others. That's how it goes."

"I hate to disappoint them." He peered

at the board with the women's pictures and names while she wondered what he was thinking.

"They'll get over it." She tapped her clipboard. "Two more."

He turned back to Elizabeth, his eyes bright. *Uh-oh.* She knew that look. "Couldn't we do a game and send the losers home?"

She shook her head. "And here I thought you wanted more control."

"I know." He read the names over and pointed to two of them. "I don't think I said two words to either of them." He sighed as if a burden had been lifted. "Now can I go back to my dessert?"

Elizabeth laughed, glad that the hard part was over. "Yes, it's your reward for being a good bachelor."

Rick glanced around the garage. "I'll stay out here for another minute, though."

Was he crazy? Stay out here in the cold? *Seriously. What is going on in his head?* "Don't want to face your adoring crowd?"

"More like wanting a few moments off camera." He shrugged. "Five years makes you forget what it's like to always be onstage. That everything you say and do is being recorded."

She sighed, relieved in a way that it wasn't

more serious. "Take your time, Rick. My crew is filming stuff for filler anyway."

Rick took a seat in her director's chair. "Any drama going on in the houses yet?"

They'd had plenty, and it hadn't been a week yet. The two houses she'd rented were side by side, allowing the women to move back and forth. And some to move again after roommate conflicts began. She crossed her arms across her chest. "I told you that we'd have some with only two bathrooms per house to split between them."

Rick laughed. "I'd love to see that."

"Well, you'll have to wait until it airs along with the audience." She pulled him up to his feet and pushed him toward the door. "Enough stalling. Enjoy your dessert. Then let's send some of them home."

He saluted her. "Fine. You are the boss."

And he'd better not forget it. She chuckled as he returned to the living room.

DESSERT ARRIVED, and they took that with coffee in the great room rather than being confined to their chairs in the dining room. Rick took the opportunity to mingle, smiling and laughing as he darted from one group to another.

He settled himself near the fireplace, mostly

because it was the one corner that was warm. Melissa, in a blue shiny dress, walked toward him. "Could we go outside for a moment?" she asked.

He nodded, then reached out and touched her bare shoulder. "Do you have a coat?"

She glanced around the room. "Not sure where it is right now."

Rick shrugged out of his coat and gave it to her. He opened the door to the patio, where fairy lights lit up the bare trees, and stepped outside. Even with his coat, the woman shivered, so Rick put his arm around her.

She looked up at him. "You really are a gentleman."

It was the way he'd been raised. Always put the other person ahead of yourself.

They sat on a stone bench after Rick wiped off the snow with one hand. He crossed his arms mostly to keep his warmth from completely escaping. He turned to Melissa. "You wanted to talk to me alone?" She shook slightly, her teeth chattering. He put both arms around her. "Is that better?"

"I wanted to let you know I'm here for the right reasons." She leaned in closer to him. "I'm not here for my career. Or to get publicity." She looked up into his face, and he could see the sincerity. "I saw the other show, and

I always felt you didn't deserve to be treated that way."

Rick took the chance to give her more than a passing glance. Her blond hair was cut short and sassy. Her eyes were deep brown pools that shone with trust and sincerity. And she had a small, compact body that told him she took care of herself. He rubbed her arm. "I'm glad you came out here with me, Melissa. I've wanted to talk to you since last night."

She laid her head on his shoulder. "It was pretty crazy."

"I already know you save lives, but what else do you do in your spare time?"

They shared a laugh. Rick thought he could use some of that in his life. Not that his life was joyless or lonely. He had friends. Family. The diner. But he wouldn't mind adding more laughter. Wasn't that part of the reason he was doing all this?

He squeezed her closer. "I hope you want to stay here for a while."

Melissa looked up at him. "I'd like that."

ELIZABETH SHOOK HER HEAD and made notes on her clipboard. She glanced behind her and saw Devon. "I think we found one of our finalists," he said.

"We'll see how it goes." She looked back

at the monitor and continued writing ideas to expand on later when she had some time.

Devon glared at her until she turned back to her notes. "Make sure she stays. They've got chemistry. And I want her in the final three, if not the finale. Got it?"

"We promised Rick that he would choose who moved on and who got sent home." She looked up. "You approved the contract yourself, so you know I can't make him do anything."

Devon leaned in closer to her. She tried not to flinch. "Looks like he trusts you. I'm sure there are ways you could influence him."

Elizabeth frowned. "What does that mean?"

"Am I the only one who thinks he shows chemistry with more than just Melissa?" Devon picked up his jacket from the back of the director's chair. "He likes you, so use it."

She shook her head. "I'm not going to use my friendship to get you what you want."

"You're on thin ice, Elizabeth. I'm not the only one who's noticed you're losing your edge with this one." He shrugged into the jacket and walked closer to her. "Prove to me you haven't lost it."

Elizabeth scowled and returned her gaze to the monitor, where she could see Rick returning to the house and chatting with a group of three women. Jumping through Devon's hoops was growing old. But she'd do it. Because what would she have without this job?

RICK STOOD AT THE FRONT of the room while the women gathered in groups of two and three. He had made a mental list of who would stay, but at the moment he couldn't recall a single name. The cameras ran, recording every word, every movement.

He hated this part of the show.

As a contestant, he'd waited to hear Brandy call his name. Waited to see if she felt the same connection he felt with her. Dreaded going home. Hoped he'd stay.

Now as the bachelor, he hated to dash anyone's dreams. Hated to be the one who would crush them by not calling their name. Dreaded the moment when he'd see the light of hope in their eyes fade.

He held twenty necklaces in his hand. Twenty women who would stay and continue to try to win his heart. Twenty chances to find love in the next three months.

He wiped his forehead. Denise, the makeup artist, added extra powder to his skin with her large pouf. "Sorry. I guess I'm more nervous than I thought."

She gave him a soft smile and continued

putting powder on his face. "Just breathe. You'll be fine."

He turned to Lizzie, who stood at the back of the room. He motioned for her to come talk to him. When she reached his side, he shook his head. "I'm not sure about my list now."

"Yes, you are. You just don't want to send anyone home." She brought up her clipboard and reviewed each name with him. "Can we do this now? You're wasting film."

He nodded and tried to swallow. Found it hard to breathe. He tugged at his tie, but Lizzie slapped his hands away. "Relax. You don't have connections with these four. It's not a judgment against them. It's just the way it is."

"They'll hate me."

"No, they won't." She smoothed his tie. "You bond with some people, not others. Fact of life." She put her hands on his shoulders and shook him slightly. "Let's do this. Like a bandage. Rip it off quick, okay?"

He nodded. She retreated to the back of the room as he cleared his throat. "Ladies, I appreciate your patience." He glanced down at the necklaces with heart charms, each one representing a possible future. "Melissa."

She stepped away from the group and approached him. He held up the necklace. "Will you accept my heart?"

"With pleasure." She dipped her head as he put the necklace around her neck. She kissed his cheek, then returned to the group.

The first necklace had been given out. With each name called, each necklace given out, the task became easier until he only had one in his hand. He glanced around the room and noticed the five women who still had bare necks. They shifted their weight. Looked at the others who already had a necklace with a bit of envy. Or kept their eyes on the floor so he couldn't see the hurt.

He held up the last necklace. "Mona."

A tall, willowy blonde approached him with a smirk. Almost as if to say she had known all along he'd pick her. "Mona, will you accept my heart?"

"Absolutely."

Rick placed the necklace around her neck. He leaned forward to kiss her cheek, but she turned and kissed him full on the mouth. Unexpected. But…kinda nice. He let his eyes drift closed for a moment.

Then stepped back. "Thanks."

Mona winked at him and returned to the group. Rick looked between those who hadn't received a necklace. "You are all beautiful and smart. And I'm sorry we didn't have a connection."

The four going home said their goodbyes and left in the waiting limousines; their luggage was already packed and loaded. Once they left, Rick handed out drinks to the twenty women who remained. He lifted his glass. "Here's to developing friendships. And finding love."

CHAPTER SEVEN

THE SPORTS COMPLEX buzzed with excitement. The regular patrons walked to the changing rooms but craned their necks to get a look at the celebrity surrounded by cameras and beautiful women dressed in softball uniforms. Elizabeth rolled her shoulders and tried to crack the tension out of her neck. She felt warm fingers trying to massage it instead.

"How did the premiere do?"

She closed her eyes and savored the feel of Rick's hands on her neck. It felt really good. She could stay like this all morning if she let herself.

Instead, she shrugged off his hands. "Shouldn't you be getting ready for the game?" She consulted the clipboard and checked off names as more women joined them from the changing rooms.

"Why? I'm not playing." He dropped his hands and walked around to face her. "Are they all here? No one dropped out because of our low ratings?"

"Who told you we got low ratings?" Elizabeth shook her head and muttered to herself. "I don't even have the numbers yet. How did the crew get them already?"

"It was a joke, Lizzie. Relax." He glanced at the cameras that pointed to the floor since they were turned off for the moment. "I don't have to be on-screen during the game, right?"

"We need reaction shots, so yeah, there will be a camera on you. But no microphone." She tapped her earpiece. "Okay, they're ready for us. Now, remember, if there's anyone on the losing team that you want to keep, just tell me. We'll make a deal or something."

Rick frowned. "That's not what we agreed to. Winning team gets immunity for the next elimination. Period."

She tried to keep the sarcasm out of her voice. "And what if Melissa is on the losing team?"

Rick smiled. "I think she's going to be around for a while. Don't you?"

Her bachelor was finding his match. Elizabeth should be thrilled. So why was part of her feeling anxious at the thought? Something to think about later. She glanced at Rick. *Much later*.

Rick flexed his muscles and rolled his

neck. "I don't think I'm sleeping very well. Are you?"

What kind of a question was that? "I'm sleeping fine. Why aren't you?"

"This finding a wife business is intense." He shrugged his shoulders. "And I'm having the strangest dreams. In fact, you were in my dream last night."

Elizabeth gulped and felt her cheeks burn. "Why are you dreaming about me?"

"It wasn't about you. But you were in it." Rick looked at the group of women. "I dreamed that I was on an auction block, and they were all bidding on me."

"Did I bid on you, too?"

Rick laughed and shook his head. "Oh, no. You were the auctioneer." He shrugged. "Guess it's not too far from reality, huh?"

"You've got more input than being sold to the highest bidder." She took a step closer and placed her hand on his shoulder. "This has to be about you and your choices. No one is pressuring you on who to keep around."

He dipped his head and glanced at her sideways. "You sure about that?"

She swallowed. Held her clipboard tight to her chest. "Positive." She patted him on the shoulder. "And don't let anyone talk you out of it. Not even me."

"Thanks." He left her and walked toward the field, where the game would be played.

Ignoring her confusing feelings, she strode into the midst of the chattering women. "Okay. Listen up. We're playing slow-pitch softball. Pinks versus greens. Three innings. Winners get to have dinner at Rick's diner plus immunity in the next elimination. Questions?" She glanced around quickly and, seeing no hands, blew her whistle. "I'll meet you on the field."

RICK SAT IN the bleachers while the teams took their places. He leaned back and tried to get comfortable. It was different sitting in the stands when he'd rather be out in the field. Made him restless. Not that he didn't watch sports. Most of his evenings were spent watching televised games or highlights from them. But he would much rather be the one playing.

Lizzie walked up to the bleachers to where he sat, then continued up two rows past his seat. He'd noticed how some of the contestants treated her as if she was some kind of interloper. He cupped his hands around his mouth. "Come on, girls."

"That isn't sexist at all."

He turned and smiled at her. "I can't exactly play favorites, so I'm cheering them all on."

She kept her eyes on her clipboard, punching things into her cell phone at the same time. Didn't she get confused working like that? "Do you love her?"

He didn't have to ask who she meant. "I don't know her enough yet. But I plan on spending a lot more time with her."

She looked up at him. "You want her to have the first one-on-one?"

He winked at her. "Oh, definitely. And make it superromantic. Over-the-top. You know. Flowers. Music. Good food. The kind of stuff you guys are known for." He looked back to the field as the first woman got up to bat. "And I want a group date, too. I need to get to know more of them better. I'm blanking on half their names."

He could hear the scratch of her pen as she made notes. "What did your mom say about the first night?"

He chuckled at the words his mom had used in describing some of the women. "She has her favorites already, but she's a good judge of character. That's why I wanted her to help me."

"Devon said the viewers like how the family is involved this time around."

Rick frowned and turned back to face her. "When did he find that out? We just aired."

"Hollywood works fast. He called me ten minutes ago with the numbers." She returned to her clipboard and made notations. Didn't look at him. "They're good."

He grimaced. "But not great."

"Do you care?"

He shrugged and turned his attention back to the game. If they wanted his reaction shots, he'd have to actually pay attention. "I know you care. What matters to me is that I meet the right woman."

"You met Melissa."

He considered this. He'd met each of the women for at least five minutes, but what could you tell in that amount of time? Sure, Melissa had intrigued him from the start. He wasn't ready to propose, but he wouldn't mind getting to know her better. See if she could be the right woman. "It's early."

She nodded. "Bachelor Kevin knew the first night which woman he would propose to."

"And how did that end? Right. He dumped her for an actress." He shook his head. "I hope I've learned some things since my last appearance. And I've been watching replays of the previous seasons. Trying to figure out what worked. What didn't."

She cocked her head to the side and peered at him. "Why?"

"It's kind of like a coach watching film of last week's game. Creating strategy for the next one." He clapped his hands, then cupped his mouth. "C'mon, batter."

Lizzie sighed and walked back down the bleachers, where she conferred with her camera operators when the umpire called the last out. The game with immunity at stake had been his idea. A way to spur competition.

He needed to make this time around different. He had to do this right. Had to do the right things to earn not only his true love but acceptance. From the television audience. From his family.

From Lizzie.

ELIZABETH KNEW NEXT to nothing about sports, but she knew what a score meant. The winning team jumped up and down, congratulating each other, while the losers looked dejected, some even pointing fingers at who had caused the loss. She approached them first. This was time to take care of business. Maybe even soothe some bruised egos. "Ladies, I'm sorry. We have a shuttle to take you back to the house, where dinner will be ready. This means you'll be at risk of going home at the next elimination. Again, I'm sorry."

She glanced around the team and sighed when she didn't see Melissa. At least one thing had gone right today. The ratings, however, told her that this was going to be an uphill struggle. They'd been good. Twelve million people had tuned in for the premiere, but they'd lost almost half of the audience after the first hour.

Why had they lost interest? Rick was a good guy. And a good-looking one to boot. He charmed not only the contestants but the audience. What had happened to make things fizzle? Was Devon right and the Goody Two-shoes act couldn't keep interest?

She made sure the losing team hit the showers first, then turned to talk to her winners. Well, Rick's winners. They still celebrated as she approached them and blew a whistle that made even the most ardent hockey fan wince. "Congratulations, ladies. Each of you has made it to the next phase of the competition. We're going to go over the schedule for the next few days. Then Rick will come over and offer his congratulations."

A hand shot up in the back. "Will there be immunity challenges all season?"

Elizabeth smiled. Obviously a fan of the show. "Yes. Rick will form favorites during the next few weeks, but this is to be a competition where hearts are at stake." Man, that sounded cheesy. Like reading from her own promotional copy. She cleared her throat. "After showers and changing, we'll meet at Rick's diner for an early dinner. You'll have free time until Tuesday night's group date. One lucky woman will have the first one-on-one date with Rick Monday afternoon. A box will arrive with her name tomorrow."

She started marking off items with her pen. "Feel free to use your off time to get to know the area. After all, you could end up married to Rick and living here. I have a list of church services if anyone is interested. Also lists of restaurants and shops. A shuttle will be available for a shopping trip tomorrow afternoon. Sign up on the board in the kitchen. Any other questions?"

Seeing no hands, she turned and motioned to Rick, who joined them on the field. He grinned widely and gave high fives to the victors. "That was a great game. Now huddle up." He motioned for them all to come in shoulder to shoulder and place their hands in

the center. "On three, we'll shout 'True love.'
Okay? One. Two. Three."

"True love!"

Even Elizabeth warmed.

CHAPTER EIGHT

RICK DOUBLE-CHECKED his ski equipment and waited. There was always a lot of waiting when filming a television show, even if the shoot took place on a snow-covered hill at the ski resort one town over. This one-on-one date plan had been Lizzie's. His choice had been tickets to a Detroit Pistons game, but this was still good. He liked skiing. Usually.

A woman dressed in pink attempted to ski toward him, but fell about halfway there. He rushed to help her to her feet again. "Sorry." Melissa looked up into his face. "I've never done this before."

"Then I'm glad I can teach you." He looked over at the crew Lizzie had sent with them. She herself was conveniently absent. Wasn't she supposed to oversee everything on this shoot? Even his first one-on-one date? They hadn't started filming yet, which gave him a few moments truly alone with his date.

Rick helped Melissa adjust the ski poles. "Did they go over everything with you? The microphone? The cameras?" She nodded but bit her lip. He put his hand on her shoulder to reassure her. "Don't worry. Like I said, I'll teach you. We're going to start on the bunny hill."

He helped her move her legs back and forth so that she had forward movement without falling on her face again. He liked that she wasn't afraid to try new things or even to fail. He might have balked at skiing for the first time on television, but Melissa was a good sport.

With cameras rolling, they spent an hour on the bunny hill until she felt comfortable enough to try something more challenging. Rick led her to the chairlift. As they rose into the sky, a camera operator turned in the seat ahead of them and filmed. He got the hint.

He leaned in closer to her. "So why did you decide to try out for the show?"

Melissa snagged a piece of hair away from her mouth. "I'm from a little town in Tennessee. Everyone in my town is either related by blood or marriage. Not many prospects, you know?"

Did he ever. That was one of the reasons he'd done this himself. "But why *True Love?*"

"My mom's a huge fan." She snuggled

into his side, either for warmth or something more, he didn't know. "It was her idea."

"Well, I'm glad you came." He rested his head on hers. "I think you're the first woman I've really connected with."

She tightened her grip and leaned closer. He cleared his throat and faced forward again. "After the last time—"

Melissa placed a hand on his arm. "You don't have to talk about it."

"I probably should. Good for the soul and all that." He glanced at her. "It's taken me over five years to get to the point where I'm open to letting someone in. Brandy…she…" He shrugged even though the camera probably couldn't see it through the layers of warm clothing. "I wanted to believe her. Wanted to trust that she loved me like I loved her."

Why was he going to that place? Hadn't he spent more than five years blocking it out? It was this show. It got to him. Made him think things, feel things. He shook his head and pulled Melissa closer. "I'm glad to have a second chance."

"There's something to be said for starting over." She rested her head on his shoulder.

Rick placed a kiss on the top of her fuzzy hat. "When we get up to the top here, we're going to push off the chair and to the right, okay?"

She nodded, and the spell of the snow and cold was broken. Rick settled farther into the chair. This was going to be okay.

ELIZABETH HURRIED to make sure all the details at the ski lodge were ready before Rick and Melissa arrived. She'd rented out the entire second floor so that they could have some privacy. A fire crackled in the fireplace. Huge overstuffed pillows were placed in front of it. Dozens of red and pink candles flickered. A vase of red and pink roses graced the dining table, where two place settings waited for an intimate dinner. It looked perfect.

So why was she still searching for flaws?

Elizabeth shook her head and consulted the clipboard that seemed to be glued to her hand lately. Even last night when she'd woken from her dream, she'd looked at her hand as if expecting her notes to be there, to tell her what to do next...every moment of her life laid out in black-and-white.

She sighed, wishing she had that kind of control. She tapped her earpiece. "How far out are they?"

"They're on the lift. You've got five minutes, give or take."

She nodded and checked everything again. It looked perfect.

Charlie had set up three cameras to capture the first intimate look at Rick. The one-on-one was more than him singling out a woman who might show up in the finale. It was about letting the audience in, as well. Giving them a taste of who he was and what he wanted.

She turned to Charlie. "We've got four minutes. What am I missing?"

Her cameraman chuckled and tested light levels once more. "I thought you never missed a thing."

"I don't because I ask my crew what I'm forgetting." She looked around the room. "If I was Melissa, would I fall under the spell of this room?"

"It looks perfect, E."

"Exactly. Looks, but doesn't feel." They couldn't pipe in music because that would interfere with editing later. They couldn't serve seafood because Melissa was allergic. She thrived on the couldn'ts of a shoot because she had to get creative. So why wasn't she feeling it this time? What was this scene missing?

Her.

Elizabeth turned as if someone had spoken. She shook her head. She was already losing it, and they still had twelve weeks of shooting and editing, then the live finale in Los Angeles in May. She tapped her earpiece. "How much longer?"

"Relax. They're heading up the stairs now."

She positioned herself in the back, and Charlie stood with a handheld camera near the entrance so they could film the couple's first reactions to the room. Everything was going according to plan.

So far.

Rick entered the room with Melissa, who made the appropriate oohs and aahs. Cliché, but Elizabeth would take it. Being a gentleman, Rick helped Melissa slip out of her coat and scarves, hat and mittens. He even held out a chair for her after they'd taken a tour of the room. Chivalry wasn't dead after all.

Servers immediately appeared with the first course, a steaming vegetable soup to warm the couple from the icy elements. From where she stood, it smelled wonderful. Her stomach growled, and she made a note to order a sandwich in a little bit. If she didn't write it down, she'd never remember.

Melissa reached for her soupspoon and took a tentative sip. "Wow."

Rick snapped his napkin open, laying it in his lap. "They have amazing chefs here."

Elizabeth closed her eyes and pushed her head against the wall. Sure, the couple had chemistry. Even mirrored each other's movements, which was a good sign. But chemistry only went so far. Elizabeth stepped forward. "Cut."

Rick and Melissa looked up at her as if just realizing they were being filmed. Good, but she didn't have time to revel in the fact that they were being natural in front of the cameras. She walked to the table and crouched between the two of them. The smell of the soup still did things to her stomach, but she concentrated on the task at hand. "The audience wants to see something special here. Give them a glimpse of yourself that you usually don't show anyone."

Rick chuckled. "What happened to being natural?"

"Your courtship is condensed into three months. We don't have time for natural." Elizabeth leaned in toward both of them. "Our audience expects to see romance. Sparks. Drama. And it's our job to give it to them."

Rick glanced around the room. "And this isn't romantic enough? All we're missing are winged cupids shooting arrows."

Melissa giggled at this while Elizabeth

rolled her eyes. "Great idea, but out of our budget. I'm being serious."

"So am I, Lizzie."

He dropped his spoon on the table, and it clattered to the floor. Elizabeth picked it up and handed it to one of the servers, who replaced it with a clean spoon. "I'm not asking the impossible here."

Rick thanked the server, then turned back to her. "All I'm saying is that I wouldn't do this in real life."

"Since when has reality TV been about real life?" She shook her head. "Rick, you need to give the audience a reason to care. Because right now? They're turning the channel to see what else is on."

"My love life is not for their viewing pleasure."

Elizabeth chuckled. "You're on *True Love,* so yeah, it is. You signed the contract. You made promises. Let me do my job."

Rick seemed to bristle slightly at this, but his calm composure took over. "You're right, Lizzie." He stood. "I need five minutes."

He pushed past her and out of the room. Once he was gone, she turned to Melissa. "When Rick comes back, tell him what you're hoping this show will bring into your life.

Show him the woman you are and the woman you want to be. Okay?"

Melissa nodded and turned in her seat to look in the direction Rick had gone. "Is he okay?"

"Don't worry. It's not you. It's me." She gave the other woman a reassuring smile, then walked off to find Rick. She waited outside the restroom door until he came out. He seemed surprised to see her.

"Can I have a moment?" she asked.

He crossed his arms over his chest and glanced around the hallway. "No cameras?"

"I told them to take a five-minute break." She sighed. "What's going on here?"

"Nothing's going on." He held up his arms so that they spanned the space around him. "I've given you complete access to my life. You're the one trying to manipulate this competition."

"It's my job to take care of the details. To create an atmosphere that invites intimacy and romance. All the things you asked for." She consulted her clipboard. "Candles. Flowers. Romantic meal. Check. Check. Check. What's your problem?"

Rick opened his mouth, then shut it. Closed his eyes and groaned. "I've been here. I've done this. And I believed it was all true. Only to find it wasn't."

"Melissa is not Brandy." He stopped fidgeting. Elizabeth stepped closer and put her hand on his shoulder. Now it made sense. Her star didn't want to get hurt again. "Is that what this is about? Don't let your past dictate your present."

"Okay, Oprah."

He joked with her, but he didn't appear any more relaxed. Elizabeth leaned in closer. "What can I do to make this easier for you?"

"I wish you could make guarantees, but…"

"I'll do my best." She gave him a quick hug. "I'll protect you as best I can, okay? Trust me."

She could feel him swallow. After a long moment, he nodded. "Okay. Tantrum over. Can I go back to my dinner? I'm starving."

He started to leave her, then turned back. "Thanks, Lizzie. You're a good friend." He returned to the dining cove.

Elizabeth took a moment to calm her nerves. Her heart beat at an alarming rate; her cheeks and chest burned. If she didn't know better, she'd think she was having a heart attack. Instead she inhaled deeply and returned to the room.

Charlie put up a finger and motioned to

the table where the couple sat. *Good.* They'd started filming without her. Melissa was telling Rick about her dreams for the future, which she hoped might include him.

AFTER THE FILMING, a car took Melissa and some of the crew back to the house. Lizzie lingered, settling up with the manager of the ski lodge while Charlie waited at the SUV. Lizzie handed the manager a check and turned to find Rick waiting by the front door, where it was warm. She sighed. "Did you need something else? Because I'm beat and looking forward to a long, hot bath. Room service. And some TV."

A vision of her bare shoulders rising above a tub full of bubbles, damp tendrils of hair clinging to her neck, flashed through his mind. He shook his head and held up his hands in innocence. "Only wanted to thank you for earlier."

She shrugged. "All part of my job. Good night."

He stepped in front of her and blocked the doorway. "There is something I wanted to talk to you about."

She closed her eyes and threw her head back. "I just want today to be over. Is that too much to ask?"

When she started walking past him, Rick reached out and grabbed her hand. "Lizzie. Please."

She stopped and turned to face him. "You have twenty seconds."

"I wanted to say I'm sorry." He looked at her, waiting. "Now is where you say you're sorry, too."

"I really don't have time for this." She walked past him, so he followed her outside.

"You can't try to make me feel things for these women. It doesn't matter how you manipulate the scene or try to invite intimacy." He hurried to catch up to her. "I thought about what we talked about earlier. I want to know it's real and not fabricated for television." He stopped walking and threw his hands in the air. "What do you want from me?"

She stopped, turned and walked back to him. "The real question is, what do you want from me? All I'm asking is that you hold up your end of the deal. Go on these dates. Keep your options open, but don't close yourself off to the possibility that you might meet the woman you're supposed to be with. And let me do my job."

"Not when you're going back on what we agreed."

She pointed at him, slashing the air with

her finger. "We agreed that you would have more input. Not complete control."

He took the few steps that separated them and looked at her. Really looked at her until he thought he was going to implode and cease to exist. The line between friendship and something more seemed to blur for just a moment. He swallowed. "Lizzie…"

She shook her head and walked away. Got in the SUV's passenger side. Didn't even glance in his direction as Charlie backed the car out and drove away.

He felt as if his best friend in the world was leaving. The confusing part was that his heart seemed to be going with her, too.

CHAPTER NINE

ICE FISHING was a logistical nightmare. The shack on ice barely held four people, and that didn't include a camera operator and sound crew. Elizabeth, however, could pull more than a rabbit out of an old hat. She had commissioned three shacks on the ice and a large heated tent on land for this group date. She had enough food to feed not only her cast and crew, but also the locals she'd hired to give authenticity to the scene.

This was going to be the best episode she'd produced.

Or the biggest disaster.

Luckily, the monitors for watching the taping were in the warmth of the tent. She made up a plate of chicken wings to eat while she took notes and barked out orders. Definitely the best part of her job.

She put her feet up on a chair across from her and groaned when someone stepped in front of the camera, where Rick baited hooks for some of the contestants. She tapped her earpiece. "Charlie, move that girl out of the way before I have to come in and do it myself."

He chuckled on the other end. "Why are you so grouchy?"

"I'm not. Just move her." The tension between her shoulder blades eased as the contestant moved.

"Problems, Ms. Maier?"

Elizabeth turned and bit back another groan. Couldn't she have peace for just a minute? "Dan, grab a plate of food and join me." She pushed a chair closer to him. He sat down and unbuttoned his long wool coat, looking every bit as if he'd stepped off the pages of a business magazine. "You're early."

"Thought I'd get the lay of the land, so to speak." He motioned to the monitors. "This is what the audience is seeing?"

"It's raw material before my editors and I cut it down to the most exciting parts." She wiped her fingers on a napkin. "The audience only gets to see about twelve hours of a total of more than a hundred that we shoot."

"So my appearance today…?"

Was he nervous? He didn't appear any different from his usual authoritative self. "Maybe five minutes."

Dan nodded and looked at his fingernails. "And the ad time we bought?"

She patted his arm. "Thirty seconds every episode, plus mentioned as a sponsor in the credits. And we're taping at the diner for several episodes."

"The diner isn't the business, okay? Mom gave Rick the diner, but Dad never meant it to be part of Allyn Pickles." He shook his head. "It's…a restaurant. Hardly a jewel in the company crown. More of a drain. I should probably just sell it."

"Doesn't Rick get any say in that?"

Dan stood and shrugged off his jacket. "Think I'll go check out the buffet."

She watched him leave. This sibling-rivalry drama would add some interest to the show. Help the audience to identify with Rick. She made a note on her clipboard and turned her attention back to the monitors. *Good.* They were having fun. Seeing Rick bait hooks reminded her of their own ill-fated fishing expedition. What would it be like to fish when there was no chance of capsizing?

Someone else entered the tent, pushing the flap aside and scanning the few people inside. The woman walked closer as Elizabeth frantically tried to recall why she looked familiar. She had long white-blond hair and wore a black peacoat with a bright pink beret. Sunglasses covered her eyes.

When she removed the glasses, Elizabeth gasped. *What in the world?* She approached Brandy. Ever the professional, Elizabeth stuck out her hand. "Good to see you again. Or should I say surprised."

Brandy shook hands with her and glanced around the tent. "Is Rick here?"

"Ice fishing on the lake." Elizabeth took a deep breath. "Forgive me for being blunt, but what are you doing here?"

The other woman shrugged. "I saw you were taping the show with Rick, and I thought I might be able to help you out or something."

Help them out with what? Adding to Rick's anxiety? Elizabeth shook her head. "Am I missing something? Did someone ask you to come here?"

Brandy turned her gaze back to Elizabeth. She frowned, marring her complexion slightly. "Mr. Scott contacted me last week. He didn't go over the details with you?"

Devon. Elizabeth frowned. "Sorry, Brandy, I need to make a quick call. Find out what's going on here." She stepped away for a moment, then tapped her earpiece. "Charlie, keep Rick out on the ice. I'm taking care of something back here. Got it?" The last thing she needed was for her star to see their new guest without preparing him. While it might make for good television, she'd promised to take care of Rick. And this time, she was going to keep her word.

With that done, she punched numbers into her cell phone. This was her show. Hers. And she wasn't giving up control to anyone.

Devon picked up on the first ring. "Did my surprise arrive?"

Elizabeth bit back a retort. "Did I miss the memo where this became your show instead of mine?"

He chuckled on the other end. "You said you welcomed ideas. Brandy's mine. And it's pretty fab, isn't it?"

Elizabeth closed her eyes and gritted her teeth. "Did Bob give you this kind of license?"

"You're not Bob."

No kidding. "Obviously. But I won't let you interfere with my job." She opened her eyes and focused on Brandy, who stood at the monitors. Was she hoping for a second chance with Rick? Or was there something more going on?

"Think about it. The old flame comes back to stir up what might have been five years ago? You brought back Rick. Why not

Brandy, too?" He chuckled again. "You want ratings gold? There it is."

She shook her head. Brandy returning would bump up their ratings. But at what cost? "Why didn't you consult with me first?"

"What's to consult? I hold the fate of your show in my hands." There was silence on the other end. "One word to the head of the studio, and we show repeats of our top-rated sitcom instead. Up to you, Elizabeth."

She took another look at Brandy. "I'll call you later."

Brandy looked around the tent, then turned her gaze back to Elizabeth. "Where is he?"

There was no way she was going to let this woman have access to Rick right now. Elizabeth had promised he could trust her. Brandy being there could ruin all that. "Why?"

The other woman looked down at her hands, which Elizabeth noted didn't have the mega-ring the show had bought for her other fiancé to give her. The engagement had lasted six weeks before a public breakup on the reunion show.

Brandy looked back up at her. "I want to apologize. Try to make him understand."

"What's there to understand? You chose someone else." Elizabeth stepped in front of the monitors. "Listen. I need time to figure this out." She gave Brandy a once-over. Five years had certainly been good to her. "Let's talk business for a bit."

Brandy tucked her hair behind her ear and nodded. "I really appreciate this chance. Mr. Scott even said if this doesn't work out for me, I could be the bachelorette again on *True Love*."

Of course he did. "Great." She put her hand on Brandy's elbow and moved them away from prying ears. "I'm thinking we'll do a dramatic reveal of your presence to the other women on the show. That way we get some great reaction shots. And that will make the audience take more notice of you. But Rick... I can't just spring you on him. I need time to prepare him for..." She sighed and glanced over her. "You."

Brandy nodded as Elizabeth made up plans off-the-cuff. Part of her job was being prepared for anything, but this definitely topped the list of surprises. "We'll have to keep you sequestered, away from the other contestants for a while. Problem is that this is a small town. Everyone knows everyone's business."

"She can stay at my mom's house. It's quiet. Remote." Dan approached them and straightened his coat. Brandy turned and seemed to lean closer to him. He gazed down into her face. "I'd be glad to keep her occupied."

Elizabeth shook her head. "You're going to be filming in a half hour."

He didn't look at her; he kept his focus on the other woman. "I can take her to my mom's now and be back in twenty minutes." He grinned wider as Brandy blushed and looked down. "Fifteen if the cop is on break."

One problem solved. Mostly. "Fine. Is that okay with you, Brandy?"

She nodded and glanced up at Dan, then back at the ground. "I wouldn't want to put you through any trouble."

He smiled at the top of Brandy's head. "No trouble at all."

Elizabeth rolled her eyes. This was worse than what she saw on her show. "Great. We'll meet later to go over any questions."

She watched them leave. She'd think about that complication later. She turned back to her crew. "Okay. Major changes coming, people. Let's stay flexible." She stretched her neck and rolled her shoulders. Stupid tension head-ache.

Two aspirin and a bottle of water later, she was ready for business. Dan even arrived ahead of schedule. The deputy must have been having lunch rather than monitoring the roads for speeders. Maybe, just maybe, things were getting better.

The question was, how was she going to tell Rick about this new development?

RICK WATCHED HIS BROTHER flit in and out of the gaggle of women, checking plates and beverage levels as if he was a born waiter. True, Dad had made them start working for their mom at the diner once they'd turned fourteen. Who knew that all those years of experience would return to Dan in only a few minutes?

Lizzie stayed on the fringes of the party, watching. For what, he wasn't sure. She had something on her mind. Not unusual for her, but whatever this was troubled her. He could tell by the way she kept her eye on him no matter where he was.

He turned back to the woman who was sharing a story of growing up in a small town with four older brothers. Nodded when he should. Laughed when it was appropriate. She was a nice enough girl, but not for him.

He turned and found Melissa in a group of four other women. He hadn't had a moment alone with her since their one-on-one date yesterday. And he wanted to see where it could lead. If the initial connection between them could turn into...something.

She raised her gaze to him, then winked.

He grinned back.

Lizzie stepped forward and clinked her champagne glass with a fork. "Ladies and gentleman." She glanced at Rick. "This concludes tonight's taping. The shuttle will be here to take you back to the house in a few minutes, but feel free to linger as long as you need to. Tomorrow's schedule is up at the house. We'll be leaving at eight sharp. Any questions?" She turned to Rick. "I need to talk to you." She glanced around the tent. "Alone."

Rick said good-night to the ladies, then joined Lizzie outside by the lakeshore. The moon shone down on the icy surface in muted silvery beams. The glow of lights from homes around the lake seemed swallowed up in the dark cold.

He observed Lizzie's back and cleared his throat. "You want to say whatever you've been holding back since we shot the ice-fishing scenes?"

She turned and opened her mouth, then abruptly shut it. "I don't know how to tell you except to just say it."

Possibilities flitted through his brain. "We've been canceled."

"No."

His shoulders sagged slightly, then tensed again. "You're fired?"

She laughed. "Don't get your hopes up just yet." She glanced at the sky. "Brandy's here."

Rick shrugged. "Brandy who?"

Lizzie stared at him until his stomach ached as if he'd been sucker punched. Which was exactly what it felt like. He bent over at the waist and rested his hands on his thighs. "Oh."

"Yeah. Oh. I didn't want to spring her on you even if that's what the suits expected. I thought you deserved to know first, so you can figure out what you want to do."

Rick tried to swallow but found it difficult with the lump growing in his throat. He hadn't signed up for this. Hadn't given them permission to play with his emotions. "Why?"

Elizabeth frowned. "Because I'm your friend. And your producer."

"I mean, why is she here?" Did that mean she still wanted him? That there was still something between them? He groaned. He'd given up on that, hadn't he? Five years was enough time to get over someone, right?

"Because the studio thinks it will add drama. Which means ratings." She took a step toward him. "What do you want to do?"

Rick gazed across the lake, then back at the tent. "What are my options?"

Lizzie closed the gap between them and waited until he looked back at her. "As your producer, it's my job to tell you that you need to get over yourself. That you signed on to do what we tell you."

Not what he wanted to hear. "And as my friend?"

She reached out and put her hand on the sleeve of his coat. "It's been over five years. Don't you want some closure? To finally shut the door on what happened?"

He wasn't sure what he wanted. Other than to run across the ice and get as far away as he could. Forget he signed on to a TV show. Start a new life being the man he'd always wanted to be. But he couldn't start with a fresh slate. His past was written on it in permanent marker, and maybe it was time to take a real look at it. "Why does she want to be here?"

"Devon's promised her her own show if things don't work out with you two."

Rick laughed. "Of course. I get a second shot, so why shouldn't she, right?" He ran his hands through his hair. The burning sensation in his gut intensified. "I never got a chance to find out why she chose him instead of me. Why everything we did turned out to be a lie." Lizzie nodded but didn't say anything. He gave a weak smile, then shrugged. "I don't want her to be here."

"I know."

He believed her. She'd promised to protect him. And she seemed as blindsided as he felt. "But it's not my choice," he said. "I gave that up when I signed your contract."

"True."

She wasn't helping him by letting him choose for himself. In a way, he wanted her to force him into a decision. Might make it easier if it all backfired later. He groaned. "How does she look?"

She shrugged. "Pretty much the same."

Which meant gorgeous. "Who else knows she's here?"

"The crew. Dan. Your mom."

Rick nodded and ignored the empty feeling in his stomach. "And they didn't tell me."

"Don't blame them. I asked to be the one." She held up a hand as if to stop his thoughts when he frowned at her. "It's my fault she's here, so why not be the one to tell you and take your anger?"

It wasn't anger. Not really. More like shock. And an old ache that hadn't healed completely. Maybe that was his answer. "It's not your idea she join us, so why is it your fault?"

"Because this is my show. And everything that happens here is my responsibility."

Rick laughed at her arrogance. "You're taking on an awful lot."

Lizzie shrugged. "It's my job. My life."

Rick sighed and reached toward her. "Lizzie, the show will never be your life."

"I'm executive producer, so you bet it is." The walls around her immediately rose up. He could see it in the way she took a step back and stood straighter. As if holding herself so stiff would make the universe fall under her control.

She didn't get it. "Your life is more than filmed bits that air on television."

"Are you talking as my friend or as my star?"

"It's all the same to me. I'll always be your friend."

Lizzie let out a long breath. "I was afraid that would change because of what I told you."

Rick took her hand in his. "That won't ever change. Friends always." They looked into each other's eyes until he got uncomfortable and glanced away. "All right. I'll do it."

Lizzie nodded. "So then we can bring Brandy on set?"

"Sure. Set up your big reveal." He toed the snow at his feet, turning it from pure white to muddy gray. She could have this, but he wanted something in return. "But I want five minutes with her. No mikes. No cameras. No crew." He looked up at her. "Not even you."

She was shaking her head before he had a chance to finish. "Rick, you know that I can't allow that."

He grinned and leaned in closer. "Not as my producer, no. But as my friend, you'll make sure I have it." He patted her shoulder. "Make it happen."

He didn't give her a chance to respond before he strode back into the tent. Dan walked up to him as soon as he entered. "Brandy's here."

A little too late, big brother. "You should have told me that before."

Dan glanced out at the lake, where Lizzie still stood at the shore. "What are you going to do?"

Rick straightened the lines of his coat. "What's expected. Like I always do."

THE YIPS AND HOWLS of the Lake Mildred Animal Refuge filled the sound track of the show as Rick led his harem into the renovated tire factory. Russell Tires had once been the largest supplier to the Big Three, but it had lain vacant for years until being repurposed. Another sign of the changing economy.

Elizabeth gathered the group around her and held up her hand until everyone quieted. "I've already had several questions about why we're here and not doing a shoot at a more glamorous location." She took the time to look at several of the women. "Rick wants you to get to know his community. By volunteering you'll not only be giving something back to this town, you'll also get a better idea of what life with Rick is like." She held up her clipboard. "I've got you all assigned into one of four teams. You'll each be given a particular task this morning here at the shelter. Feeding, cleaning, walking, whatever. Rick will move between the groups. Any questions?"

One woman raised her hand. "What if we're allergic?"

Already planned. "You're assigned to the front office to answer phones and help with filing. Anyone else?" Seeing no hands, she nodded at her crew. "Okay, we've got a camera assigned to each team. But let's remember why we're here. Volunteers are scarce, and these animals need your love and attention."

She handed out assignment sheets, then watched as everyone did as planned. Cameras whirred. Women chatted. Dogs pranced around at the attention.

Rick approached her, and she grimaced. He looked haggard. "Didn't get much sleep? Still having strange dreams?"

"More like nightmares." He chuckled and attempted to put the microphone on under his sweater. "Maybe Denise can put some cover-up on my dark circles before I go in front of the cameras."

Uh-oh. Here it comes.

"I think you should reveal Brandy after the elimination tonight. Bring her in without telling the other women she's here or why." He shrugged as if it was no big deal. As if he didn't care or hurt. "Make it dramatic. A cliff-hanger for the next episode."

Impressive. "You're talking like a producer."

One eyebrow rose at that; then he grinned. "Guess you're rubbing off on me."

She looked around, then leaned in close enough to smell the lingering soap from his morning shower. "You've got your five minutes." She winced and helped him get the microphone wire connected to the unit on his belt clip. "Well, three because of today's shooting schedule. But you've got it. Just you two."

Rick nodded. "When?"

"After we send everyone to lunch."

He glanced around the shelter. "I remember when this place made the best tires in Michigan. Now it houses those whom others have forgotten."

She nodded and rubbed one arm. Had the temperature dropped? "We've all been in a place similar to this at some point."

Rick turned and peered at her. "What was yours?"

The bench of a bus station holding on to the leg of her well-loved but battered stuffed elephant.

Elizabeth shivered and shook her head to clear the memory. "Doesn't matter. We all have them." She gestured to the group assigned to clean out the cages. "You might want to get your hands dirty, too."

Rick left to join the squealing women, who held trash bags for soiled newspaper shreds.

Elizabeth crossed her arms, trying to stay warm. The director of the animal shelter approached her with a stack of release forms. "Thank you for doing this."

"It was Rick's idea to advertise the pets available for adoption." She took the forms and added them to the back of her clipboard. "We want to help."

The director chuckled. "If that's really the case, I have a finicky kitten who still demands being bottle-fed."

Elizabeth shook her head. She didn't do animals. They represented complications and obligations she didn't have time for right now. Maybe someday. But now? "Thanks, but I have to keep an eye on my show."

The director nodded, but Elizabeth soon found herself sitting on the concrete floor holding a black-and-white kitten that hungrily sucked on a baby bottle. She could imagine taking this little guy with her. Surely a cat could adjust to her bohemian life on set, right?

And for a moment, she could envision a normal life. One where it wasn't all about her job. Where something, or someone, could join her.

The thought warmed her.

RICK HELD THE LEASH of a German shepherd pup that seemed determined to outrun all the other dogs. "Whoa, fella. Why don't we let the girls catch up to us?"

He tugged on the leash, but the pup kept pulling him along. One of the contestants, Vanessa, put her fingers in her mouth and gave a loud whistle. The dog stopped midtrot, and Rick almost tripped over him.

Vanessa caught up with her own dog on a leash, a small Yorkie mix. "He really had you going."

Rick bent over at the waist, trying to catch his breath. "Yes. Thanks."

The other women in their group started to catch up with them at the end of the driveway. Vanessa glanced back and slipped her arm through Rick's. "Ready to walk again?" she asked and tugged on his arm.

Rick shrugged. "Sure. I take it you want me alone?"

Vanessa tossed her head back and gave a hearty laugh. "You might say that. I'm willing to go after what I want." The look she gave him made him think he was on that list. "Let's take that path to the right."

Rick tugged on the leash so the pup would stay with them. "There's a view of the lake up ahead."

Vanessa nodded and pulled him and her dog along. "I've been hoping to get some one-on-one time with you for a few days. Get to know you better."

He could identify with that. When he'd first been on the show, time alone with Brandy at the beginning had been rare and precious. Maybe he needed to spread himself out more among them. "I'd like to get to know you better, too."

He glanced behind them and saw that the group of women held back but a cameraman ran after them. "I think they want to film this."

"Oh, right." She stopped walking. "It's hard to do this on camera, isn't it? Dating is tough enough without having an audience."

"Life in a small town is kind of like that." He chuckled. "Everyone knows your business and has an opinion."

"Do they approve of this show?"

The camera operator reached them. "Sorry, guys. Can we back up and start over?" Eddie asked. He pressed a button on the camera and walked backward to film them while they made their way down the path with the dogs.

Rick cleared his throat, struggling to find a topic that the audience would find interesting. "So, Vanessa, are you an animal lover?"

She laughed. "My dad's a veterinarian and my brother followed in his footsteps. We always had a bunch of animals around the house. Some injured or sick. Some temporary until they found a permanent home." She leaned down and petted the Yorkie. "I just wuv my animal fwends."

Rick tried not to wince at the baby voice. It seemed a bit much. Maybe she was acting natural, though. He didn't know her well enough to know for sure. But when she began to kiss the dog on the mouth, he fought hard to keep his face neutral. Yeah, he wouldn't be kissing her mouth after that.

Rick glanced at Eddie, who raised his eyebrows and shook his head.

One of the other contestants, Jennifer, ran up to them. "I thought I'd never find you."

Grateful for the distraction, Rick tugged on his dog's leash. "You know, it's getting colder by the minute out here. Why don't we take everyone back inside?"

Rick led the group as they returned to the shelter.

AFTER LIZZIE CALLED for lunch, the hornets in Rick's stomach buzzed louder and angrier. Brandy was near. He could feel it. Always could when they were on set before. Lizzie had laughed when he'd told her, said it was his imagination.

But once the bus had driven the rest of the

production crew and contestants away, he knew she lingered close.

Lizzie tied things up with the shelter director, then joined him by the dog cages, where Rick patted the head of the German shepherd. "You two look good together."

Rick glanced down at the dog. "My life currently doesn't allow room for a pet, but I'm open to the possibility."

Lizzie shrugged. "I know the feeling." She glanced in the direction of the cat room. "But every once in a while, I wonder."

Rick nodded as Lizzie removed his earpiece and microphone; she avoided his gaze. "I'll be waiting in my car." She glanced at her watch, then him. "Three minutes."

He didn't know what to say. Didn't trust his voice.

As Lizzie left the shelter, a familiar blonde walked in and scanned the room before settling her ocean-blue eyes on him.

His heart squeezed but it felt…different. Not like five years ago. Not when he saw a future every time he looked at her. Now he felt as if everything he'd planned on could change in the next few moments. All his plans would turn upside down until he didn't remember what they were in the first place.

He swallowed. *Nope. Not good.*

He walked toward her, but she remained frozen where she was. Was it fear keeping her from moving? He opened his arms then, and she rushed toward him. "Ricky."

When he put his arms around her, she sighed and snuggled closer. "I thought you'd never talk to me again."

He held her out to look at her. She looked good. Too good. Hard to remember she'd once broken his heart. "You look as fabulous as ever."

Brandy blushed and pushed his shoulder. It felt familiar and normal. As if they'd been in touch all this time. "Always the charmer."

"Things don't change much," he observed.

She nodded, then looked at the ground. When she brought her gaze back to his, her eyes were filled with tears. "I'm so, so sorry."

Rick let out a big sigh. *Please, not the tears.* He could handle anything but those. "I am, too."

She shook her head furiously. "But you're not the one who broke my heart."

"But he did." He took her hand and led her to a bench near the front door. The feel of her hand in his was warm. Again, familiar. "I only wanted you to be happy." He looked down at their hands, then back at her. "But I had hoped it would be with me."

Brandy shook her head. "I wanted it to be you so badly. But when it came to that moment, I knew my heart had already chosen someone else."

"Even though we all kept warning you he was a player."

She squeezed his hand. "When it's your turn, you'll understand. You'll know that no matter how much you should choose the perfect woman, it comes down to who's climbed into your heart and made a home there."

"Are you here for a second chance with me or with the audience?"

Brandy peered into his eyes intensely until he could feel a piece of himself starting to come loose and fall away. "Maybe both? I want to make things right with you. And I hope you'll give me that chance."

Rick's cell phone chirped, ruining the moment. "I think time's up." He rose to his feet, still hanging on to her hand. Unwilling to let her go just yet. "Why don't we take things as they come? No promises. No lies. Just whatever happens, happens."

Brandy turned into his arms. "It's a deal."

A BRUNETTE WITH a short blue dress approached Rick after dinner at the house. He had decisions on his mind. Who to send home? Who to keep? How would they take the addition of Brandy to the house? *Distracted* put it mildly.

"Can we talk outside?" the brunette asked.

Always the talking outside. Couldn't they stay where it was warm by the fire? Instead of suggesting that, he nodded. "But let's take our coats."

In the foyer, they both grabbed coats, then stepped out onto the porch. Rick could see his breath as soon as they walked into the cold. He crossed his arms more for the warmth than anything. One of the cameramen turned on lights and gave a thumbs-up before either one said a word. "How are things going, Britney?"

She glanced at the camera, then at Rick. "Um…"

Rick addressed the cameraman. "Eddie, why don't you take a five-minute break? I think we need some privacy." He motioned with his head toward the garage. "I promise you won't miss anything juicy."

"No can do, Rick. Boss lady would have my hide."

Britney shook her head and took a seat on the stone bench. "It's fine. I signed up for this. And it's not something I can't say on camera."

Rick nodded and focused his attention on the young woman. "What's wrong, Brit?"

She stayed quiet for so long that he thought she wouldn't share what was on her mind. Finally, she began, "Rick, you're a nice guy, but—"

Really? That was what she wanted to talk about? He chuckled. "You're giving me the 'It's not you, it's me' speech? Wow."

"I grew up in a town just like this and promised I'd never go back." Britney took a deep breath and shook her head. "I can't do this. Not even for a catch like you."

What was so wrong with his town? Everyone seemed to want to get away from it. But Rick liked it. Loved it. It was friends. And family. It was home. "We want different things is all." He put a hand on her shoulder. "I won't give you a necklace tonight, okay?"

"Thanks, Rick. If it was anywhere else…"

He leaned over and kissed her cheek. "I wish you the best."

Britney threw her arms around him. "You, too." She started to rise. Then she sat back down. "Don't trust Mona."

What? He'd only had a brief conversation with Mona. They certainly weren't picking out china patterns at this point. "Why shouldn't I?"

Britney bit her lip. "I don't think she's in this for the right reasons." She leaned in closer. "None of us do. Just be careful, okay?"

Rick nodded, still stunned. Someone cleared her throat behind them, and he turned to see Lizzie. He patted Britney's shoulder. "Why don't you go back inside and get warm? I have something to take care of."

Once Britney shut the front door, Lizzie stared at Eddie until he turned the camera off and returned to the garage. Rick stood and started to open the door. Lizzie took a step in front of it, barring his way. The hits kept coming. "Liz, I'm freezing. What do you want?"

"Brandy's waiting in the garage until we're ready." She stepped closer to him, touched his arm. "You're sure that you're okay with this?"

He shrugged. "You said it would give me closure, so why not?"

She held up her clipboard. "Want to go over the contestants and narrow down who you're sending home tonight?"

Rick shook his head. "I think I'll do this one on my own."

"Oh." She tried to keep the hurt out of her voice, but Rick heard it all the same. "I only wanted to help."

"I've got to make these decisions on my own eventually." He gave a shrug and a grin he didn't really feel, then opened the door to the house and walked inside.

ELIZABETH COULD TELL that Rick hated the elimination. His brow was damp, his eyes wide. If his coughing was any indication, he had a dry throat, too. No one liked rejection, and he hated being the one who handed it out.

Rick stood in front of the refurbished fireplace with twelve necklaces in his hands. "Ah…ladies?"

Immediately, the conversation dropped to a lull and the remaining contestants gathered in a semicircle in front of Rick. Elizabeth gripped her clipboard. In the past, Rick had discussed the women with her and given a hint about who he was sending home. But this time he'd kept the decision close to his chest, which meant that she was as clueless as the rest of their viewing audience. And she didn't like that one bit.

Elizabeth closed her eyes and mumbled, "Pick Melissa. You like her. So pick her. Please."

On the monitor, Rick looked at each woman a moment. "This is always the toughest part of our time here. Choosing who will stay and who goes home." He cleared his throat. "So…" He took one gold necklace and dangled the heart charm. Glanced at each woman. "Melissa."

Elizabeth went limp with relief.

Melissa walked to stand in front of Rick. He unclasped the necklace and held it out. "Melissa, will you accept my heart?"

The woman smiled and nodded. Dipped her head so that Rick could place the necklace around her neck. Touched the charm to her chest. Leaned in toward him and kissed his cheek. "Thank you."

The ceremony continued until eleven more women had joined Melissa next to Rick. Elizabeth examined them on the monitor. Melissa was definitely the nice girl in the bunch. He'd also chosen two women who had already fought at the house over bathroom space, a loud smart aleck who made him laugh and several who could blend in anywhere. They'd probably be the next to leave.

Rick took the time to say goodbye to each contestant he hadn't chosen while Elizabeth prepared for the surprise. Brandy returning may have been Devon's idea, but it was Rick's brilliant plan to introduce her after the goodbye ceremony. Making it a cliff-hanger for the next episode ensured ratings for both shows.

One of her cameramen hopped up. "We got a crier on the porch. I'm on it."

He ran out of the garage before Elizabeth could stop him. While the crying women often made ratings, she personally hated seeing it happen. She grabbed her coat and ran after Eddie.

The young woman saw them coming and turned away. Eddie already had the camera running before he reached the porch. Elizabeth put her hand on his shoulder and shook her head. "Give us a moment?"

Eddie sighed a little too loudly. "The audience loves these scenes."

"Only because Bob insisted on exploiting them. I'm in charge here now." When her cameraman walked away grumbling about missed opportunities, Elizabeth approached the woman. "Kayla, are you all right?"

She squinted at Elizabeth through tears. "Do I look all right to you?"

Not with those red eyes and stained cheeks. Elizabeth dropped her voice. "Listen, Rick's a great guy, which is why he's on the show, but he's not the only one out there. Just because it didn't work out this time doesn't mean your life is over." She placed a hand on Kayla's shoulder, hoping it would bring some comfort.

Instead the young woman whirled on her. "What would you know about it?"

Elizabeth gave a soft chuckle. "I know plenty about men, good and bad. But I also know that life doesn't stop after a breakup. You're going to be okay."

Kayla shook her head, unwilling to listen. "What if he was the one? I thought that we had a chance...."

"Every woman does. But the reality is that there's someone else out there who is perfect for you. In the meantime, worry less about a prince to rescue you and focus on making the best of yourself."

Kayla glanced at Elizabeth's left hand. "I don't see a ring on your finger, so what would you know about it?"

"My prince is this job. That's what I wake up for every day. It's what saves me from the dragons out there."

Kayla shook her head and walked off the porch. "Whatever."

How many times had she had this conversation with those going home? How many more times would she before someone believed her? She turned to go back to the garage. She spotted Rick watching her. "Kayla was upset."

He nodded and turned his attention to the house. "They're waiting for you before we bring in Brandy."

Back to business. "Right. How do you think it went?"

He turned to look at her. Shrugged, though she knew it took more effort than he had. "I hate telling someone that we didn't click. But that's all a part of life, right?" He gave a soft laugh, but she could tell he took no pleasure in it. "Now, let's go knock the socks off this game."

Elizabeth turned to watch Kayla get in the waiting car. She held up a hand, but the other woman ignored it and slammed the door shut.

From inside, she could hear the murmurs of voices reach a fever pitch. So much for waiting for her to spring Brandy on them.

"But you can't! She can't!"

Here we go.... Elizabeth stepped inside and glanced at the remaining contestants. "Is there a problem?"

Brandy raised her hand from the corner. "I guess that would be me."

"If you want someone to be angry with, pick me." Rick stepped forward. "This show is about second chances for me, and I figured she deserved one, too."

The contestants looked at each other; most of them didn't seem happy about it. Finally, Melissa said, "You're welcome to room with me if you'd like. My roommate, Britney, got sent home tonight."

Brandy nodded but didn't say anything. Neither did anyone else until Rick clapped his hands together. "Well, I don't know about you, but I could use some more of that fabulous chocolate mousse we had at dinner. Any other takers?"

The women slowly followed him back into the kitchen. That man could probably get them to do almost anything, Elizabeth marveled.

Brandy stayed behind. "I didn't think my being here would upset them so much."

"It's a competition. Remember the feud between Wade and Larry? Anything that could get in your way is immediately viewed with suspicion and anger." Elizabeth consulted her clipboard. "I'll make sure your luggage gets moved to the house tonight."

"Thanks." Brandy started to leave but turned back. "Why don't you want me here?"

"I never said I didn't."

"Right."

Elizabeth called after her, "He's a good man. He doesn't deserve to get hurt. By you or anyone else."

The other woman turned and shook her head. "I don't want to hurt him." She shrugged.

"Guess I'll try to get in on some of that dessert, too."

Elizabeth watched her leave and took a deep breath. She needed to get a better handle on hiding her feelings.

CHAPTER TEN

RICK LET HIMSELF into the back door of the house where the remaining women were staying—they no longer needed both places. He'd gotten a key from one of the crew members to plan this surprise breakfast. If Lizzie knew about it, she'd probably have his hide. So the less she knew, the better. This was something he wanted to do for the women, not the camera.

Silence greeted him in the kitchen as he set down the plastic bags of groceries that he'd brought with him. He took off his coat and tossed it on the back of one of the stools. Searching, he found the supplies he needed: whisk, bowls, pans, spatula. As well as a frilly apron that he was sure looked better on the sleeping inhabitants of the house than it did on him.

By the time the coffee had finished brewing, Rick had been joined by two of the contestants, Jenny and Becky. He used some flair to flip a perfect golden pancake onto a plate, then topped it with another. He added a few pieces of bacon to the side. And the first plate was served.

Becky murmured her thanks as Rick started on Jenny's plate. "You guys are up awfully early."

Jenny watched him. "Hard to sleep when the aroma of fresh coffee hits my nose." She took her plate from him. "This looks fabulous. Thanks."

"My pleasure." He winked at her and started preparing another plate. "Everyone else still sleeping?"

The women nodded but continued eating. Rick topped off their mugs of coffee, then poured himself one. He started brewing another pot so it would be fresh for whoever came downstairs next. "So what do you think of my town?"

Becky swallowed. "It's cute. But small." She cut her pancake into tiny bites. "Kind of like me."

Rick raised his coffee cup. "Hear, hear." He heard feet on the stairs and started pouring pancake batter onto the griddle. "Sounds like we have more customers."

When the women saw him standing there, some left to go upstairs and change. Put on makeup. Do whatever it was that women did before facing the world. He thought they already looked beautiful. Rick stopped them. "It's a pj's breakfast. Come as you are."

Soon the kitchen couldn't hold them all, so the women who already had breakfast took their plates into the dining room while Rick brought out more for those who had arrived later as he did at the diner. Sometimes, he couldn't escape it. Once they had all been served, he took a seat at the head of the table. They looked at him as if waiting for him to say something. He stalled and took a sip of his coffee. They still waited. "So what's on the agenda today?"

"We thought you'd know," Brandy said.

She'd been the last to join them, the last at the table. He'd noticed how some had turned their chairs as if to shut her out. He caught her gaze then nodded at her, hoping it reassured her. "I'm as clueless as you. Lizzie usually posts a schedule around here somewhere, right?"

"Yes, I do."

The woman in question stood in the doorway of the dining room. Anger and tension seemed to radiate from her. And the look that she gave him could have scorched the apron off him. "Did I miss the invitation for breakfast?"

Rick stood and held up his hands. "I wanted to do something just for them. A surprise breakfast."

"Oh, it's a surprise, all right." She crossed her arms as she took in the scene. Then she zeroed in on him. "A word alone?"

He poured his producer a cup of coffee, then joined her in the living room.

ELIZABETH COULDN'T believe it. Why was Rick at the house? Where was the camera? The crew? "What were you thinking?"

Rick held out a mug of coffee. "Like I said, I wanted to do something nice for them. What's the big deal?"

"The big deal?" She shook her head. And peeled her coat off and tossed it over the back of one of the love seats. "You're robbing the audience of special moments like that."

"I didn't do it to score points with the audience." He placed the cup of coffee in her hands, then ran his hands through his hair. "I wanted to do this to thank the women who are still here. Just from me to them. Nothing else."

She looked around the room. "How did you get in?"

Rick colored slightly as he dug a key out of his jeans pocket. "Don't get mad."

"I'm beyond that." Elizabeth held out her hand and closed it around the warm key when he placed it there. "I was already dreading holding my meeting this morning, and you being here isn't making my job easier."

"I wasn't thinking about you when I made these plans."

"Obviously." That was the problem. He had only thought about doing something nice for these women. So why was she jumping down his back? Something she didn't want to think about. Not right now. "Any other surprises you need to tell me about?"

Rick dropped his gaze to his feet and shook his head. Elizabeth sighed and touched his arm. "Making breakfast for them was really sweet. But next time can we show it on air?"

"Deal." He glanced at her face. "You look like you haven't slept or eaten. Want me to make you a plate?"

Rather than fight him, she agreed. She joined the women in the dining room and took Rick's spot at the head of the table.

When Rick returned to the dining room with her breakfast, Elizabeth thanked him. "Sweet of Rick to surprise you this morning, huh?" Might as well start things out nice. Because the rest of the meeting wouldn't be.

There was light applause and words of

thanks. Elizabeth smiled at him. "Thank you. Now we girls have some things to discuss without you."

"Dismissed just like that?" Rick chuckled as if to show he didn't care. But the look in his eyes told her he might. "I'll see you all later."

Once he left, Elizabeth pulled her clipboard closer. "Just some quick notes, and then I need to see Mona and Leslie alone."

With efficiency, she laid out the day's schedule and stressed how important it was to explore the town. "Who knows, you could end up living here. Any questions?" No one raised a hand. "Details for those of you going on the trip to the winery this afternoon are posted on the whiteboard in the kitchen. Otherwise, you're free."

They got up and left, and the two she needed to talk to stayed behind. Elizabeth waited until the room was empty, then moved down the table to sit closer to the two women. Mona had her arms crossed already, as if she knew what they were going to discuss, while Leslie kept her gaze on her hands.

She waited for them both to look at her. "Listen. I know space is precious with all of you living here in cramped quarters. But I will absolutely not tolerate any kind of turf war on set."

Leslie frowned and Mona narrowed her eyes at the other woman. "It's hardly a turf war. She's a thief."

"I am not!" Leslie stood. She slowly sat back down as Elizabeth kept her gaze on her. "I didn't know it was hers."

"Regardless, the fighting has to stop." Elizabeth leaned forward. "Although it does get us better ratings on the show, it's not good for you or for the others living here."

"The show?" Mona wrinkled her nose. "She took my necklace, and you're worried about the show?" She scowled at Leslie. "You better be worried about the police."

Every show had one of these meetings. Every bachelor had a group of women who couldn't live together without a fight. Or several. "The necklaces that Rick gives out all look alike. It's a simple misunderstanding."

Mona leaned back in her chair. "She wants me off the show. Her and everybody else in this house."

"Rick decides who leaves, Mona. So can we cut the drama?" She reached for her clipboard and glanced at her notes. "But I think we need to separate you two. Jenny has a free bed in her room. Who wants it?"

Mona stared at Leslie until the woman raised her hand. "I do."

"Good. I'll let you get your things moved."

Leslie rose to her feet, then glanced at Mona. "I'm sorry about the necklace. I thought it was mine."

"Whatever."

Elizabeth let Leslie pass. She turned to Mona. "Now you have the room to yourself. That should satisfy you. So stop the threats." She got to her feet. "Maybe there's a reason they don't want you here. Something to think about."

Mona rolled her eyes. "All I need to think about is that ring on my finger at the end of this show."

Elizabeth left, shaking her head. There was one of those every season, too.

His mom piped lemon filling into the tiny pastry cups, concentration making her tongue peep out at the side of her mouth. "Ma, they're not expecting perfection." He reached out to take one from the tray but got his hand slapped away.

"These are for the ladies. Not you." She started on the next one, looked up at him and sighed. "Fine. But only one."

Rick took one of the first she'd made,

which looked a little lopsided. He bit into it and closed his eyes. "These are fabulous."

She continued filling the pastries. "Of course they are. I made them."

He leaned on the counter and licked off his fingers, watching her for a moment. "Is there something I can do to help you out?"

"Can you count the plates and silverware? Make sure I got them all out?"

Rick pushed off the counter and walked to the kitchen table, where stacks of china and rows of forks and spoons were laid out in precision. "I think it's nice that you're doing this for the ladies," he said.

"And filming it."

He shrugged. "You didn't have to agree to that, you know." He fingered the top of one fork. "But I'm sure Lizzie appreciates it."

His mom placed the last pastry cup on the tray, surveying her work. "I'm doing this for you, not her." She glanced at the clock. "The mini quiches come out in ten minutes. Salads are made." She looked around the kitchen. "Can you arrange the cookies on the trays when you finish? I'll start brewing the tea and making the coffee."

Rick enjoyed working with his mom like this in the kitchen. On holidays, he'd been her little helper, mashing potatoes or preparing salads. In high school, he'd worked for his parents at the diner, then rejoined her staff after the accident that had robbed him of his baseball career. She'd taught him everything he knew, then handed her dream over to him. He loved her for that.

He pulled tubs of homemade cookies from the pantry and started to fill crystal trays with them. He wished he'd inherited her baking gene. It would make life more interesting at the diner. Though Ernesto did have a talented hand with pies. Taking a quick glance to see if the coast was clear, he popped one of the cookies into his mouth. His mom sighed. "At least leave some for your ladies."

"You made enough for them, the crew and the rest of the town if they show up for tea." He continued putting cookies on the tray, then paused. "What do you think of Brandy coming back?"

His mom stopped scooping coffee into the percolator and looked out the window for a moment. "She seems willing to try a second time. Why?"

He shrugged. "I don't know. I thought her coming back might rekindle what we had, but that's gone. Replaced by something...different, I guess."

His mom tilted her head to the side. "Different bad or different good?"

"I don't know. Just different." He resumed putting the cookies on the tray. "I still like her, but I don't trust her. Does that make sense?"

He felt his mom put her hand on his shoulder. Turned to see her watching him, love shining at him. He knew that had never changed. Would never change. He gave her a soft smile. "None of this makes sense, right?"

"Son, I stopped trying to make sense of things a long time ago." He chuckled as she continued, "What matters to me is that you are happy. That you are healthy." She started to walk away. "And that you make me a grandmother."

Thanks, Mom. Nothing like adding more pressure to the process. He cleared his throat. "Can you keep your eyes and ears open today? Let me know what you think? I need help this time. And I'm not afraid to ask."

She walked back to his side, then kissed his cheek. "Of course. Love you." She glanced at the clock on the wall. "Now, finish that tray and get out of here. It's ladies only."

He returned her smile and kept arranging cookies.

ELIZABETH WAS OUT of ideas. Rick wanted to
showcase the community more on air, but
her creative well had run dry. They'd danced
with the seniors. Played with the animals.
The only other logistical nightmare left was
doing something with kids. And as a rule,
she steered her production away from them.
Kids might look cute on film, but they were
too unpredictable. But then, when had that
stopped her before?

Rick sat across from her in the back booth
at the diner after a long day of shooting interviews, his least favorite thing on the show
besides the elimination ceremonies. He had
his arms draped across the back of the booth,
head back, eyes closed. She studied him,
wondering what else she could do to help him
find the right woman. She felt as if she was
failing. And he deserved so much more. To
be loved and cared for. She reached across the
table and smoothed a stray lock of hair that
had fallen across his forehead.

He woke with a start and found her staring
at him. "See something you like?"

"What do you think about kids?"

"Having them? I'm for it." He stretched his
legs out so that his feet rested on the seat beside her. "You volunteering?"

"No way." She shook her head furiously at the suggestion. Her, a mother? What did she know about raising a child? Not as if she had any strong role models in that area. "I meant on the show."

"Don't they say never to work with animals or kids in show business?"

"Only the wimps say that." She drew large circles on her clipboard, willing the ideas to come. Hoping they'd come. Because she needed a lot of them and soon. "I thought you being around kids might raise your appeal."

He leaned across the table. "Aren't I appealing enough?" He held out his arms. "I mean, look at me. I'm every mother's dream future son-in-law."

"You've got some ego on you tonight." She started making X's to match her circles on the paper.

"Must be all this sharing about myself." He stood. "You hungry? I know the diner's closed, but I can whip us up something. A sandwich? Or I think Ernesto has some chicken pie left over."

Elizabeth shook her head, but her stomach growled in response. Rick raised an eyebrow until she sighed. "Fine. But a little piece. I'm going to need bigger clothes the way you feed me."

"That's not a bad thing, Lizzie." Rick disappeared into the kitchen while she doodled some more. They were halfway through filming here, and most of the time left would be devoted to dates. But she'd hoped to have one more group activity. One more chance to make a statement about this town. Maybe some kind of civic cleanup duty? Or volunteer opportunity? Volunteering with kids?

She groaned and rested her head on the back of the seat. Get off the kid track. She closed her eyes and pictured a woman sitting on the couch watching the show. What was she interested in? What did she want to see?

The clink of a plate set before her ended her reverie. That and the heavenly smell wafting toward her. She opened her eyes. "Thanks. I think I ate sometime this morning."

"You need to take better care of yourself." He set his own plate down and handed her silverware wrapped in a paper napkin. "Don't think I haven't noticed the dark circles under your eyes."

"Maybe I should have Denise put makeup on me in the morning, too." She grinned and opened the napkin. Grabbed the fork and speared a thick piece of chicken. Took a bite. "Man, can you cook."

"Can't take credit for Ernesto's potpie, but thanks."

He sat across from her, and they ate in silence for a while. He motioned with his fork to her notes. "Get any ideas?"

"Not any good ones."

"Read them to me. Maybe we can come up with something together." He took a bite of his dinner and spoke with his mouth full. "What can it hurt?"

"Besides your manners, can't think of a thing." She set her fork down and picked up the clipboard. "'Cleanup. Volunteer. Kids.'" She looked up at him. "That's all I got."

He motioned with his free hand for her to give him the clipboard. She ate while he looked it over, waiting for a response. Finally, he sighed and placed the clipboard on the table between them. "It's good."

"That's all you've got?" She grabbed the clipboard and scanned it. "It's good? It's not good. It's reaching." She groaned and rested her head on the table. "I'm better than this."

"You're hungry and can't think." He pushed her plate toward her. "Your creativity needs fuel. Eat."

She lifted her head and sat back up. Took her fork and ate a few bites. When Rick looked satisfied, she stopped. "We haven't had much time to talk lately. How do you think things are going?"

"With the girls, fine." He finished his meal and sat back in the seat. "I'm beginning to see who might make it to the end." He grinned. "I think."

"Melissa?" She mentally crossed her fingers. They had chemistry together. She was a nice woman who was pretty and sweet. She thought of the other woman he had chemistry with. "What about Brandy?"

"Melissa's nice." He nodded, his eyes getting a far-off look. "I can see myself with her."

"But…"

He shrugged. "There is no but." Elizabeth pierced him with her eyes until he sighed and leaned forward. "Okay, there is. I don't feel a lot of sparks with her."

It was her turn to sigh. How many times had her bachelors told her the same thing? How many had believed in the sparks only to find out later that they didn't last? "Sparks are overrated."

Rick shrugged again. "Maybe." He closed his eyes and rubbed his forehead. "Now, with Brandy, there's plenty of sparks."

"But…"

"But I don't know how much I can trust

them. Or her." He opened his eyes and looked at her. "What do you think?"

The big question. Did she think either one of these women deserved Rick or his love? Rather than answer that question, she wiped her mouth and placed her napkin on the table. "Doesn't matter what I think. I'm not marrying them."

Rick laughed. "True." He glanced at their empty plates. "How about some dessert?"

She rubbed her full belly. "No, thanks."

"I've got cheesecake."

Elizabeth groaned and held up her hands in surrender. "Fine. But—"

"Little piece. I know." Rick laughed as he left to get their desserts. He returned quickly with two pieces. "I can make coffee."

"Are you trying to spoil me? This is fine." She took a bite of the cheesecake and moaned. "Your diner will ruin me."

He again took his seat across from her. "It's kinda nice. Just the two of us. No camera. No crew."

She nodded as she finished her bite. "Hard to remember what real life is like without the cameras."

"Exactly." They ate in silence, then Rick asked, "Why aren't you married?"

Where had that come from? She choked on her food. "What? Why?"

He looked her over. "You're pretty. Smart. Successful. Are they blind or just stupid?"

How did they get on this topic? "Doesn't matter. I'm not getting married."

"Ever?"

"Never wanted to."

"So, no kids. No marriage." He leaned forward. "I know you love your job, but don't you want more?"

She searched for a way to change the topic but failed. He looked at her with those warm brown eyes that invited someone to trust him. To tell him everything. She shook her head. "It doesn't matter."

"It does to me. C'mon, Lizzie. What kind of guy could make you change your mind?"

"Why do you want to know?"

"You spent three hours asking me questions, so now it's my turn." He tapped the table. "Fess up. What's your dream guy like?"

She scowled at him. "He wouldn't be pushy."

Rick laughed and leaned back. "Okay, what else?"

It had been so long since she'd thought of this. She couldn't remember anything she used to dream about. Well, mostly. "He'd have a good job. Security. Strong principles."

"Now we're getting somewhere." Rick frowned. "But he sounds kind of…I don't know. Boring."

"Boring can be good." She polished off the last bite of cheesecake. "Thanks for the late dinner, but I've got to get going." She stood and grabbed her clipboard. She turned to find Rick helping her into her coat. It was almost like being on a date. Almost like… She shook her head. "You are a true gentleman. Those are rare."

He turned her around and kissed her on the cheek. "Good night, Lizzie." He put his arms around her shoulders, and they looked at each other.

Too long. Until she flinched and hurried away.

"Night," she croaked, then ducked out of the restaurant.

ELIZABETH'S PHONE RANG from the bedside table. She groaned and rolled over. Peered at the digital clock. Who in the world would be calling her at four in the morning? She jabbed her finger at the offensive phone. "This better be good."

"Have you taken a look outside?"

She frowned. *What?* Slowly getting to her feet, she walked to the curtains that led to the balcony. Opened them slowly. And groaned even louder. All she could see was white. At least a foot and a half of it against the glass doors.

"I knew there was snow in the forecast, but not a blizzard."

Charlie chuckled. "So much for the hockey game in Detroit tonight. Hope you had a plan B."

"And C and D, if needed." She turned on a light and located her clipboard where she'd left it the night before by the television. "Give me a few hours. I'll make some phone calls. Check some websites. We can still make this work."

"It's a little after four. Most people will be sleeping."

"Which makes me wonder why you called me right now. This couldn't wait?" She turned on her laptop and waited for it to boot. Waited for the real reason Charlie had called her. "What else do you need to tell me?"

"I spotted Wally Ray at a local bar last night."

Elizabeth's heart fell into her stomach, and she rubbed her forehead. "Did you talk to him?"

"He approached me. Told me he's on an explosive scoop." Charlie got quiet. "What else is here in this teeny town besides us? He's got some inside story on the show, E. What else could it be?"

No.

No, no, no.

She picked up the hotel phone and dialed Devon's cell phone. "Charlie, I'll call you back with details later." She hung up her cell phone and wrapped her finger around the hotel phone's cord. When Devon didn't pick up, not that she expected he would, she growled, "You'd better call me in ten minutes. *Hollywood Insider* is here investigating us. What is going on?"

She slammed the phone on the cradle and picked up her cell phone. Dialed a friend's phone number. "Jeremy, I need some answers that I know you have. Please call me back."

Without anyone to talk to, she brought up the internet and scanned her list of secondary plans on the clipboard. They wouldn't be able to drive to Detroit in this weather for the game, but could they find one closer to home? A local team perhaps?

Her cell phone chirped. She glanced at the caller ID before answering it. "Tell me what you know about this."

"Elizabeth, sweetheart, there's nothing to know." Devon sounded as if he'd enjoyed too much whiskey. "You're worrying about nothing."

This topped her list of things to worry about. "Wally Ray is in town. He doesn't show up unless the story brings in high five figures. Tell me what you know."

Silence. *Great.*

Elizabeth printed out the new itinerary for tonight's date while she waited for Devon to come up with some excuse. Some reason why a Hollywood reporter would come snooping in their very own backyard. "Is it because we added Brandy?"

Nothing.

"Devon, did you pass out or are you avoiding me?"

"Beth, baby…"

She sighed. "Good night, Devon. I'll put out the fires like I always do. Glad to know they pay you the big bucks for all my hard work." She threw her phone on the bed. Then picked it back up and called Charlie back. "Did he say anything about the story he's on?"

"That's why I called you. It's obviously us, but I don't know the angle."

"Did he say where he's staying?"

Charlie gave her the directions as she pulled on jeans and a sweatshirt. She wasn't going to look the greatest, but this wasn't a time for vanity. It was a time for action. She had to get answers and quick. Had to protect her show. No matter what.

Wally Ray's hotel was definitely several rungs lower than those she'd put her crew up in. She slammed her hand on the door until he answered.

"Beth."

She wrinkled her nose at the smell of him, but moved past him and into the hotel room. Glanced around at the disheveled queen-size bed. The empty bottles on the bedside table. The open suitcase that could hold clues. "You alone?"

"You could have had me anytime, princess. I've been waiting for you to beg." He shut the door behind him and locked it. Lounged against it as if posing for a magazine cover.

She whirled around and stalked toward him. "What's your story?"

"I ain't got one, sweetheart, but if you give me a few minutes, I'll make one up for you." He licked his lips. "For a price."

She pushed him against the door. "Why *True Love?* What have you got?"

"Oh, that story." Wally Ray chuckled and

moved over to the bed. He picked up a cigarette butt from the ashtray and relit it. "Is that what's got you so hot? It's nothing."

"Really? That's not what I heard."

He laughed again and took a long drag. "Even if there was a story, why would I go and spill it to you? Unless you've got a hundred large to outbid my employer."

A hundred thousand dollars. Elizabeth paled. It had to be huge. She switched tactics. "Wally, you know I have a soft spot for you. Maybe we could help each other. You don't get more on the inside than with me."

"You're on the inside all right." He blew out the smoke so that it drifted in her face.

Her cheeks grew warm. "Leave Rick alone. He's a nice guy, not like the others I've worked with."

"Like I said, unless you can outbid my employer…"

Sweet-talking him didn't work. Neither did appealing to any compassion he might have. She shook her head and grabbed the sleeve of his plaid shirt. "You little opportunistic weasel. You're messing with people's lives. There's nothing going on here."

"That's not what my source says."

She let him go and wiped her hands off. "Do what you want. Say what you want. But you'll be hearing from the network's legal department."

"Freedom of the press, baby."

She unlocked the door and slammed it shut behind her. Just what she didn't need.

RICK CHEERED ON the Lightning Bolts as they scored another goal. Although he would have loved to see the Red Wings play, it felt good to be in the stands rooting for his old high school team. The women on each side of him took up the shouting and clapping. Now, this was his kind of date. He glanced at his three dates. "Anyone want hot dogs? Popcorn?"

He took their orders and walked down the bleachers to the concession stand. Charlie filmed him as he ordered their food, but he noticed that the man seemed a little stressed. "You okay, man?"

"Don't worry about me."

Rick paid the cashier for the food. "What about Lizzie? She as tense as you?"

Charlie lowered the camera. Looked around, then nodded. "There's a reporter in town."

"There's a lot of those. So what's different about this one?"

Charlie leaned in closer. "It's *Hollywood Insider*."

Rick accepted the box of food from the cashier and walked away from the stand. He waited for Charlie to catch up. "What's the story?"

"We don't know."

Rick stopped walking and stared at Charlie. "C'mon. Lizzie knows everything. What's the story?"

Charlie looked him square in the eyes. "The former producer's affair with the bachelorette is becoming old news. Now they want something juicy going on set here."

Rick glanced at the food, then up at the stands where his dates waited. "The reporter will go home when he sees there's no scandal." He looked back at Charlie. "And there is no story. Right? We're all playing our roles. Doing our jobs."

The other man nodded and put the camera back on his shoulder. "Glad we could come to an understanding."

Rick returned to his dates. He handed out hot dogs, popcorn and sodas to the women, then settled in between Becky and Jenny. "This is some game, isn't it? And I have a surprise for you all after the game. We're ice-skating."

His dates squealed, and Rick forced a smile onto his face. He would have fun if his life depended on it.

CHAPTER ELEVEN

RICK WORKED LIKE a magician behind the grill, flipping pancakes, scrambling eggs and frying bacon. His two breakfast dates, Mona and Melissa, watched him with huge eyes much like Elizabeth had when she'd first seen him cook. They sat on stools in the kitchen while the rest of the town tried to peek through the windows of the diner to see what was going on with their favorite citizen.

Rick flipped two pancakes onto a plate, then slid three slices of bacon next to it alongside a scoop of scrambled eggs. With a flourish, he placed the plate in front of Mona. "Here you are, my dear. Compliments of the chef."

Mona wrinkled her nose. "You don't have egg whites?"

Elizabeth rolled her eyes and made notes on her clipboard. When Rick placed a similar plate in front of Melissa, she looked up and thanked him. She got a wink from the handsome chef.

The talk during breakfast centered on their morning plans—a sleigh ride through the town. Elizabeth had found a local farmer who owned not only a cutter but two roans to pull her cast through town. It would be a picturesque tour of Lake Mildred, and her audience would love it. Maybe Rick was right and the show would bring in much-needed tourism.

Jeffy showed up to clear the plates and bumped Mona's elbow, sloshing coffee on her lap. "Hey, watch it. These jeans cost more than your life."

Rick's head snapped up, and he frowned at her. "It was an accident."

"Then he should be more careful. If he can't do his job right, then he shouldn't do it at all." Mona mopped at the dark stain with napkins. "I'd fire him."

Jeffy looked at Rick, then ran outside. Rick dropped the volume of his voice. "He is careful. He's also sweet and kind and wouldn't hurt a fly. He's a good employee. And my friend."

Mona suddenly turned sweet under Rick's glare. "It's okay, sugar. I know he didn't mean to."

Rick glanced at Elizabeth, who turned to Eddie. "Let's take five." She ushered the crew out to the dining room. She returned to discover Rick had left to find Jeffy. She glanced at Mona and Melissa. "Everything okay?"

"Everything was fine until he ruined my outfit." Mona still dabbed at the brown stain on her jeans. "Do you know how much these cost?"

Elizabeth rolled her eyes. "And what about the cost of your tirade to that sweet boy?"

Mona gave a big sigh. "I apologized."

Elizabeth raised an eyebrow. "When? I certainly didn't hear it." She turned to the other woman. "Did you, Melissa?"

She shook her head slightly but didn't say a word. Rick returned to the kitchen and slapped the towel on the counter. He glowered at Mona. "I wouldn't get too comfortable here."

She stood up and straightened her sweater. "Don't worry. This town isn't my type, and neither are you. Whatever happened to defending the woman you love?"

"The woman I love wouldn't come down so hard on a kid. She'd be compassionate. Understanding." He narrowed his eyes at her. "Not cold like you."

Mona turned to Elizabeth. "I want to go back to the house." She glanced at Melissa. "He's all yours."

Melissa smiled brightly. "Gladly." She got

up from her chair and walked beside Rick, linking her arm in his. "The man I love would defend those who can't do it themselves." She looked up at Rick. "You're amazing."

He grinned down at her, and Elizabeth fought the feeling that rose up from her stomach. Anger? Jealousy? She shook her head. This was crazy. He was her friend. Nothing more.

Mona stormed out of the kitchen and into the dining room. Elizabeth groaned. "You two couldn't have waited until cameras were on for that display? We could re-create it."

Rick shook his head. "The moment's over, Lizzie. Besides…" He hugged the woman next to him. "It wouldn't be real. I think you're amazing, too, Missy."

Elizabeth turned on her heel and walked out to the dining room, leaving the two lovebirds. That was what she wanted, right? She wanted Rick to find a wife, and if the moment in the kitchen was any indication, he had. The perfect partner.

Eddie squeezed up next to her. "I'll set up the handheld for the sleigh ride." He pulled his coat on and walked out of the diner.

She surveyed the crew left in the dining room and found the SUV driver finishing his breakfast. "Lou, Mona's going back to the house and we'll be done here around noon."

He wiped his mouth with a napkin, then slid out of the booth. "Noon it is." He left the diner without a word to Mona. Obviously, her little fit in the kitchen hadn't gone unnoticed.

Rick and Melissa walked out of the kitchen holding hands. Elizabeth should be cheering, but instead alarm bells started ringing in her head. She watched the couple for a moment, then sighed. "Ready for that ride?"

WHAT SHOULD HAVE been a quiet sleigh ride through the countryside had turned into a slippery, wet mess in a blizzard. Eddie kept wiping the camera lens. Rick felt cold and miserable. If he didn't have the warm woman snuggled against his side, it would be a disaster.

He put his arms around Melissa and squeezed. "Not exactly the sleigh ride you expected, huh?"

"Does it always snow like this?" Her teeth chattering almost drowned out her words.

"Pretty much, from November through April. Do you think a Southern belle like you could adjust?"

She looked up at him and tried to smile.

"For someone I love, I'd turn my world up-side down."

Rick held her closer. She said all the right things. She was beautiful and warm and funny. She was perfect.

Wasn't she? Or was she playing for the cameras like Brandy had? How could he tell what was real?

They took a turn at the end of the road, and the frozen lake the town was named after came into view. The ice-fishing shacks still dotted the icy surface. Long tracks beside the road meant cross-country skiers had recently been along this trek. Despite the cold, wet snow, Rick loved it.

He leaned forward past Eddie, who seemed determined to film everything, and shouted to the driver, "Take a left up here. I want to show Melissa something."

Lizzie glanced around them and shook her head. She held up her clipboard. "That's not on the schedule."

"You can't do everything by the book, Lizzie." He leaned back and pulled the quilts higher. "Let's shake it up a little."

When they reached the family home, Eddie was the first to hop out of the sleigh. Rick held out a hand to Melissa and helped her down, then turned to give Lizzie the same courtesy. As soon as their hands clasped, electricity sparked and he brought his eyes up to meet her own startled expression.

Not good.

His mom met them at the front door, holding it open and sending shards of light onto the covered porch. She looked as if she'd been busy with a book; her reading glasses rested on top of her head. "Come in and get warm."

He reached over and kissed her cheek. "Sorry to barge in like this. I thought I'd show Melissa around. If you don't mind."

She turned to Melissa. "Not at all. I'll make us some coffee while you do that. Warm you all up from the inside out."

Rick helped Melissa out of her coat and hung it on the rack near the front door. He took Melissa's hand and led her into the spacious living room. "This is where I grew up."

"I remember from the tea party your mom hosted." She released his hand and walked over to the fireplace, looking up at the framed pictures that graced the mantel. "You certainly were a handsome young man."

"Still am." He winked at her and took down the picture of his parents on their wedding day. "This was my dad. I wish he was still around to meet you. He'd have loved you."

Melissa looked up at him, her cheeks pink,

obviously pleased by his words. "I remember him from the first time you were on the show."

"It was his idea for me to go on." He replaced the picture. Touched the frame. "He said it was for the company, but I think he knew I needed a wife."

"And now?"

Rick glanced at the camera behind him. "Still do. But I'm willing to take the time to make sure I do it right."

She nodded and turned back to the fireplace. She picked up the recent picture of his family, without his dad. "Do you miss him?"

Every day.

Rick cleared his throat and took her elbow. "I'll give you the tour that you didn't get before."

He took her upstairs to the bedroom where he'd grown up. Trophies and posters still decorated the room. The quilt his mom had made him still covered the twin bed. The books on the shelves above the bed were mostly biographies of sports heroes.

He showed her the bathroom he'd shared with Dan. The corner of the tub where he'd hit his head and needed stitches after he'd been horsing around with his brother. Even after his dad had warned them.

Dan's room and the tiny cubbyhole underneath the floorboards that his brother had thought no one else knew about. The journal he'd kept in high school still waited there. He told Melissa how he'd read it aloud one night over dinner. How Dan had paid him back by running a pair of his boxers up the flagpole at school. Typical brother stuff.

He took her up to the third level that entirely contained his parents' bedroom suite. They'd shared almost thirty years of marriage before his dad had died. Clothes still hung in his dad's walk-in closet.

Melissa looked around the spacious bedroom with the large bathroom and his mom's sewing room jutting off of it. "This house is huge. Unlike anything I've ever seen."

Rick nodded. "My dad designed it. If granddad hadn't died and left him the pickle company, I think he might have become an architect. But we all have to give up dreams sometimes to do the right thing."

Melissa put her hand on his arm. "What about your dreams? What have you given up?"

Rick rubbed his left leg and shrugged. "It doesn't matter. We get the life we deserve."

"Or we can take our circumstances and find new dreams."

Where had Lizzie found this woman? Rick reached out and touched her cheek. Noticed the cameraman recording them and cleared his throat. "If you like the house, you'll love the kitchen. It's really the heart of this place."

The tour ended in the kitchen, where he found his mom and Lizzie sipping coffee. His mom sprang to action and poured mugs for both him and Melissa. "It's not fine china, but it's what's inside the cup that counts." She gave him a pointed look.

Rick put cream and sugar in Melissa's mug, then handed it to her. "Just the way you like it."

Melissa took a sip and nodded. "Perfection," she said, looking at him rather than her cup.

Lizzie shook her head and walked out of the kitchen, mumbling about needing to revise their schedule.

THE CONTESTANTS EACH paired up with a preschooler; Rick had his own rambunctious four-year-old to deal with. He tried to get comfortable in the tiny seat, but his knees came up almost to his shoulders sitting that way. He adjusted and moved until little Wesley turned and frowned at him. "Miss Tompkins don't like it when we wiggle."

Rick leaned in and dropped his voice. "How do you get comfy in these chairs, then?"

Wesley scrunched up his face and put a finger to his mouth. Then he leaned in so close that Rick could smell the shampoo from his bath. "We wiggle when she's not looking."

Miss Tompkins must have seen them. "Wesley, do you have a question?"

Rick raised his head. "No, Miss Tompkins. Just waiting for your directions." He turned to Wesley, and they shared a grin.

Lizzie stood in the corner of the room, checking the releases each parent had signed to get their little one on the show. Rick noticed some parents were determined to get their child more airtime, too. Luckily, Lizzie shepherded them out to the other room with the crew. Rick gave a sigh of relief.

Miss Tompkins passed out old shirts and had the adults help their child partners into theirs after putting on their own. She then passed out large pieces of newsprint paper and paper plates with large splotches of paints in bright primary colors. Some of the women paled as they saw the paint and the eager expressions on their partners. Rick chuckled and nudged Wesley. "What are we gonna paint?"

"Miss Tompkins ain't said yet." Wesley

looked at the colors. "Probably another rainbow. Or butterflies. She really likes those."

"And you don't?"

"I like cars."

Miss Tompkins returned to the front of the classroom. "Boys and girls. Ladies and gentleman. I want you to paint what love looks like. Whatever you imagine love is, paint that."

A little girl near the front raised her hand. "Like hearts?"

Miss Tompkins nodded. "If love looks like hearts to you, Ashley, then yes. Paint hearts."

Rick's tiny partner groaned and crossed his arms. Rick ruffled his hair. "Wesley, what do you love?"

"Cars." He shrugged. "And my mom."

"So maybe love looks like your mom driving a new car?" Rick looked up to find Melissa watching him. He winked, then turned back to his painting partner. "I think love is more than just flowers and hearts, too. Sometimes it's the people we care about."

"Like girls?" Wesley wrinkled his nose.

Rick laughed. "Sometimes. But wait until you're older."

Satisfied with his answer, Wesley set about painting a large red car with big blue wheels. Rick peered at his own blank sheet. What did love look like? He closed his eyes and could see his family. His friends. Even the diner.

Funny how none of the women vying for his heart had made it into the picture.

BRANDY'S FIRST ONE-ON-ONE date with Rick took place in his apartment. He'd made dinner for the two of them and created a romantic atmosphere down to flickering red candles and Ernesto's apple pie.

Charlie set up lights and cameras as both Rick and Brandy got their microphones checked and pinned to them. Elizabeth glanced at the clipboard as if the answers would be there. Answers to questions she didn't want to ask.

What was she doing?

Was she falling for someone she was being paid to marry off to someone else?

What if he found a wife at the end of this? Wasn't that what she wanted? Or was she just fooling herself? Had she engineered this whole thing so she could spend more time with Rick?

She shook her head at the last question. Fought the panic that bubbled in her belly. She was here for a job, not a man. That was her life. That was what she planned.

Not some crazy idea that maybe her friendship with Rick could lead somewhere.

"We're ready."

Her head snapped up at Charlie's words. Leave it to her camera operator to keep her on task. He'd done it before and promised to do it again. "Great." She approached the couple, who nervously adjusted their clothes and hair. "Relax. You two have both been here before. This should be old hat."

She consulted her clipboard. "Dinner here. Then a moonlit walk down Main Street. Romantic. Intimate."

Rick shivered. "Freezing."

She crooked one eyebrow at Rick. "The forecaster said we might hit twenty tonight."

"And the weatherman's always right." Rick grinned at Brandy. "But then we midwesterners know how to handle cold, right?"

Brandy chuckled.

"We're all set up, E." Charlie took a spot behind the camera. "Ready when you are."

She clapped her hands once, then gestured at the table that was set for two. "What do you say we start this date?" She held up the clapboard for the camera as they got settled into their chairs.

Rick pulled out the chair for his date, then brought their salads to the table. "I left off the green peppers on yours."

Brandy froze, the fork halfway to her mouth. Her face broke into a grin. "You remembered."

Rick winked at her. "Hard to forget someone like you."

Brandy swallowed and wiped her mouth delicately. "We haven't talked much about what you've been doing the past five years. Do you like running the diner?"

Rick took his seat and placed the napkin on his lap. "After I lost my contract with the major league, it was my lifeline. The reason I got up in the morning. It saved my life a thousand times. I know I don't have to be there from open to close, but I love it. It's my life." He grabbed his fork. "But that's a talk for another time. Let's eat."

They ate quietly for a moment while Elizabeth took a seat on Rick's sofa and pretended to pay attention to the scene in front of her. There was way too much déjà vu for her. She stood and crossed the room to gaze out the front windows that overlooked the downtown strip. What if she were the one sitting across from Rick? What would her life here be like? She gazed back at the couple enjoying dinner. Would she die of boredom? Or would the charm of this town bring new experiences? A new life?

After the salads, Rick brought out the pot

roast with fixings. Elizabeth's stomach grumbled, which made him smirk. He prepared two plates, brought them to her and Charlie, turned back and made two more. Elizabeth accepted hers with a nod of thanks and began to eat while she watched the date continue.

Brandy gracefully sliced her meat and put a bit of gravy on it. She took a bite, and her eyes closed as she chewed. "Oh, wow. Is that rosemary?"

"And garlic, yes." Rick took a bite of his own meal. "Plus a little coffee added to the gravy to make it hearty."

Brandy licked her fork. "Fabulous."

Elizabeth agreed. Who wouldn't want a husband who could cook like this?

Rick laid his fork next to his plate and glanced at Brandy. "Do you mind if I ask you something?" She sighed but waited for the question. He paused a second, then asked, "Why choose Wade?"

Elizabeth held her breath. It was the question the audience would be asking themselves. Why hadn't she chosen the nice guy? Why choose the bad boy who broke her heart instead?

Brandy dabbed her mouth, then laid the napkin in her lap. "I've been expecting that question."

"Do you mind answering it?"

"The heart wants what it wants." She reached out and touched Rick's hand. "I loved you, too, but it was different."

Rick scooted his chair back from the table. "So what's changed now?" He paused, then tipped his head to the side; one lock of hair fell across his forehead at a rakish angle. "Do you think there's a chance for us this time?"

Brandy shrugged. "Before I didn't know what I wanted."

"And now you do?"

Elizabeth leaned forward. Rick was asking the questions America wanted to know, too. She gave a silent prayer that viewers were tuning in to hear Brandy's answers.

Brandy nodded. "I know better now. I'm ready to be better this time."

It was an answer that would be quoted ad nauseam after they aired, Elizabeth knew. One she would make sure was posted on their website. It was an answer that sounded good, despite the fact that she doubted it. Maybe Brandy really did want to be better this time.

And maybe Elizabeth was wrong about the attraction she'd sensed between Brandy and Dan.

Brandy gave a soft smile, then raised her

water glass. "To Rick, a new man with a new mission."

He raised his own glass and clinked it with hers. After they had taken a sip, Rick kept his gaze on hers and nodded. "To second chances."

Elizabeth hoped the same thing for Rick, a man who deserved another chance.

RICK PUT HIS ARM around Brandy's shoulder as they took their moonlit walk down Main Street. The darkened storefronts added a hint of mystery and romance with the glow of the streetlamps lighting their path only a few steps at a time.

Being with Brandy felt comfortable. Familiar. He'd been here before. He could easily fall back into love again. After all, five years could be nothing.

Brandy leaned her head on his shoulder, and Rick pulled her in tighter. "I'm glad you're here."

She sighed, and her body seemed to melt further into his. "I'm glad I came."

They walked to the end of the street, then turned back. Rick could see a dark sedan parked in front of the diner. "Looks like my brother wants to see me."

Brandy's body tensed but remained glued

to his side. She looked away from the car and focused on him. "Dan seems nice."

"He can be. But then he's my older brother so I remember all the lame things he did growing up." He chuckled and pulled her closer. Tried to ignore the fact that she didn't respond as quickly as she had earlier. "Before we get back, I'd like to talk to you about something."

She didn't say anything. Seemed to wait on his next words.

He held out the small jewelry box. "If I give you the immunity charm—"

"Rick, don't." She pushed the box back into his hands and stepped away from him.

He frowned and stopped walking. Waited until she looked up at him. "Don't you want to stay?"

"Of course I do." She bit her lip, a habit that had enthralled and frustrated him before. "But I need to earn my place here just like all the other girls."

Rick held the box out again. "You already have. I want you to have this." She shook her head and started walking back to the diner. Rick had to sprint to keep up with her fast little legs. "Brandy, I want you to stay."

She turned and faced him. "Give the charm to someone else this week."

He thought he understood. He could remember what it was like returning from one of their dates with the charm. It made things tense with the other guys, even those he'd become friends with. He put the box back into his pocket. "Are things bad back at the house?"

She shrugged, then nodded. "They don't like me. Well, except Melissa. She's a sweetheart." She picked at her mittens. "Giving me the charm this week would only make it worse. Please don't."

Rick nodded, then pulled her back into his arms. "Okay. You're the boss."

Brandy giggled, and the heaviness in his heart lightened slightly.

CHAPTER TWELVE

RICK TURNED the open sign and unlocked the doors to the diner. After several weeks playing bachelor, he welcomed the chance to get back to a seminormal schedule.

Last night's elimination hadn't been a surprise to anyone. Mona needed to go home, and he had been more than happy to send her. They were down to six women—Melissa, Brandy, Becky, Jenn, Leslie and Vanessa. The only one he wasn't sure was meant for small-town life was the last. They'd barely spoken except for that moment by the lake with their dogs, but tonight's one-on-one would change that.

The bell over the door tinkled, and Mr. Crosby walked in followed by his pals Mr. Teetum and Mr. White. "Hey, fellas, I've got fresh coffee."

They waved their agreement and took their usual spot at a table near the back, where they'd spend the next four hours discussing sports and politics and drinking coffee. Rick snagged three mugs and the carafe.

Once the men were settled, Rick discovered that Lizzie had called a crew meeting at the front of his diner. Troy, Charlie, Eddie and Nick, the sound guy, perused menus while Lizzie chirped on the phone. He grabbed four mugs and met them at the table. "Gentlemen, lady, can I interest you in some coffee?"

Charlie accepted a mug, as did Nick. Eddie shook his head. "I'll take an espresso, though. Elizabeth told me you got the new machine."

Rick raised an eyebrow and shrugged. "It's been over a month, so it's hardly new. Single or double?"

Eddie grinned. "Surprise me."

Rick turned to Lizzie, who held up her finger at him as she hissed into the phone. Obviously a bad morning. He poured her a cup of regular coffee, then left to get Eddie's espresso order.

When he returned with Eddie's drink, Lizzie had finished her call and was going over notes with her crew. "The set looks dark on air. Charlie, that's your expertise. Brighten it up. Bring in more lamps. I don't care. Fix it."

Charlie nodded and took notes on his napkin.

Lizzie turned to Eddie, who guzzled the espresso, then held his tiny cup out for Rick to refill. "I'm also not happy that you're choosing your own footage. You've got your shot list. Stick to it."

"Then we lose the candid moments." Eddie leaned in. "Like the criers the past few weeks. The audience eats that stuff up, you know."

"So you're producing the show, too, now?" Lizzie shook her head. "Stick to your list. And leave the editing decisions to Troy and me."

"I'm trying to make this tired show into something magnificent." Eddie stood and slammed down his cup. "If you're done yelling, I'm outta here."

Lizzie stood and glared at her cameraman. Rick took a step closer in case she needed him to knock some sense into the kid. She shook her head at Rick and he took a step back. "We're done when I say we're done. And these are just the beginning of the notes I have from last night's show."

Rick passed out menus. "Why don't you order some food to go with those notes? Everybody feels better with some food in their stomach."

Lizzie seemed to sigh in relief. "Thanks, Rick. That's a great idea."

After they had made their selections, Rick left to give their order to Ernesto. The diner was still short a waitress, and Rick had interviews scheduled for later that week. Which gave him an idea.

As he delivered their breakfasts, he leaned against their table. "I've got another great idea."

Lizzie groaned, which made her crew grin. "What's it going to cost me?"

"That's the beauty. Not a thing." He leaned down, inviting them to draw in. "What about putting the remaining six in a waitressing competition? See who's got the stuff to work here, be a true partner."

Lizzie whistled. "When you get good ideas, you really do. I like it." She turned to her crew. "How much of a logistical nightmare would it be to film?"

Charlie glanced around the diner. "Lighting's an issue. Sound might be another story, but it could work."

"Thanks, Rick. We'll schedule it just before the next elimination."

Rick hummed a tune as he returned to the kitchen.

ELIZABETH WAS SMART enough to know when someone had a better idea and to use it. She liked the idea of having the women wearing waitress outfits and being put through the same test Rick had put her through before agreeing to do the show. It was character building. And it made great television. She'd made a list of items she needed to pick up as well as a schedule of what needed to be done and where.

She picked at her cold piece of toast. Her crew had left a few minutes ago, after being given their assignments for the day. Charlie was filming tonight's one-on-one with Rick and Vanessa, while Eddie got assigned the women's house and candid interviews. She reviewed her clipboard, then rose to her feet to find Rick.

He sat at the counter in the kitchen eating hash browns loaded with sour cream and green onions. She wrinkled her nose. "You really eat that?"

Rick motioned her closer and held up a fork. "Taste it first. Then tell me what you think."

She approached him and opened her mouth. The first taste was creamy and tangy followed by the bite and snap of the onion. She closed her eyes and swallowed. "Oh, my, that is good."

Rick smirked and returned to eating his breakfast. "You needed something?"

"That idea of yours is inspired." She leaned against the counter, facing him. "I should listen to you more."

"I do have good ideas every once and a while." He shrugged. "Not that many people listen to them."

Probably thinking of his brother. "Then they're really missing out."

Rick reached up and wiped the side of her mouth with one finger. Her skin tingled at his touch, and her mouth opened slightly.

He held out his finger. "Sour cream."

She wiped the side of her mouth he'd just touched. "Right. Thanks."

A noise outside the kitchen door caught her attention, but no one was there. Probably her imagination. "Good luck tonight. Vanessa might be a hard sell on the whole small-town-living thing."

"Maybe she has reason to be."

"You cut people a lot of slack. Whether they deserve it or not." She stood and adjusted her coat. "That's what makes you one of the nice guys."

"I try." He motioned to the pile of dirty dishes near the sink. "Feel like washing some for old times' sake?"

She held up her hands. "I need these today. But thanks." She laughed and walked out of the kitchen. Made a note to finally get him that industrial dishwasher.

VANESSA LOOKED LOVELY in a red satin dress. The fact that it was strapless and the weather was more suitable for sweaters didn't seem to faze her. Rick glanced at the program. It constantly amazed him that Lizzie could come up with fresh ideas for dates in such a small town. Tonight's date was a play put on by a nearby community theater. It wouldn't be Broadway, but it promised to be entertaining.

Rick leaned closer to Vanessa, catching a hint of orange blossoms. "So you're a dental hygienist?"

She looked up at him and considered him before answering. "Actually, I had to quit to come on the show."

He frowned. Not a smart move in a shaky economy. "Why would you quit a job?"

"Why would you come back on television to find a wife?" She adjusted the top of her dress. "I felt I had no other choice."

He swallowed at the sudden pressure in his throat. Wanted to wipe at the moisture he was sure gathered at his temples. Had they turned up the heat in the theater? "And what if this doesn't work out?"

Vanessa shrugged. "I'll find another job. I might not get another chance like this with a nice guy." She placed her hand on his arm.

"You don't date nice guys?"

She gave a soft smile but it had a tinge of bitterness. "I have the bad habit of dating the wrong ones."

Rick understood. Hadn't he had his own share of dates with women who were definitely wrong? "So what are you looking for in a man?"

She removed her hand from his arm and placed it on his thigh, caressing his leg. Rick didn't move away despite the panic it brought him. "Nice. Good-looking. Someone who makes me laugh."

He chuckled. "Have I told you the one about a duck that walks into a bar?"

Vanessa laughed harder than was necessary. Rick frowned at the response. He was looking for something real, but this wasn't it.

Real was Melissa. Maybe even Brandy.

Or Lizzie.

He welcomed the anonymity of the darkened theater as the production began onstage. Gave him time to consider that last name.

ELIZABETH STARED at the images on the computer screen.

No. Not possible.

Yet there they were. In Rick's kitchen. They appeared cozy. Intimate. She paled as she saw the picture of Rick touching the corner of her mouth. This looked bad.

Her cell phone chirped, but she ignored it. She searched Rick's name on Google and grimaced when six websites came up boasting the same pictures. Headlines of True Love for Producer and Bachelor? and It's Getting Hot in the Kitchen screamed from her computer screen.

Obviously someone had been spying on them and taking pictures. But who? Someone in town? One of her own crew? Wally Ray?

She picked up her cell phone and saw she'd missed Devon's call. So she wasn't the only one who had seen these. Instead of calling him back, however, she grabbed her jacket and headed out the door. Time to talk to the weasel himself.

Wally Ray didn't answer when she pounded on his motel door. A glimpse under the door and through the crack of the drapes revealed no lights inside. She walked back to the parking lot and glanced up and down the street. Wally Ray was a drunk, but he wasn't an idiot. He'd walk to the nearest bar rather than risk driving anywhere farther out.

She found him at the Rusty Nail, nursing a beer and yelling at the television. She stood in front of him, blocking his view. "Hey, I got money on that game."

She stayed where she was and crossed her arms. "Who gave you those pictures?"

Wally Ray took a sip of his beer. "Saw them, huh? They're good. And I got paid coupla times over for them, too." He snickered. "Everyone loves a scandal."

She grimaced and shook her head. "There's nothing going on."

Wally Ray licked his lips. "You sure? 'Cuz it looked like a big something to me."

She leaned down and tried not to tip his chair over. He wouldn't get away with this. "Rick is a good guy. Decent. Leave him alone."

"Is that why you're with him?"

She stood and shook her head. "I'm not. We're not." She ran a hand through her hair. "We're friends."

"I gotta get me a friend like you, then." He started to sip his beer, but she took it from him. "Hey, I paid for that."

"Who took those pictures?" When he tried

to take his glass back, she held it higher. "Tell me and you get it back."

"I can order another."

He held up his hand to the bartender. But Elizabeth waved him off. "Be the nice guy for a change. Where did you get these photos?"

"Sweetheart, I get paid well for those photos. And I get paid more to keep my mouth shut." He stood and looked up at her. "Now, unless you have a nice big figure in mind, I'm gonna find me a drink."

Elizabeth growled and left the bar. Her cell phone sang a Diana Ross song, and she prepared herself for bad news. "What happened this time, Mom?"

But the gruff voice that answered didn't belong to her mother. "Ms. Maier, your mother is in the hospital."

CHARLIE PUT THE CAMERA equipment in the back of the limo, then joined Rick and Vanessa inside. The performance had been good, but hardly prizewinning. Still, Rick made a note to see more of these productions. Support some of the local theater. Might be nice to support someone else's dreams for once.

Charlie's phone rang. While he answered it, Rick glanced at Vanessa. She patted her hair into place despite the fact that it looked perfect. He tried to imagine what a future with her would be like. "Did you enjoy the play?"

She shrugged and gazed out the window. Rick sighed and tried to find something to talk about. "Ernesto made Italian cream cake today at the diner. I've got three pieces with our names on them. What do you say?"

Charlie snapped his phone shut. "Can't. E needs to see you right away."

That didn't sound good. "Everything okay?"

Charlie didn't answer; he leaned toward the driver and changed their destination to the house where the women lived. The rest of the car ride was silent. Rick tried to figure out why he felt as if he were a child waiting for his father to come home and discipline him. Something wasn't right. And he had no idea what it could be.

The driver let Vanessa out at the women's house, then sped off toward the hotel where Lizzie and the crew were staying. Rick turned to Charlie. "Not even a hint about what's going on?"

"E will go over it with you." The cameraman didn't elaborate, but by the grim set of his mouth, it wasn't good.

"Okay." Rick settled back into the seat, gazing out the window as they passed through Lake Mildred. He glanced at his dark apartment and diner, wishing he could end the night alone. Maybe catch the sports report on the news.

They arrived at the hotel, and Charlie quietly escorted Rick to one of the conference rooms, where crew members milled around talking on phones, typing on computers, ignoring them. Rick spotted Lizzie across the room on the phone. He didn't need to hear the words to know that she was upset. She paced. Shouted. Shook her head. Talked with her hands even though the person on the other side couldn't see them.

When she looked up and saw him and Charlie, she stalked toward them. Charlie patted Rick's shoulder and left. Rick glanced at his retreating figure and swallowed at the panic rising in his throat. What happened to sticking together?

Lizzie grabbed a stack of photos from one of the tables and thrust them at Rick. "What do you know about these?"

Rick glanced through them and frowned. "Who's taking pictures at my diner?"

"That's what I want to know." Lizzie pointed to the top one. "Who's trying to sabotage your life and my show?"

"And you think I know the answer?" He stopped at the one where he was wiping sour cream from her mouth. Winced. "This looks bad."

"You think?" She snatched the photos from him and slammed them on the desk. "Who in town needs money bad enough that they would sell these?"

Wait. No one he knew could do this. Would do this. Rick frowned. "You think it's one of my friends?"

Lizzie glared at him, probably hoping it would wither him. Make him confess something. "Hollywood coming to town doesn't happen every day. Maybe someone thought they could make an easy buck."

"No one I know would sell me out." He crossed his arms and looked her over. "But I'm sure you know a few who would."

"This is why I wanted it done the regular way. A closed set. Controlled." She rubbed her forehead. "Those pictures are all over the internet. It's the lead story on tonight's news. I got calls from the tabloids. It's like the scandal with Bob all over again. This is a nightmare."

Rick looked at the pictures again and tried to chuckle. "It's not like they're nude photos."

Lizzie pointed at him. "Don't make a joke of this. They're damaging enough."

She stalked away from him. Rick grabbed

the top photo and perused it. Anyone with half a brain could see they had chemistry together. Even if there was nothing going on, his confusing feelings were now out there in glossy eight-by-tens. He followed Lizzie to a computer and pulled up a chair next to her.

He sighed and folded his hands in his lap. "So what do we do now?"

"We spin it." She kept her focus on the computer monitor. Refused to look at him. "And we hope that a bigger story comes to take its place quick."

Rick nodded. "Sounds like a plan."

"And you stay away from me. We're never alone. We don't even have to talk to each other." She glanced up at him, then back at her laptop. "If we're not seen together, there's no story."

They worked together. How in the world were they going to avoid each other? "But you're my producer."

"Not for the next couple of days." She clicked off her laptop and shoved it into a messenger bag. "I have something personal to take care of."

When she started to step away, Rick grabbed her arm. "Won't it look even more suspicious if you suddenly disappear from the set?"

She shook his hand off. "There's nothing

to see if I'm gone. And it's only for a couple of days. Maybe a week."

Rick looked around the room at the crew, who scurried here and there, answering phones, typing on laptops. "And who's going to do the day-to-day producing when you're gone?"

Lizzie nodded at a young man surrounded by crew members. He held a familiar clipboard. "I've promoted Troy. For now."

Rick shuddered. "That guy rubs me the wrong way."

"At least there won't be incriminating pictures of you two all over the internet." She hitched the bag higher on her shoulder.

"Those pictures only captured innocent moments between friends." He wanted to tell her it was going to be okay. That they weren't going to be driven apart by this. "You're making a big deal out of nothing."

Lizzie looked up at him, tears threatening. "This might be my last season with the show. I'm on notice."

He winced at the tears. He could handle anything but that. "Then you'll get a new show."

She shook her head. "If the network fires me, no one in Hollywood will hire me."

"They're not that powerful." Only in her

mind. Maybe he could help her see that. Maybe he could convince her that there was more to life than the show. The network.

Lizzie snatched the pictures from the table and shook them in his face. "These will ruin any chance for me. Who's going to hire a producer who can't keep scandal away from her show?" She slammed them back onto the table. "This is not a game to me, Rick. This is my life."

He reached out and touched her arm. "It's your job, Lizzie. Not your life."

"It's the same thing."

"Then I feel sad for you." He started to walk away.

Lizzie followed him. Practically stepped on his heels. "You don't get to tell me how to live my life."

He whirled around and faced her. "You've done a pretty good job of telling me how to live mine." He motioned to everyone in the room, who had stopped talking to watch them. "I was fine before you all came here. I had a life before the show, and I'll have one that's just fine after."

Lizzie smirked. "If your life was so great, why did I find you still stuck here after five years? What happened to your plans of getting out?"

Plans changed. Dreams did, too. Rick seethed and gritted his teeth. "When my dad died—"

"Right. He died. Not you."

He opened his mouth to say something. Shut it. Then turned and walked out of the conference room.

CHAPTER THIRTEEN

Rick sat in front of the camera and rolled his head from side to side. Rubbed his knee, which had begun to ache. Troy had been doing interviews for the past two hours non-stop. What was he trying to do? Kill the show with boredom?

"Seriously. Can't we plan one of the dates? Or plan the next elimination?" Rick glanced at Charlie, who looked as bored as he was.

Troy shook his head and consulted the clip-board. "The problem with Elizabeth was she focused on the dates, but the audience connects with the bachelor because of the interviews."

"Have you ever watched the show? They love the conflict and the romance." Rick stood and stretched to get feeling back in his arms and legs. "Trust me. They fast-forward the interviews."

Troy frowned. "Well, Elizabeth said—"

"Lizzie's not here." Rick glanced at Charlie. "Sorry, man. I need to stretch my legs or something."

Rick left his apartment and walked down to the diner. The lunch crowd had already thinned out, but he found Jeffy sitting at the counter, eating a plate of fries. Rick took the seat next to him. "Mind if I have one?"

Jeffy pushed his plate toward him. "Mr. Rick, we've missed you."

Rick snagged a fry and dipped it in ketchup. "I've missed you, too, buddy. They keep me pretty busy."

"When will this be over? I want to work with you again."

"A few more weeks." Rick ate another fry, then motioned to Shirley. "Can you get me a club sandwich and fries?"

"Sure, Rick." She wrote his order down and leaned on the counter next to him. "Please tell me this show is almost done."

He touched his chest. "You guys miss me that much? I'm touched."

Shirley groaned and rubbed her lower back. "The lunch crowds are killing me. I deserve a raise."

Rick shouted after her as she left, "You'll get one." He turned back to Jeffy and helped himself to another fry. "So what have I missed?"

"Shirley's feet hurt and make her cranky. Mr. Ernesto is tired." Jeffy bit his lip, then shrugged. "Did Mr. Eddie give you the picture?"

Rick stopped eating the French fry and frowned. "What are you talking about, buddy?"

"He took a picture of you and Miss Lizzie. Said he was going to give it to you. Like a surprise."

Rick closed his eyes. *Right.* "Yes, those pictures were a surprise. Thanks for telling me." He got to his feet and motioned to Shirley. "Can you wrap my sandwich to go? I have a phone call to make."

ELIZABETH HAD ELEVEN missed calls on her cell phone when the plane landed in San Francisco. While in the air, she'd glanced out the window and marveled at the clouds that covered any view of the land below. Too bad she couldn't live up there where problems wouldn't find her. Where temperamental cast members wouldn't make her life miserable. And internet rumors wouldn't make her run away.

As if that was the problem.

The longer she'd thought about it, the more she'd come to believe that the photographer who had started all this was someone she knew. Perhaps someone she'd hired. The fact that they knew who to give the pictures to pointed to someone with inside knowledge of tabloids. Someone who knew the business. Someone who could get in touch with Wally Ray, promising a big story.

She regretted now the way she'd jumped all over Rick. He hadn't deserved that, but he'd been there. Earnest and handsome as ever. She'd wanted to protect him from the press, but it turned out that she needed to protect him from herself.

She searched the concourse for a coffee shop that didn't have a mile-long line. These endless days and sleepless nights were getting to her.

While she waited in line for coffee, she dialed her voice mail and entered her password. She listened to the first three before hanging up and dialing Devon. "I want that weasel off my set."

"Elizabeth, you obviously got my message."

The line moved up one step. If she didn't get coffee soon... "Tell me I can fire him."

"It's not that simple."

Frustrated, Elizabeth left the coffee shop and strode down the hall of the terminal, hiking her carry-on higher over her shoulder. "Eddie compromised the show for a couple of bucks. I should have known—"

"No one knew."

She walked in the direction of the ticket counters. "Well, now that we do, I'm going back to take care of this." She checked her watch and read the signs to see when the next flight back left.

"You have more important things to take care of right now."

"I know." She stopped walking and closed her eyes. "If I didn't have to go take care of my mom, you know I'd be back on the next plane. This is my show."

"Knowing it was Eddie doesn't change the fact that you're getting too close to Rick."

She scanned the crowded hall and lowered her voice. "Rick is a good friend. There's nothing going on. How many times do I have to say it?"

There was silence on the other end of the line. Elizabeth almost felt triumphant to make Devon speechless.

"You're off set for a week, Elizabeth. Let the scandal blow over." He paused while she let her carry-on sag to the floor. "In the meantime, keep doing what you planned. Take care of your mom."

Elizabeth hung up with Devon and massaged her forehead. *Right.* Take care of her mom. Truth was, she had no idea what she'd find once she got to the hospital.

RICK SAT IN one of the booths as the six women raced to serve their tables. Ernesto had mixed orders to see which women could keep them straight and which could handle the stress while staying positive. Melissa appeared to be handling it the best, providing the best service with a smile. Brandy, on the other hand, could spot the switches and change it back to the way her orders read.

If anyone had doubts about who would fit into Rick's life, this competition was clearing any of that confusion.

Once the orders were served, they all joined Rick at the booth. Jeffy brought over plates of salads with little cups of dressing. Rick gave each of the women a wide grin. "You all did very well. My life can sometimes get like what you just did. What did you think?"

Melissa placed her fork on the table. "It would be a challenge to learn, but I think I could adjust."

Rick agreed. She'd handled it really well. He could see her in the diner. He could see her living with him in the apartment up-stairs, too. They'd probably want to find a house soon after the wedding. The place was crowded with just him.

Brandy shrugged. "It was fun to do, but I don't think I could handle working at the diner day after day. Is that really your life?"

"For now." Rick poured some French dressing over his salad while he changed Melissa with Brandy in the picture of his future. Even if she didn't help out at the diner every day, she could still fit into his world. But then he'd always seen her here in Lake Mildred. "My whole life is the diner at the moment. And that means early mornings and long days. I wouldn't expect my wife to work here unless she wanted to, but I do view our life together as a partnership."

They considered that as they finished their salads. Jeffy brought out their turkey dinners and a basket of rolls. "Enjoy."

After dinner, they drove back to the house for the elimination. Rick didn't have any doubts which women were going home this time. Looked as if he was going to pull another surprise out of the bag.

RICK STOOD IN FRONT of the women. He knew what he had to do. Knew he had to make the right decision. And that was what this was. The necklaces felt heavy in his hand. As if they knew they meant more than a gold chain with a charm. He looked between them then nodded. "Brandy."

She stepped forward. "Brandy, will you accept my heart?"

She gave him that smile that made him want to drop to his knees and hold on to her. "Absolutely."

He placed the necklace around her neck, then kissed her cheek before she turned and joined the rest of the women. He separated the next necklace. "Melissa."

Melissa also smiled as she approached him. He could lose himself in her beautiful face. No doubt. He found comfort in her. Peace. None of the soul-troubling passion he had once felt for Brandy, but he felt safe with that. As if he wouldn't lose himself by loving her. "Melissa, will you accept my heart?"

She reached up and kissed his cheek. "Yes." After the necklace rested around her neck, they embraced tightly. He almost didn't want to let her go.

He looked at the necklaces in his hand then surveyed the rest of them. He pulled another necklace away from the other two then looked out and nodded again. "Becky."

She practically ran up to him and threw her arms around him. "Yes, yes, yes."

He chuckled at her exuberance. She would be joy and light in his life. She would bring laughter and fun. He put the necklace around her neck and kissed her cheek. "I'm glad you're willing."

She winked at him. "You have no idea."

She joined the rest of the contestants, who watched him. Waiting for the next name. Wanting it to be theirs.

He looked down at the necklaces. "I'm sorry, ladies. I won't be giving out any more tonight." When they protested, he shook his head. "I've enjoyed my time with you, but it would be unfair to drag this out any longer. Each of you is beautiful. Amazing. And deserving of love. But I don't feel that you can find that with me."

He approached them and took his time telling the other three goodbye. Leslie tried to hide her tears, but he could still see them glistening. "You'll find the guy who's right for you. I know it."

She shook her head and walked away from him.

Man, he hated this part of the show.

ELIZABETH APPROACHED the hospital room but paused before entering, unsure of what she'd find on the other side of the door. A nurse whisked past her into the room while she stood trying to decide. In a moment, the nurse came back out. "She's awake if you want to see her."

Elizabeth steeled herself and then stepped inside.

She let out all her air at the sight of her mother hooked up to machines. Both eyes were black with bruises, and a bandage covered her chest from what the cop had said was a slash from a butcher's knife.

This couldn't be happening. Shouldn't be. *No, no, no.*

She took a step forward and clutched the end of the bed. She hung her head and cried silently until the woman in the bed stirred. "Bethie?"

"Oh, Mom." She walked to the head of the bed and collapsed into a chair beside it. Grasped her mother's hand. "What happened?"

"I thought he loved me." Tears squeezed from her mother's bruised eyes. "But this… It's not love."

"No, Mom. It never is." She leaned her forehead on her mother's hand. "When are they releasing you? Do you have somewhere to go?"

Her mother stayed silent. Watching her. Finally, she said, "I was hoping I could stay with you."

Mild panic rose in Elizabeth's chest. With her? Could her mother fit into her life now? They hadn't been close in years. Hadn't lived together since she was sixteen and her mom had wanted to move to Arizona. She shook her head. "I'm not at home right now. I'm on assignment."

Her mother swallowed. "You always are."

"Because that's my life." It was always her life. In the past year, she'd been home a total of thirty-two days. If she didn't need somewhere to go back to, she'd get rid of her apartment altogether and live out of a suitcase. Much like she already did.

Her mom closed her eyes and faintly squeezed her hand. "Oh, Bethie, I wanted more for you than some job."

"This is not some job. This is a major show on network television. This is what I've worked for my whole life."

"And what about love?"

The woman tethered to machines was going to lecture her about relationships? "We both can see where love can get you." Elizabeth winced. "Sorry, Mom. I didn't—"

"I know." Her mother squeezed her hand again. "I haven't been the best example."

"Not even close." Elizabeth swallowed and removed her hand from her mother's. "Why did he always come first?"

"He didn't—"

"I was six, and you left me at a bus station while you went off who knows where doing whatever it was with your new boyfriend." Elizabeth shuddered, pulled her arms closer to her sides and crossed them. Whether to keep out the chill or to protect herself, she wasn't sure. She only felt the need to hug herself. "I thought you'd left me. I thought you were never coming back. I thought you stopped loving me."

"I could never stop that."

"You only call me when you need something. Not to say hi or to find out how I'm doing." She stood. "You call me when your new man dumps you and you have to move out again. You ask me for money when he steals all of yours. You want to move in with me when you have nowhere else to go." The tiny beeps of the machines filled the air between them. Elizabeth shook her head. "That's not love, either, Mom."

"Neither is your job."

"My job makes sure I have somewhere to

live. And food in my belly. Which is more than you did." She hiked her purse higher on her shoulder. "I'm sorry that he did this to you. And I'll pay for your hospital bills. But I can't let you go home with me right now."

Elizabeth's cell phone chirped, but she ignored it. "I can help you find somewhere to go."

Her mom turned away. "Just go answer your phone."

She walked out of the hospital room, shut the door and dialed Troy's number. "What now?"

"You need to come back."

As if she didn't want to. She needed this job even more now. The proof of that was lying in a hospital bed. "I'm dealing with some personal things. What is it?"

"Your boyfriend just changed our entire schedule."

Elizabeth shut her eyes and tapped the cell phone on her forehead. She replaced it to her ear. "Is Rick there?"

A few seconds later, a warm voice came on the other end. "Lizzie."

"Don't 'Lizzie' me. What did you do?"

There was a pause, then a long sigh. "Tonight was the elimination."

No kidding. She may not be on set, but she

was still very aware of what was happening on her show. "Yes..."

"And I sent Vanessa home."

She took a deep breath. "Okay. I had a feeling she wouldn't last."

"And Jenny. And Leslie."

He'd just removed two weeks from their schedule. "Then you ask two of them to come back."

"I'm not doing that."

"We have schedules for a reason, Rick. We have to fill so many weeks with episodes, and when you change it up, we lose whole weeks of programming." She rested her head against the wall. "We're locked into an agreement with the network about how many we'll deliver." She fought to keep her voice calm. "And you just screwed that up."

"You might see it like that."

Might? He had no idea what he'd done. "Because that's how it is."

"Or you could see that I want more time with the finalists. Give me a chance to really know them." He paused. "How can you expect me to know who I want to spend the rest of my life with when I barely know her? I need more time."

"Well, you just got it. Put Troy back on the line." There was an exchange on the other side, and Troy came back on. She started marking things off with her fingers. "Do you have your clipboard? Good. Move the family dinner to this weekend and eliminate the bingo night. It was a logistics nightmare anyway. And I'll figure out the rest. Have you got that?"

"When are you coming back?"

Elizabeth pulled her planner out of her purse and consulted her calendar. "I'll be there by Friday night. Make sure you have a car to pick me up. And, Troy? No more surprises."

She snapped her phone shut and tossed it into her purse. No more surprises at all.

RICK DELIVERED a veggie stir-fry to Troy's table, then took a seat across from him. "Can we talk?"

Troy looked up from his cell phone and frowned. "Is something wrong?"

"You tell me. Lizzie's been gone for days, and I need her." He lounged back in the booth. He'd missed her these past few days. He'd been busy with the show, planning for the family dinner this weekend, but his thoughts drifted to her often. He missed her laugh, her smile, her presence. He rubbed his face. "Why isn't she back yet?"

His producer placed his cell phone on the table and unrolled the napkin surrounding his silverware. Adjusted his water glass. Fiddled with his fork. Stalling.

Rick sighed. "Why did she leave?"

"She'll be back tomorrow afternoon. Then you can make *her* life miserable instead of mine."

Rick rose to his feet. "Enjoy your dinner."

He left Troy and saw Charlie sitting at the counter. Rick took the seat next to the cameraman. "Did you need anything else?"

Charlie looked down at his empty plate and shook his head. "I think I've gained ten pounds eating here every day."

Rick nodded and grinned. "Appreciate the business, man."

"Pretty easy to do when you're one of the only restaurants in town." Charlie picked up his coffee cup and took a long swallow.

Rick rose to his feet and retrieved the coffee carafe, topped off Charlie's cup and poured one for himself. Sure, it was late, but he hadn't slept much the past few nights anyway. He returned to his stool and doctored his coffee with cream and sugar. "Who's going to pick Lizzie up from the airport tomorrow?"

Charlie shrugged. "Probably Troy. They

have some things to go over, and you know how E hates to waste time."

Rick chuckled at that. Very true. "Think I could hitch along on that ride? I have some things of my own to discuss with her."

"I don't think that's a good idea."

Rick turned and looked over the cameraman. "And why is that?"

"Listen, I'm not supposed to know this, but she's feeling fragile right now." Charlie paused, as if to let the words sink in, then shook his head. "Sorry, I shouldn't have said anything. Never mind."

"You can't start talking and then just stop like that." Rick leaned in. "I consider her my friend, too, and I'm worried about her. What happened?"

Charlie glanced around, then dropped his voice to a whisper. "I'm only telling you because she's going to need a friend when she gets back. And you're the best one she has right now."

That meant a lot, especially coming from him. Rick held up two fingers. "I won't share what you tell me. Scout's honor."

The cameraman looked him over, then sighed. "Her mom got hurt pretty bad, and E flew out to check on her, to take care of things."

Rick sat back and absorbed the information. "She doesn't talk about her mom."

"She's got reason not to." He picked up his cup and took a swallow. "And that's all I'm saying."

Rick nodded and toyed with his coffee cup. His heart ached for her. He remembered watching his father in the hospital. Praying that he'd recover, accepting the inevitable when the doctors gave them no hope.

He stood and clapped Charlie on the shoulder. "Thanks for being honest with me, man. Lizzie means a lot to me."

And in that moment, he realized how much. And he needed to find a way to be the one to pick her up from the airport. Because there were some things that needed to be said between them before it was too late.

ELIZABETH SCANNED the luggage-retrieval area for her ride. Lou, Troy, whoever. It didn't matter. She'd told Troy no more surprises, and she'd meant it. And being stood up at the airport didn't work for her.

"Lizzie, over here."

She turned and saw Rick waving. But then maybe surprises were a good thing.

She grabbed the handle of her rolling suitcase and headed in his direction. Once she was a few feet from him, he jogged up and took the handle from her. "Here. Let me."

Always a gentleman.

She handed him the suitcase, and he led her out to the sidewalk, where Lou waited with one of the SUVs. Rick opened the door and helped her inside, then ran to the back and loaded her suitcase. He was being so solicitous. She wondered if he was buttering her up to get something. Probably something she wasn't willing to give.

He opened the door and slid in next to her. Leaned over and gave the driver the signal to leave. Then settled back and fastened his seat belt.

He looked tired, she thought. Puffy eyes. Tension lines in his forehead. Jaw clenched. She reached out and touched his hand. "What's going on?"

He shrugged. "What do you mean?"

"Why are you here instead of Troy?"

He opened his mouth, then shook his head. "I bribed Troy into letting me be the one to pick you up. That's all."

That's all? There was more to it, she was sure of it. "Okay, then." He'd tell her when he was ready. She settled into the seat and turned on her cell phone. Scrolled through her email. Checked her phone log.

Rick sighed. "I know about your mom."

Her eyes snapped up to meet his. She scowled, hating the pity she saw there. "How did you…?"

"Charlie let it slip," he said. "But you should have been the one to tell me."

"It's none of your business." And it wasn't. Never would be. Why did he have to be so comforting, so welcoming? Why couldn't he let her keep her personal problems to herself and not bring them out for everyone to see?

"It is when it takes you away from my show."

Elizabeth chuckled. "Your show? Interesting."

"You know what I mean." He reached out and took her hand. "I thought we were friends. I thought we could tell each other anything. And then you leave town…"

"I had to leave town." She removed her hand from his grip. "Things were getting too…" Her voice trailed off, and she stared out the window at the passing highway. "We needed to put some space between us."

"I don't want space. I want…"

Elizabeth turned to look at him. Saw the different emotions playing in his eyes. She felt a pull toward him. The need to reach out and smooth the hair by his forehead that was sticking up at an odd angle. Instead, she clenched her fists. "You want to find your wife. And I'm here to help you do that."

He swallowed and searched her eyes. "What if my wife isn't one of them? What if she's someone else entirely?"

The air in the truck warmed as they gazed at each other. Finally, she shook her head. "Rick…" Her voice broke, so she cleared her throat. "It's cold feet. I've seen it every season. It gets down to the last three contestants, and the bachelor starts to get nervous. That's all this is. Nerves."

"We both know it's more than that." He leaned forward and touched her cheek.

Her eyes drifted closed, and her breath caught as Rick pressed his lips against hers, so softly she thought she thought she must be imagining it. But the pressure on her lips stayed until she turned away.

"Don't." She rubbed her lips with the back of her hand, trying to stop the tingling sensation his kiss had ignited.

Rick's brow furrowed with hurt. And to build up the wall between them, she gave a bitter chuckle. "My bachelors usually try that about now, too."

She watched him pull away from her. She wanted to call him back, to wrap her arms around him and taste his lips again. She realized now that it was what she had wanted all along. But she knew this was for the best. It was better for him and for the show if she kept her feelings to herself.

She turned and gazed out the window again. Reminded herself that it didn't matter what she wanted. Or felt.

The show had to go on.

RICK STARED OUT the window of the SUV and watched as cars passed them on the highway back to Lake Mildred.

He shouldn't have come. Shouldn't have expected that Lizzie would return his feelings. Because at the moment, all he felt was embarrassment. Well, that and a little confusion.

Okay, a lot of confusion.

He had three women waiting at home for him, each of them beautiful and smart and loving. Yet he was hung up on the woman sitting next to him.

When had it changed? They'd been friends, confidants. He could tell her anything and found himself saving up tidbits to tell her the next time they saw each other. He looked forward to their morning meetings going over the schedule so he could watch the hair fall over her shoulder as she focused on her clipboard. He enjoyed the way her green eyes lit up with excitement during brainstorming sessions. He loved the way she laughed, throwing her head back and giving her entire body over to the joy.

He snuck a glance over his shoulder and found that she stared out the opposite window. She couldn't even look at him after he kissed her.

He had to fix this. The thought of not having her in his life at all left an empty ache in the middle of his chest. But how?

He cleared his throat and reached across the seat to touch her hand. It startled Lizzie, and she withdrew her hand. He looked down. "Sorry, Lizzie. I shouldn't have done that."

"No, you shouldn't have."

Her words were clipped. Short. Her tone icy.

"Maybe you're right. This is cold feet." He searched her eyes to gauge her reaction, but they were wary, guarded. "So help me figure this out. You're really good at that." He took a deep breath. "What do you tell your other bachelors?"

She stared at him for a moment, then seemed to snap out of it. "Why don't we go over what you like about each woman? You must be attracted to them, or you would have sent them home long ago." She flexed her fingers as if trying to reach for her clipboard. "First, Melissa."

"Ah, Melissa." Rick closed her eyes and imagined her. "She's one of those rare women who is gorgeous and genuinely kind. As my wife, she'd be an asset, watching over me and making sure I take care of myself." He could see how wonderful she was, but he wished they had more sparks, more chemistry together.

"And Becky?"

The picture in his mind changed to the brunette with an infectious laugh. "She's funny and makes me laugh." He opened his eyes and glanced at Lizzie. "But are laughs enough to make a marriage?"

Lizzie swallowed and looked away. "I don't know. I'm not exactly an expert on marriage."

"But you are on engagements. What does a couple need to last?"

"You're asking the wrong person."

Rick shook his head. "You're wrong. You've seen enough people getting together to get a sense of who will make it."

"Well, my instincts must be off, because none of the couples I got together have lasted." She sighed. "I must be the world's worst matchmaker."

"It's not like you can control the contestants' hearts or ensure success for the rest of their lives." He shrugged and tried to make light of it. "They make their own choices, and you're not responsible for those."

"Still…"

They stayed silent for a moment. Finally, Lizzie asked, "And what about Brandy?"

Rick's eyes drifted closed and he saw her in his mind. But the feelings from five years ago had changed. "I don't know about her." He opened his eyes and gazed at Lizzie. "I feel as if she's holding herself back somehow. Like she's got a secret that she's afraid to share with me."

She glanced down at her hands. "Rick, I should tell you…"

"She's secretly married to someone else? I knew it."

He shot her a grin, but she didn't return it. Instead, her expression seemed to turn sad. "I knew five years ago that she was going to choose Wade, and I didn't tell you. I couldn't because of my job. But I wanted to." She reached out and touched his shoulder. He warmed at her touch and longed for her to keep it there, but she dropped her hand. "Be cautious with her this time. She's hurt you once, and I'd hate to see her do it again."

He frowned at her words. "Is there something you know and aren't telling me?"

"I don't know anything, but I have this... feeling." She shrugged and laughed it off. "Maybe it's nothing. Maybe I'm wrong."

"You're never wrong."

"Thanks, but we both know that's not true."

They fell silent once more until Rick chuckled. "I like this much better. I've never been able to talk about things with someone like I can with you. It was true before, but it's even more so now."

She returned his smile. "I'll always be your friend. No matter what."

And maybe that was what he needed to hang on to.

He nodded and returned to looking out the window. He'd go back to Lake Mildred and make the best of this situation. Put aside his feelings for Lizzie and try to figure out how he felt for the last three contestants. The finale loomed, and he needed to know who would make the best partner in his life.

RICK WASHED ANOTHER dish and handed it to his mom, who dried it. He glanced out at the dining room, where the three remaining contestants sat talking to Dan. "So what do you think?"

Mom put the dish up in the cupboard, then reached for the next plate he handed her. "I like them."

He turned off the faucet. "But?"

"It doesn't matter what I think. What counts is how you feel."

How he felt. *Right.*

He returned his hands to the soapy water and wiped the remains of their dinner from a bowl. "How did you know that you wanted to marry Dad and not Mr. Henderson?"

She chuckled softly. "Did your father tell you about that?" She took a glass from the counter and dried it. "Your dad was the only one who got my pulse humming. That made me feel alive. Loved. Wanted." She stood on tiptoe and put the glass in the cupboard, then turned to him. "That's what I want for you boys. A wife who makes your life more than you imagined."

Rick glanced toward the dining room again. "There is someone, Mom, but...I don't know."

"You don't know that you love her?"

He shook his head. "It's complicated." He handed her some dripping silverware. "She's unlike anyone I've ever known. But I don't think we can be together."

She put the towel with the silverware on the

counter and approached him. Put her hands on his cheeks. Forced him to look down at her. "Nothing is impossible if you know what you want. Do you love her?"

Lizzie walked into the room with more dirty dishes, and Rick moved away from his mom. He pointed to the coconut cake displayed under the glass dome. "We're just finishing up the dishes. Then we'll have dessert in the family room."

"Great." She smiled at his mom. "Dinner was fabulous, Mrs. Allyn. Rick obviously learned how to cook from you."

"He begged me to show him how to make his favorite pancakes when he was four." She glanced at Rick with a grin. "Been teaching him my secrets ever since."

"Your hard work paid off." Lizzie put the dishes on the counter and returned to the dining room.

Rick followed her with his eyes before turning to his mom, whose smile had faded. "Oh, honey. What have you done?"

Rick frowned. "I haven't done a thing. We're just friends."

He turned back to the dishes and rinsed off a platter. When he tried to hand it to his mom, she reached up and hugged him instead. "Is she what your heart wants?"

"More than my heart, Ma." He peered into his mom's eyes. "What am I gonna do?"

RICK GLANCED AROUND the dining room table at his family, then at his three dates. He stood and held out his hand to Becky. "Want to go for a little walk?"

Becky nodded and took his hand. He hated to do this. Didn't want her to go home yet, but he knew that more time wouldn't change how he felt. He helped Becky into her coat, then took her hand again and led her outside. He waited a moment for Charlie to check lights and turn on the handheld. He gave a nod, so Rick walked with Becky to the end of the dock.

The thick layer of ice that once crusted the lake had thawed into a cracked surface that would soon melt. Winter would be a memory.

He turned to his date. "Becky…"

She took a deep breath. Held it in. Then let it out in a big sigh. "I know what you're going to say."

"I wish things could have been different. You're amazing." He reached out and touched her cheek. "There's some guy out there who's going to be a very lucky man someday."

She backed up slightly so that his hand fell to his side. She turned and looked out at the lights from the houses across the lake. "Time will heal. There are other fish in the sea. It's not you, it's me." She turned back. "Any other clichés you'd like to add to your speech?"

"Becky, I—"

"Don't." She took another step back and crossed her arms over her chest. "I thought we had something special."

He closed his eyes. He knew what she meant. Knew what she was thinking. Hadn't he been saying similar things when Brandy had left him? "I don't think I'm the right man for you. You need someone—"

"Don't tell me what I need, because you have no clue." She shook her head. "If you did, you wouldn't be saying these things to me."

Rick winced. Gone was the sweet, funny Becky. Replaced by a hurt, angry one. "I'm sorry."

"I bet you are." She turned and left, brushing past Charlie and his camera.

Rick glanced at the cameraman. "That went well."

"You know women."

Rick nodded, but in truth he was learning he knew very little. He'd thought Becky would be gracious. Maybe tear up a little but otherwise accept his goodbyes.

He knew nothing.

ELIZABETH WATCHED FROM the kitchen window as Becky stormed to the waiting limousine and slammed the door shut once inside. She consulted her clipboard before Rick could return and they planned their next steps. So the hometown dates would be Brandy and Melissa. Chicago and Tennessee. City and country.

Rick opened the back door and shut it quietly behind him. Elizabeth walked over and rubbed his shoulder. "She take it hard?"

He nodded but didn't explain. He looked around the empty room. "Melissa and Brandy?"

"I sent them back to the house to pack." She held up the clipboard. "We really need to go over these plans."

"Not tonight." He walked past her into the family room, turned off lamps and checked the fireplace to make sure that the fire had been put out. When he looked back up at her, she walked toward him. He backed away. "Seriously, Lizzie. It's been a long night. I've had to break another heart. I'm in no mood to talk about schedules and dates and finales, okay?"

She tilted her head to the side and watched him. "This is about more than Becky going home."

He walked out of the family room and into

the kitchen. Elizabeth followed him closely. "Rick, talk to me."

He turned and faced her. "Why?"

"Because I thought we were friends." She looked into his eyes. "Was I wrong about that, too?"

"What we are seems to go back and forth from colleagues to friends to more." He started to put dishes from the dish rack away in the cupboards. "You made it clear that we need to keep our distance. And yet here you are. Alone. With me." He turned and faced her. "So what is it that you want? For me to open up and talk or to stay away? Because, frankly, I'm getting whiplash with your mood swings."

"Mood swings!"

He shrugged. "You have a better word for it?"

You bet there's a better word. "How about I'm trying to help you? I'm trying to find you a wife." Didn't he get it?

"And keep your job while you're at it."

"I never made it a secret that my whole life is this show." She crossed her arms over her chest. "Especially now."

He stalked toward her. "And maybe my job is to show you that there's more."

He pulled her into his arms and looked

down into her eyes. She wanted this. She didn't want this. Finally, he released her.

Elizabeth bit her lip and struggled to pull her emotions together. She bowed her head and stared at her feet while Rick finished putting dishes away and started to turn lights out in the kitchen. They stood in the dark, silent room. He walked to the back door and opened it. "Goodbye, Lizzie. I'll see you in Chicago."

"Why are you so upset?"

He handed her the car keys. "Drive carefully. It's starting to snow."

"I care about you, Rick." More than she should, if she wanted to admit it. She walked closer and took the keys from his hands. "But you're right. I need to stay away from you."

"Fine."

"Fall in love, Rick. Just not with me." She gave him one last look, then stepped out into the cold night.

RICK LOCKED THE FRONT door and stood quietly for a while. He turned to head to bed, when he saw movement on the porch. The sheriff had mentioned that there had been a break-in a few streets over on Lawn. Well, it wasn't happening on his watch. He whipped open the door. "Gotcha."

Dan and Brandy jumped apart. Rick stared

at them, then walked back into the house and slammed the door.

"Ricky, wait."

He turned to his brother, who stood alone in the foyer. "For what? So you and Brandy can stage a repeat performance?"

"We weren't doing anything."

Rick doubted his words. "Then why act guilty?" He returned to the kitchen and locked the back door.

Dan followed him. "I think I love her."

Rick stared at his older brother. Was he kidding him with this? "I chose her tonight because I thought she and I might still have something." He held up his hands. "But she wants to be with you instead? How did I end up here again?" He shook his head and closed his eyes. Five years was definitely not long enough. "I should have known. Should have seen."

"We didn't even see it until tonight." Dan took a few steps toward his brother, then stopped when Rick backed away. "I thought it was just me. That she couldn't…" He groaned. "I'm not the marrying type, but when I look at her, I see her in a white dress in a church. Heaven help me."

"This isn't helping me."

Dan shook his head. "My plan was to wait until the end. When you picked Melissa."

"What makes you think I was going to pick her?"

"Because she's perfect for you. We all see it."

Rick nodded, not because he agreed but because he didn't know what else to do. "I'm glad you're deciding my life for me."

"Someone has to. Because you seem to be completely willing to sail through without going after what you want." Dan stood taller, reminding Rick of his father. "I know what I want. And I'll go after it. But I'll wait. And then she'll be mine."

"And she feels the same way?"

Dan nodded. "I think so. It's what we were talking about when you interrupted."

Rick leaned against the kitchen counter and gazed at his feet. "How did you know you wanted her?"

"When you know, you know."

THE NEXT MORNING, Rick knocked on the door to Lizzie's hotel room. She'd called him an hour earlier, requesting a meeting. Didn't say why. And he didn't ask. But his damp palms and the warmth spreading across his chest made him think that his life could change when she opened the door.

The door opened, and she ushered him inside. Before she could say anything, Rick started. "Lizzie, I don't know why I'm here, but I have to tell you something."

A second knock at the door stopped him from telling her. He'd been so sure about what he had to say, but Brandy walking into the room changed that. He shook his head and started to leave. "I don't need to be here for this."

Lizzie blocked the doorway. "Oh, yes, you do." She pointed to the bed. "Sit." She turned to Brandy and pointed at the chair by the window. "You, too."

He had no choice but to obey with that authority in her voice. He sat on the edge of the bed and turned to face Lizzie rather than looking at Brandy. Ever since seeing her with Dan last night, he'd felt as he had five years ago. Betrayed. Bewildered. And wondering what was wrong with him. Was he really that bad a catch that she would keep choosing someone else? He'd thought they had something again. And again he'd been wrong. So wrong.

Lizzie looked at them both, then sighed. "Does someone want to tell me what happened after I left last night? Or do I have to fill in the blanks myself?"

Rick glared at Brandy. "Why don't you ask her? She's the one who's been lying this entire time."

Brandy stood and faced him. "It wasn't lying."

Rick stood, as well. "Then what else would you call sneaking around behind my back?"

"We didn't do anything!"

Lizzie stepped between them and held up her hands. "Stop. Both of you." She snapped her fingers, and they both sat again. "Brandy, do you want to continue on the show?"

Rick jumped to his feet. "Why should it be her choice? I'm the one looking for a wife here. She's the one who lied and cheated. Again."

Brandy looked over at him, then down at her hands, remaining silent. Lizzie looked at Rick until he sat back down on the bed. She buried her face in her hands. When she looked up at them, she seemed tired. Ready for this to be over. Rick knew exactly how she might feel.

Lizzie looked at Rick. "If you want to send Brandy home and bring Becky back, we can reshoot the last episode. Make it look as if you had in the first place."

He shook his head. "I sent Becky home because I didn't see a future with her." He turned and glanced at Brandy. "I saw one with you, though. Always thought that's the way it was supposed to be."

"Rick, I'm sorry—"

He held up his hand to stop whatever she might say next. "What if the reason I saw you in my future was because it was supposed to be you with Dan, and not with me?"

Lizzie turned to him and opened her mouth but stayed silent.

He continued, "I'm not saying I'm not hurt. And a little angry. I still feel like you lied to me."

"I didn't think the feelings I had for Dan could go anywhere. I didn't know he felt the same way." Brandy closed her eyes. "I like you, Rick, but maybe I should drop out. Give you a chance to find real love."

Lizzie threw her hands up in the air. "So where does that leave us? Is Brandy going home? Is Becky coming back? How do you want to handle this?" Lizzie looked between them both. "I'd like to hear some suggestions because I'm out of them."

Rick glanced between both women. "I don't think Melissa would like to know she won by default. It's not fair to her or the audience."

He rose and walked toward Brandy. "Would you be willing to stay on? We can pretend for the cameras for the last few shows."

She bit her lip. "But is that fair to you?"

He shrugged. "I guess I'm proposing to Melissa." But even as he said the words, he knew he didn't mean them. If he did, he would be more excited. More certain. If anything, he only felt more confused. "What else am I supposed to do? What do you want from me, Lizzie?"

"I want you to be happy. Does this decision make you happy?"

"The fact that my brother is in love with one of my contestants?" He shook his head. "Nope. Not happy about that. But I can't do anything to change it, can I?"

The room started to close in on him. He held up his hands. "I need some air."

He left them behind.

ELIZABETH WATCHED Rick go. Wished she could ease his pain. Instead, she turned to Brandy. "You should have told him from the beginning about Dan."

Brandy frowned. Almost pouted, which Elizabeth thought was more annoying than anything. The woman shook her head. "I thought my feelings were one-sided. I didn't know he felt the same."

"Then you should have told Rick you were having feelings about someone else. You've done this to him twice, Brandy. Don't take this the wrong way, but I hope he kicks your butt to the curb for this." She walked to the door and held it open. "Unfortunately, Rick is a nice guy, so he won't. He'll forgive you and accept you. And let you get away with it."

Brandy walked through the door, then stopped and turned. "What about the show?"

"That's up to Rick now. But I'd start packing my bags." She slammed the door in the other woman's face.

Her heart reached out to Rick. It was bad enough that Brandy had rejected him before, but now this? Small comfort in the fact that it had been done behind closed doors rather than on live television.

She picked up her cell phone and dialed Rick's number. Wasn't surprised that her call got directed straight to voice mail. She hung up the phone and considered the possibilities.

Without the sense that the proposal could go two different ways, much of the drama and romance would be left out of the last dates. As well as the live finale. If the audience knew who Rick had chosen, why would they tune in?

She sank to the bed, head in her hands. Should she call Becky and ask her to come back? Give them a chance to redeem the show?

Or keep all this quiet and proceed with Brandy and Melissa?

Again she thought of Rick. He didn't deserve to be treated like this. He deserved love. True love. The kind that poets wrote about and singers sang about. The kind that made her show popular.

The kind that just maybe she deserved, too.

She sighed, not wanting to think about that, grabbed her phone and dialed another number. When he picked up, she held her breath. "Will you meet me in an hour at the factory? We need to talk."

DAN MET HER in the pickle factory parking lot, leaning against his car as if the gray skies and melting snow on the ground didn't affect him. She'd asked him to meet her here thinking he'd be more comfortable on his own turf, and since it was Sunday there wouldn't be too many unwanted eyes and ears for their conversation. Elizabeth got out of her SUV and walked toward him. He held up his hands. "We haven't done anything yet."

She nodded and removed her sunglasses to

look at him. "But you haven't made this easy on me. Especially with Rick." She shook her head. "What were you thinking?"

"For once, I was thinking about myself. Not Rick. Or the company. Or the town." Dan turned up the collar of his coat. "I love her."

"I knew it. I could see it happening right in front of my eyes. But I thought I could control it. Just like everything else."

"No offense, Elizabeth, but you can't control love."

She looked at him and slowly nodded. "I think I'm finally realizing that." She crooked her head at the factory. "Mind if we continue this conversation somewhere warmer?"

Dan led her inside the factory, where the hissing and whirring of machines and conveyor belts filled most of the space. He walked her down the hallway to his office and held open the door for her.

She surveyed the room. It was much like Dan. No-nonsense. Neat. Organized. And focused on business. She turned and leaned against his desk. "What do we do about Rick?"

Dan frowned and looked at her as if she'd asked about climate change. "He'll honor his commitment to the show, of course."

"I meant about his heart." She pushed off

the desk and approached Dan. "He's really hurting right now, and I need to find him."

"Well, he's not answering my phone calls." Dan held up his cell. "I've called him every fifteen minutes this morning. No response."

Elizabeth nodded. "I'm worried about him. If he was hurting, where would he go to think?"

Dan considered this. "Our cottage is closed in the winter. Otherwise I'd send you there. He'd be alone." He shrugged. "Other than that, I'd say your best bet is the Penalty Box. It's past Main Street before you get to the lake."

"Thanks, Dan." She left to find Rick. Had to find him. Because he should know he wasn't alone.

RICK BIT INTO another nacho and cheered as someone scored a goal on the television. He wasn't quite sure who was playing, but it didn't matter. At least someone was winning.

The door to the bar opened, and Lizzie walked in, scanning the room until her eyes locked on his. *Great*. The one person he didn't want to see.

Well, maybe there were two or three.

He returned to eating his early lunch, piling the chip with two jalapeño peppers. Bit into it. Welcomed the sting and burn.

Lizzie sat in the seat across from him. Folded her hands and placed them on the table. He nudged the plate toward her. "Want one?"

"No, thanks."

She glanced at his mug and raised an eyebrow. He shrugged. "It's pop. Too early for anything stronger."

She motioned to the bartender to get her a pop, then turned back to him. "We need to talk."

"Do what you want about the show, okay? I don't care." He took a swig of his drink.

"I don't care about the show, either, right now," she said, leaning forward into his sight line. "You're the one I care about."

"Why?" When she raised one eyebrow at him, he winced. "I don't do the wallowing thing very well. But I desperately want to wallow."

"Rick, you're an amazing guy, but you've got to stop acting like a victim." When he started to protest, she continued, "Brandy doesn't love you. So what? Give Melissa a chance. Or find someone else. But don't act like your life is over."

Where was the sympathy? The reassurance? He glowered at her. "Aren't you supposed to be comforting me? Supporting me in my time of need?"

She shook her head and waited as the bartender placed the drink in front of her. She handed him her credit card. "I'm picking up his tab, too." Once he was gone, she leaned in closer. "Is that enough support for you?"

"You don't get it, Liz." He closed his eyes and shoved the plate of nachos away. They sat heavily in his belly, the burn of the spices no longer welcome. "I let her into my life, and she hurt me again."

"So you made yourself vulnerable. What's wrong with that?" She reached out and grabbed his hand. "Part of loving someone means you open yourself up to getting hurt by them. It's a risk. Sure. But isn't it worth it?"

Why did she have to make sense? Couldn't she let him enjoy the pity party before getting back to his promises? "I'm still alone."

She looked at him hard. "Are you really? You have your family. Your friends." She glanced around the bar at the few patrons who watched the game. "You even told me yourself that this town won't let anyone be alone. I'm sure any one of them would join you for lunch."

"I'm tired of going home alone." *There.*

He'd said it. The thing that weighed on him every night as he tried to ignore the ache and emptiness. "I'd hoped that this time would be different."

"And it is different. You still have Melissa."

He looked up at Lizzie. "But is she the one I want?"

Lizzie swallowed and turned her gaze elsewhere. Watched the game for a few seconds. Then she faced him. "I'll support whatever you want to do going forward. But I think you should give Melissa a chance. I know you like her."

He did like her. Which was the problem. He never wanted to hurt her. "But what if I'm not in love with her?"

"Then open your heart and take a chance." She squeezed his hand. "It'll be worth it in the end. I promise."

CHAPTER FOURTEEN

Rick stood outside Brandy's Chicago apartment, hand raised to knock on the door. Was he doing the right thing? Should he even be there alone? Before he could lose his nerve, he knocked and waited for her to answer.

He should have called first. She might not be home. But he wanted to surprise her so she couldn't run away. They needed to talk. They had to get this thing figured out before cameras started rolling again.

He knocked again. Maybe she hadn't heard the first time.

This was crazy. He could have done this over the phone, but he thought being face-to-face would make the truth easier to see. To say.

He hung his head and debated knocking again. She obviously wasn't home.

He'd turned to leave when the door opened. Brandy looked at him, then up and down the hallway. "You're alone?"

He held up his hands. "I wanted us to talk,

just the two of us. No cameras. No producers. No Dan. Just us."

She nodded and stepped aside, letting him brush past her into the apartment. He looked around. It was on the small side, but she paid more for the address than the space. She still kept things neat and homey. It was a place where he wouldn't mind curling up on the couch and watching TV or cooking for her in the galley kitchen.

He shook his head. He had to stop thinking about Brandy that way. He turned to her. "It's a nice place."

She shrugged and motioned to the love seat. "Can I get you something to drink? I can make coffee."

He shook his head and patted the sofa next to him. "I only want to talk."

She took a seat in a rocking chair across from him. Folded her hands and kept them in her lap. Her casual wear told him that she'd planned for an easy day; her blond hair was pulled up into a messy ponytail. He sighed. Again, he had to stop looking.

"I've told Lizzie that I want you to stay on the show." He watched for her reaction, but she didn't give one. She waited for him to continue. "It wouldn't be fair to Becky to bring her back when I've already decided she's not the one for me."

"And Melissa?"

He thought of the blonde and softly smiled. "I've also asked that they shorten our week together so that I can spend more time with Melissa in Tennessee." He shrugged. "Might as well get to know my future wife, right?"

Brandy rose and took the seat right next to him. "Do you love her?"

"I like her. A lot." He chuckled. "Guess I have to do more than just like her if I'm going to marry her, huh?"

"No one says you have to marry her just because she's the last woman standing." She touched his hand, and he tried not to flinch. "It's just a show. But marriage is your life. Can you see yourself with her?"

Rick shifted on the sofa, then stood and walked to the entertainment center. Brandy had a much smaller television than most, but he remembered she'd preferred spending time out with friends rather than at home. He turned and faced her. "Can you see yourself with Dan?"

Her head shot up, and her eyebrows knit together. "Do you really want to talk about that?"

He'd rather have a root canal, but this conversation had to happen. He noted the boxes stacked by the wall. "You planning on moving?"

"My lease is up next month. I'm ready to make a change." She stood and approached him. "I'm moving to Lake Mildred."

Huh. Hadn't seen that coming. "Does Dan know?"

She shook her head. "We've agreed that we won't contact each other until after the show. But I know this is what I want."

"Dan. You want Dan." He put his hands on his hips and looked at her. "What's wrong with me?"

"Nothing."

He crooked his eyebrow. "Really? Because twice you've dated me, then chosen someone else." He shook his head. "Why couldn't it have been me?"

She shrugged. "I tried, Rick. I really did. You're a nice guy. Everything a woman could want for a husband." She turned and walked to the balcony that overlooked the shore of Lake Michigan. "But when I saw Dan…" She turned back and looked at him. "Sorry."

Rick took the few steps to reach her. "No matter what happened with us, I always wanted you to be happy. That's no lie." He took her hands in his. "If Dan is what makes you happy, then I say go for it. Move to Michigan. Find a future with him. And be happy."

She hugged him, and he let her linger in his arms for a moment. When she stepped back, he put his hands in his jeans pockets. "I should go. But I'll see you tomorrow with your mom and best friend."

She nodded and walked him to the door. Opened it. Waited until he passed through before she gave balm to his hurting heart. "I want you to be happy, too. And you deserve someone special. If that's Melissa, then great. But if there's someone else…"

He shook his head. "Doesn't matter. I can't have her."

RICK MET LIZZIE in the lobby before the limousine would take them to the restaurant. She again wore a suit, this time navy. But her hair looked a bit shorter. He reached out to touch it, but she backed away. "It looks good on you."

She nodded and turned her gaze to the parking lot. "You talked to Brandy alone."

"Thought I should. Had to clear up some things before shooting today's home visit." He sighed. "Believe me, it was not a conversation for the audience to be a part of."

Lizzie gave a short nod. All business. "I've

rearranged the schedule with Melissa. We'll go over my notes on the plane there."

Rick watched her for a moment. "Have I done something wrong? You're ignoring me."

"I'm your producer, so I can't avoid you, can I?" She glanced down at her clipboard, then back out to the parking lot.

"But you're doing exactly that." He stepped closer to her. Put a hand on her arm. Which she brushed off. "What did I do?"

"Nothing. The limo's here." She walked out the revolving doors.

Rick followed her. Took a seat in the limo beside her and gazed out the window. On the ride, Rick relaxed for the first time since this crazy show had started. He didn't have to pursue Brandy because her heart already belonged to another.

Just like his.

Problem was, she didn't belong to him. Never would.

Though his heart was filled with regret, Rick couldn't help enjoying the view of Chicago. He watched as buildings passed, people walked by and other cars tried to get to their destination faster than anyone else on the road. He even caught a glimpse of the El and grinned like a kid. He loved this town.

They arrived at Willis Tower, though in

Rick's mind it would always belong to Sears. He got out of the car, then craned his neck, trying to see the top of the soaring skyscraper. He remembered coming here as a kid with his family. His dad had let Uncle Larry take over the company while they explored Chicago for a week. It was one of the best vacations he could remember. Probably because it was the only one they'd had.

Brandy stood next to a young woman with dark hair and an older woman with dyed blond hair and dark roots. She looked like an older version of Brandy that had been crumpled up and left in a dark corner. Rick approached her and held out his hand. "Mrs. Mathews, it's good to see you again."

"Just call me Rita. Never saw a reason to get hitched myself." She glanced at Brandy. "But this girl has been planning her wedding since she was a flower girl for my sister when she was ten." She looked back at him and perused his face as if trying to place it. "Baby, he's different from the picture you sent me."

Brandy colored. "That wasn't him," she said in a hushed voice.

"Well, you sure are a good-looking man." She put a hand in the crook of his elbow. "Let's go. I'm dying for a drink."

Lizzie had made arrangements beforehand,

so they sat at a table near one of the windows. Salads waited for them as well as a bottle of wine for Rita. Rick passed around the basket of freshly baked bread as they talked about movies, the show. It was a nice dinner.

Until Rita asked, "So you gonna marry her this time or what?"

Charlie turned his camera in Rick's direction. He shook his head. "I can't really answer that question now. There's still one more woman in the picture."

Rita leaned her head on one hand. "But do you think you might? I mean, what's wrong with her?"

Rick sighed as the waiter brought their pasta dinners. As Rita continued to stare, he shrugged. "Nothing's wrong with her."

Brandy nudged her mother. "Mama, just drink your wine."

"My glass is empty and so's the bottle." She held up a hand to a passing waiter who didn't belong to their table. "Another house white."

Brandy leaned closer. "Then maybe you've had enough."

Rita glared at her. "You're right. I've had enough of your thinking you know what's best for me. You don't know. Never have and never will."

Brandy winced. "Mama..."

"Rita…"

Rita stood up, and Brandy's friend Lil took her elbow when she wobbled. "I think I'll take your mom home." She turned to Rick. "Good luck with the show."

Brandy rose and gave Lil a quick hug. "Thanks. You're the best."

After they left, Rick had no idea what to say. And by Brandy's silence, he guessed she didn't, either.

Finally Charlie cleared his throat. Rick sat up straighter. "Right. We have some time to sightsee if you're in the mood."

Brandy nodded but didn't say anything. She kept her gaze on the full plate of lobster ravioli in front of her.

Rick reached across the table and touched her hand. "I'm sure they'll edit it to put our time together in the best light."

Brandy glanced up at him. "She's having a bad day." She tried to smile.

Rick nodded. "I know."

She chuckled glumly. "Actually, she's having a bad life." She put her face in her hands, and her shoulders started to shake.

Rick looked at Charlie and made a slashing movement near his throat. The red light on the camera turned off, and Charlie excused himself. Once he left, Rick took the seat next to Brandy and touched her shoulder. "It's just us now." Brandy looked at him through her fingers. "Families aren't easy, are they?" He reached up and wiped a tear from her cheek. "Why don't you take a moment, okay? Maybe go to the bathroom and freshen up or whatever it is you ladies do in there."

She kissed his cheek before leaving the table. Lizzie walked over and sat in the chair next to him. She took his hand in hers. "She doesn't deserve you."

"Well, she's not getting me, is she?" He took a deep breath and looked her over. "Thanks for understanding about my needing to talk to Brandy alone yesterday."

She nodded. "You were right."

Rick touched his chest and waved Charlie over. "Did you hear that? Ms. Producer said I was right. We should have recorded that for posterity."

Even Charlie chuckled at that. He took a seat next to them and cleaned off the camera lens while they waited for Brandy's return. Rick watched Lizzie, who kept looking in the direction of the bathrooms. He nudged her shoulder. "Do you want to go check on her?"

"I probably should." She stood and put her hand on his arm. "I'm sorry about the attitude earlier. To be honest, I was hurt you didn't include me. But I understand now."

Rick patted her hand as she walked away. He glanced at Charlie. "Does life ever get easy?"

The cameraman stood and switched the camera on. Rick turned and saw Brandy walking back to their table. He stood and pulled her chair out for her. She looked more composed and pulled together. He swore women could perform miracles in the ladies' room.

Once they were seated, Brandy picked up her fork and resumed eating her meal. Rick followed suit and placed the napkin back on his lap. He cleared his throat. "I think after dinner we should go all the way to the top of the tower. You game?"

RICK LOOKED OUT the windows and tried to see if he could catch a glimpse of the Michigan shore. It was a cloudy day, so what appeared to be land on the other side of the lake was probably just fog. Brandy brushed against his sleeve. "Trying to see home?"

He turned and smiled at her. "Can you see where you live from here?"

She grabbed his hand and pulled him to the south side of the building and pointed. "I grew up in one of those houses. But I try not to go there often."

"Hard to go home?"

She nodded. "You saw what my mom is like. Would you want to be around that day after day?"

"She wasn't like that the last time we met."

"It was a good day, I guess. I don't know." She shrugged and wrapped her arms around herself, then stood off to the side. "There's good and bad, and you never know what you're going to get until she shows up."

To break the somber mood, Rick snatched her hand and pulled her onto the glass floor that jutted out over the side of the building and made him feel as if he were walking on air. Brandy squealed and closed her eyes. "I can't look down. I feel like I could fall at any moment."

Rick glanced at his feet and marveled that glass could hold him up all fourteen hundred and fifty feet in the air. He squeezed her hand. "If you fall, I'll catch you."

RICK HELD A BOUQUET of daisies. Lizzie checked him over. "You couldn't have worn something nicer?"

He glanced down at his jeans. "This is my nice pair. Besides, what she sees is what she gets with me. Why dress up to look like something I'm not?"

Lizzie glanced up at the hospital. "My source told me she's working on the third floor today. Cameras are set up to record your surprise visit. She thinks you're not arriving until next week."

Rick nodded as he took in the information. Today's plan to surprise Melissa at work had been his attempt to keep part of this real. Besides, he really wanted to see her. Especially after everything with Brandy. He sniffed the flowers. "Daisies are a nice touch."

"You said she seemed like a daisy girl. Not roses." Lizzie consulted her clipboard, then sighed. "Please give her a chance, Rick. I'm not saying you have to marry her, but open yourself up to that possibility."

"Melissa is a wonderful woman. I'd be lucky to have her. But I need to make sure it's really love before I can promise anything."

"Agreed." She glanced behind her at the camera crew, who waited for her to give the cue to start filming. "We ready for this?"

Rick wanted this to work. Wanted to give her a chance. He'd worked so hard to turn off his feelings for Brandy, but now needed to turn them on for Melissa. She might be his future bride. "Let's do this."

Cameras followed him as he entered the hospital and found the page who would escort him to Melissa's ward. Patients and families gave them odd stares as they got in the elevator and even more when they reached the third floor and started walking down the halls. One woman approached Rick. "You're from *True Love! Honey*." She motioned to a man in the waiting room. "He's from that show."

Rick grinned at her. Held his finger up to his mouth. "We're surprising Melissa."

The woman's eyes got big and she nodded and allowed them to pass down the hallway and approach Melissa's nurses' station. He spotted her walking out of a room and quickly turned away. He held the daisy bouquet over his face as if that would hide him and the cameras, then glanced behind at Lizzie. She mouthed, *Go.*

He ran down the hall. "Missy."

She turned and took a moment to realize it was him. Smiling widely, she ran toward him. They embraced tightly, the flowers smacking Rick in the face as he pulled her closer. "I've missed you." And he realized he meant it. He took a step back and held the bouquet out. "These are for you."

Melissa took the bouquet and held it up to

her face. Inhaled deeply. "Daisies are my favorite. How did you know?"

Rick shrugged. "I guessed." He glanced around at the crowd that had started to gather. "When's your break? Maybe we can have lunch."

She sighed. "Not for two more hours. You're sure you want to wait around that long?"

"For you, I'd wait even longer." He touched the tip of her nose.

A nurse in purple scrubs approached them. "Why don't we switch breaks for today? I'd hate for you to keep your man waiting."

Melissa beamed at the other woman. "That's so sweet of you. Thanks." She glanced at her watch. "Can we meet in ten minutes?"

"Absolutely." Rick rubbed her arm. "I brought us a picnic."

ELIZABETH FOLLOWED RICK and Melissa as they took a seat on the bench in the park adjacent to the hospital. The trees and flowers had budded, and the scent of spring was in the air. Which should make a young man's attention turn to love. Or so the poets said.

Rick opened the basket and brought out the salads she'd ordered for them. He'd told her nothing fancy or over the top, so she'd chosen a simple grilled chicken over greens with balsamic vinaigrette. She'd ordered one for herself and sandwiches for the crew while she was at it.

They talked quietly between bites of lunch, and the cameras filmed every word. Every glance. They looked like a young couple in love enjoying a brief moment together.

This was what she wanted for Rick. After everything else that he'd gone through, he deserved some happiness. He needed love in his life. And if the scene playing out in front of her was any indication, he could find it with Melissa given some time.

Rick wiped his mouth with his napkin. "I know this is short notice, but I was hoping you were free tonight. Maybe we could go see a movie?"

Melissa smiled. "That sounds so...normal."

Rick shrugged. "I could use a little normal right now. Especially before I meet your family this weekend." He reached up and touched a flyaway strand of Melissa's hair. "So what do you say to dinner and a movie?"

"I'd love it." She leaned across to kiss his cheek.

But Rick turned at the last moment so that they kissed on the mouth. Lingered for a moment. Then they sat back and acted as if nothing had changed.

But it had.

He hadn't willingly kissed anyone on camera this season. Had told Elizabeth he wouldn't until it meant something. She should be thrilled that he'd waited for Melissa.

So why did her heart ache?

RICK SHOOK HANDS with each of Melissa's four brothers. By the time he reached her father, his hand and shoulder hurt from the vigorous workout they had received. "Mr. Weskitt."

"Rick."

The two men nodded and shook hands briefly. Rick turned to greet her mom. She was the same height and build as Melissa. "You two could be sisters."

Her mom blushed while Melissa laughed and linked her arm through his. "Mom's putting on our Sunday best for dinner tonight. Fried chicken. Mashed potatoes. Biscuits."

Rick's stomach growled in response. "Sounds fabulous." He turned to Mrs. Weskitt and rubbed his hands together. "Why don't I give you a hand in the kitchen and you can give me some pointers?"

He soon found himself elbow deep in flour and buttermilk as Barbara showed him how to dredge the chicken in milk before adding it to the flour. The pieces turned golden in the oil as they fried.

He peeled potatoes, grated carrots and cabbage, and talked up a storm to Melissa and her mom while Charlie recorded every moment and asked for tastes between takes. Rick felt at home with them. Not for the first time, he felt something for the beauty smiling and laughing beside him. It could be love. It would make life easier if it was. But then he'd usually chosen the road less traveled.

Once dinner was placed on the dining room table, Rick had to admit he could eat a bear if he had the opportunity. The family gathered around the table. Yes, he would fit in here.

But was it enough?

Over dinner, they discussed religion, politics and the show. Her dad brought up Rick's plans for Melissa. Rick deflected by asking about the family business. They didn't lack for topics.

After dinner, Rick helped clear the table, then took a dish towel and dried dishes while Melissa washed. Once the kitchen was clean, he put an arm around her shoulder. "We make a good team."

She nodded and stepped closer. "You make it easy."

"I could say the same thing about you." He tapped her on the nose. "What say you show me how to ride a horse?"

"You never have?"

He shrugged. "I was more a bike rider growing up."

She smiled and took his hand. They went out the back door and followed the path to the stables. With an expert hand, Melissa showed him how to talk to the horse before putting a saddle on it. "You want her to trust you first. Then she'll let you take her anywhere."

Rick pulled her closer. "And what about you? Do you trust me?"

Melissa looked down and took a deep breath. "I want to."

"I want you to, too." He kissed the top of her head. "So how do I climb on?"

They followed a path alongside the river that bordered the Weskitts' land. The landscape glowed in golds and greens as the sun began to set. Rick knew that it would look magnificent on television. And as long as it looked good, everything would be fine.

But inside, nothing was fine with him. He glanced at Melissa, who rode next to him. He could see a life with her. It would be comfortable like a pair of his favorite jeans. He could be happy. Right?

To find out that answer, he pulled his horse up next to hers, then leaned over and kissed her. She brought her hand up to the back of his neck to pull him closer. He sighed into her mouth.

And waited for the fireworks to start.

CHAPTER FIFTEEN

FOR RICK AND BRANDY'S last date, Lizzie had scored tickets to a sold-out concert at the Hollywood Bowl. Before the concert, they enjoyed a picnic on the lawn as the musicians warmed up. They feasted on cheese and crackers, fruit salad and brownies.

After they ate and filmed what they needed to, the crew left so they could enjoy the concert. Brandy leaned back and looked up at the sky while the music flowed over them and out into the stars. Rick nudged her arm. "What are you thinking about?"

She ducked her head and checked to make sure that the crew was truly gone. "Your brother. He'd love this."

"He'd never come out here. Hasn't been on vacation since Dad died." Rick sat up. "Brandy, if you really like Dan, you have to know he's serious about his work. He needs someone like you to show him there's more to the world than spreadsheets and production schedules." He nudged her shoulder. "I think you could make his life magnificent."

Brandy nodded. "I can try."

"I figured you would."

They sat listening to the music for a while. Brandy turned to him. "Have you decided what you're going to do at the finale?"

He swallowed as if something got caught in his throat. "I don't know."

"Melissa is a wonderful woman."

Yes, she was. But she wasn't the one for him. He didn't trust his voice, so he nodded. Perceptive as always, Brandy frowned. "You do love her, right?"

"I think we could have a good life together. But is it enough?"

Brandy took his hand. "I've been there, re-member? Always go with your heart."

"Your heart led to you getting dumped."

She sighed. "But for those six weeks I had, it was marvelous." She settled back on the blanket. "And now my heart is leading me to your family. So it can't all be bad, right?"

Rick fell back next to her and looked at the faint stars that tried to break through the lights and smog of this town. "If you say so."

RICK TOOK MELISSA to the Santa Monica Pier for their last date. They ate hot dogs on the boardwalk, then took a ride on the Ferris wheel. Melissa sat next to him and gasped as they reached the top and saw the city dressed in twinkling lights. "They look like jewels in a crown."

Rick pulled her tighter to his side. She was the jewel tonight. He hated to hurt this amazing woman next to him. "Melissa, about tomorrow—"

"I know you can't tell me what you're going to do. But I want to tell you…" She sighed and turned to face him head-on. "No matter what, I love you and want what's best for you. Whatever makes you happy makes me happy."

It could have been word for word what he'd told Brandy on their last date more than five years before. Was this sinking feeling in his stomach how she had felt that night? He shook his head. "What if that means someone else?"

"Then I hope she makes you happy." She put her head on his shoulder. "But I think you should know that I love you. We could be good together. We could make a wonderful life. If you just give me the chance."

She looked up at him, her heart shining out of her eyes. And he couldn't help it.

He touched her cheek and leaned in. Softly kissed her.

And thought maybe it could be her...if he kept his eyes closed long enough.

Once the date was over, Charlie put his equipment in the trunk and glanced at Rick. They'd seen Melissa off in the limo, and just the two of them remained. "Tomorrow's the big day."

Rick rubbed the back of his neck. "What am I gonna do?"

"I've done enough of these shows to know when two people should be together." Charlie slammed the trunk closed, then slipped a piece of paper into Rick's hand. "Don't tell her I gave this to you."

Charlie got in the car and left. Rick looked at the paper in his hand. He unfolded it, unsure what it could be.

Lizzie's address.

ELIZABETH UNPACKED ONE suitcase as she started to pack another. After tomorrow's finale, she was scheduled to fly out to Dallas, where she would begin interviews with the next bachelorette for the show. It would never end. She'd always be working on the show. Sometimes she dreamed of a different job.

A different life.

A knock at her front door startled her out of her thoughts. She needed to stop thinking about changing her life and get more focused. On her career. On the balance in her checkbook. And on the bills waiting to be paid.

She opened the door and found Rick standing there with grocery bags in his hands. She glared at him. "How did you... Never mind. What do you want?"

He grinned, and it almost melted her resolve. "You."

"Rick—"

"You missed my date with Melissa."

She nodded and planted her fists on her hips. "I told you before that Troy was taking over that shoot. I had a meeting with the suits that I couldn't get out of." She looked him over again. "Now, what are you really doing here?"

"I want to make you dinner." He pushed past her into the apartment and whistled. "Now, this is some place."

"It's okay."

Rick crossed the living room to look out the windows into the darkness. "I always wondered how you lived. I bet you have an ocean view."

"More like an alley view." She clenched her

hands and wondered what he was doing there and how he'd gotten her address.

Rick continued to look out the window. "You have the best life, I swear."

"Didn't your mother ever tell you not to swear?"

He turned back to her, one eyebrow lifted at her attempt at humor. "Cute." He lifted the bags. "Where do you keep your pans?"

"Why?"

He walked past her and into the tiny kitchen. "Knowing you, you forgot to eat and now you're starving. Am I right?" He started poking his head through the cupboards.

Her stomach rumbled. Rick chuckled and made himself at home in her kitchen. He searched the cabinets and found her pans. Opened drawers and found her knives. Unlatched her pantry door and found her food stash. He glanced over his shoulder at Elizabeth, who moved in between him and the pantry door, attempting to shield the contents from his view. "Stay out of there."

Rick whistled softly. "That's a lot of macaroni and cheese."

"Don't. Start. With. Me."

Rick glanced back at the shelves of cans and boxes of food. "Are you expecting a food shortage? You could live a year off the stuff in there."

"Eighteen months." Elizabeth crossed her arms tightly over her chest.

"You don't even cook."

"And you don't know what it's like to go hungry." She shut the door and leaned against it—keeping him out of the pantry and that part of her life.

"And you do?"

So much for keeping him out. She bit her lip. "My mom wasn't known for hanging on to a job. And sometimes there was no money. Which meant no food." She stood taller. "I won't go through that again. No matter what, I won't be hungry."

Rick took a step back. "I didn't know."

"No one does. It's not something I brag about." She walked away from the door and away from him. "There's a reason I keep that door shut, Rick. Don't open it."

"If you can't open it with me, then who?" He took a step closer to her. "Who are you going to let into your heart?"

She broke off eye contact. "I thought you were making me dinner."

"Yep." Rick rubbed his hands together. "The way to a woman's heart is through her stomach, right?"

He took packages out of grocery bags and laid them on her kitchen counter. Ground beef. Cheese. Onion rolls. Lettuce. Tomato. Onion.

She glanced at the ingredients. "You're making me a cheeseburger?"

"Not just any cheeseburger. It's my specialty." He motioned for her to step closer. "And I'm going to teach you how to make it."

She shook her head and held up her hands. "I told you before. I'm no cook."

"You can learn just like I did." When she didn't move, he grabbed her hand and pulled her to the kitchen counter. "First wash your hands. Very important."

He led her to the kitchen sink, pumped soap into his hands, then massaged it into hers. Elizabeth swallowed, trying to will her feelings away and hoping that as he turned on the faucet to rinse off the soap, her fears would go down the drain with it.

Rick dried her hands off. He found a mixing bowl in the cupboard and handed her the package of meat. "Put that in the bowl while I get out your ketchup and mustard."

She opened the package and dumped the pink meat into the bowl. Rick squirted the condiments on top, then added chopped onion and shredded cheese to the mixture. He then took her hands in his and helped her knead the mixture together. "Make sure it's mixed well. Then we'll form patties."

His hands on hers distracted her again, but she did as instructed. She took a palm full of meat and flattened it into a round disk. "Like this?"

"Perfect." Rick winked at her and placed his own patty next to hers. "Now we preheat the pan. We want to make it hot enough that it will sear the meat and make almost a crust on the outside to keep the juices inside."

Once their hamburgers were fried and the vegetables sliced, Rick took two buns from the package and warmed them in the microwave. Placed more shredded cheese on each burger. Then began the process of stacking the burgers to perfection. More ketchup and mustard on top. Then placed them each on a plate.

"And that is how you make my cheeseburgers." He held his up in a toast. "To you, Lizzie. You can do anything you set your mind to."

She smiled and tapped her cheeseburger to his. Then took a bite.

Oh, my.

She closed her eyes and chewed slowly, letting the flavors play on her tongue. She swallowed to let her stomach in on the experience. He'd taught her how to make the perfect cheeseburger.

She opened her eyes and found Rick watching her. She set the burger back on the plate, then put her arms around Rick's shoulders and kissed him. The man tasted even better than the burger.

The fact that she shouldn't be doing this started to flare in her mind, but she ignored it.

"Lizzie," Rick said softly against her lips and pulled her body closer to his. He started to kiss her neck. "I think I'm in love with you."

That brought her back to reality. "Don't. We can't." She pushed him away. "What were you thinking?"

"Me? You were the one who kissed me."

She shook her head and crossed the room to the kitchen sink and leaned against it. "This is ridiculous. You need to leave."

"I came here tonight so we could figure out whatever this is." He motioned between the two of them.

"There is no this. You're probably going to be proposing to another woman tomorrow." Elizabeth laughed when she'd rather start crying. "What were you thinking?"

"I'm wondering the same thing about you."

He stepped closer to her, but she retreated to the living room. He followed her. "We have something between us. I know it. And you do, too. Otherwise you wouldn't be so scared."

"There can't be anything between us. That's reality." She shook her head and glared at the ceiling. "I can't believe I'm so stupid."

"The only stupid thing you've done is convince yourself that you don't love me. But we both know the truth. That kiss proved it."

"That kiss was a mistake."

"The best mistake of my life." He stalked toward her and grabbed her shoulders. "I love you, Lizzie. More than I want to. And I know that messes up your plans, but it's the truth. And you love me, too."

"The show—"

Rick groaned. "It's just television. It's not real life no matter how you want to package it. The fact is that I don't love Brandy or Melissa. I don't want to spend the rest of my life with either of them." He looked into her eyes. "You're the one I want to wake up next to every morning. The one I want to sleep next to every night. It's you I want to see across the dinner table. And our baby I want to hold in my arms."

"Rick, don't."

"It's too late. Because I do." He pulled her in and kissed her.

She closed her eyes and pretended for a minute that she could have this. That this could be her life. Then she pushed him away. "I don't love you."

Rick just shook his head. "Right."

"Don't make a mistake tomorrow. It's not just your future it affects, but mine, too. Don't do something we'll both regret."

"My only regret would be proposing to someone who I know is wrong for me."

"I asked you to leave."

He snuck a quick kiss, then winked at her. "See you in the morning."

CHAPTER SIXTEEN

ELIZABETH REACHED UP and straightened Rick's tie. "Are you ready?"

"You feeling the big déjà vu vibe here?" He grinned at her and peered into her eyes. "I'll be making television history again today."

"So you're sure about your choice?" She swallowed at the lump in her throat as he nodded once. "And you still won't tell me if you're going to propose?"

"Is the suspense killing you?"

She gave a half shrug. "Not that I'd let you know."

"Of course not."

She reached up to fix his tie again, but he slapped her hands away. "It's fine."

"I just want everything to be perfect for you this time."

"It will be."

"I wish I was as confident as you." She glanced at her clipboard. "The finale is always a nightmare, but these changes you gave me? I'll be lucky not to find myself without a job in the morning."

"Lizzie, about last night…"

She looked up at him and shook her head. "Nothing happened last night. End of story."

Rick smiled at her again, and her heart caught in her throat. Was she really going to stand back and watch him make the same mistake? "Listen, Rick, what if we forgot all this? You can go back and live your life the way you want to. I won't bother you again. How can you be so certain that you found the one right for you?"

"Sometimes, Lizzie, you just have to have faith."

She rolled her eyes and pushed her earpiece tighter into her ear to hear better. She glanced at Rick. "They're ready for you."

Rick reached out and touched her cheek. "If I don't get a chance to say this later, thank you."

She frowned. He was thanking her for making his life miserable yet again? "What did I do?"

"More than you know."

With that cryptic answer, he stalked away and took his position at the end of the rose-strewn path. Elizabeth thought she was going to get sick all over the red petals and white satin carpet. It would cost big bucks to get it cleaned, but she doubted that she'd care. She had to stop this. Had to keep him from making a huge mistake.

She glanced at the people around her, each waiting to see true love play out on her carefully created stage. And if they believed that, they didn't know what love was, because it certainly wasn't what she'd tried to produce on this show.

And it wasn't watching the man she loved make a big mistake. She should stop him. She should tell him.

Instead, she nodded at Charlie. "Roll cameras."

RICK WATCHED the patio doors open, and the two finalists dressed in their finest walked toward him. He kissed each on their cheek and turned to the main camera.

"Over five years ago, I stood on this stage and made a mistake. I proposed to a woman I now realize was wrong for me. I won't make that same mistake today."

He cleared his throat, mentally reviewing what he'd practiced in the mirror that morning. This had to work. He didn't know what would happen to him if it didn't.

"I found my true love. She inspires me yet

infuriates me. She makes my life amazing and completely crazy. She reminds me of why I still seek something better than what I have. She's moved into my heart and made it her home." He reached into his pocket for the ring and started walking past Brandy and Melissa toward the cameras.

Lizzie whispered, "Follow him."

He stopped in front of her, then dropped to one knee. "Elizabeth, would you marry me?"

Everyone's eyes bulged and mouths dropped. He could hear the whir of the camera trained on him but not a word fell from his beloved's mouth. He gave a quick grin to hide his nerves. "I know. This is sudden. And completely different from what you were expecting. But isn't that what life should be?"

The execs watching the filming stood and started to whisper among themselves. Lizzie glanced back at them and scanned the cast and crew. She turned to Rick. He smiled in encouragement because he knew this was what they both wanted.

Her mouth opened. "I can't."

CHAPTER SEVENTEEN

ELIZABETH POUNDED ON the hotel room door. "I know you're in there. The front-desk clerk said he saw you." No answer. She rested her palm on the door as if she could heal the problem with her touch. "Rick, please. I need to explain."

Still no answer.

She hung her head. What had she expected? She'd turned him down. Live. On national television. In front of an estimated twenty million viewers.

She knocked once more. "Please. I'm so, so sorry."

She heard the chain on the other side of the door move. She took a step back. A deep breath. Which she blew out in a rush at the sight of Rick's mother. "Mrs. Allyn—"

She held up a finger. "Don't." She closed the door behind her and stepped out into the hallway. "I asked you to make sure my son wouldn't get hurt. I begged you to protect him. I didn't realize you were the one I should be protecting him from."

"Mrs. Allyn—"

"I'm not finished." She put her hands on her hips like a schoolmarm scolding a misbehaving student. "When he told me he loved you, I warned him. Warned him that it would only come to pain. I wanted to be wrong, but you certainly proved me right."

"Mrs. Allyn—"

"You can speak when I'm through." She clutched her hands in front of her. "He loves you, Miss Maier. More than he can say. Now, what can you possibly say that would make this better?"

Elizabeth opened her mouth, a thousand retorts in her brain but none that would journey to her vocal cords. She dropped her gaze to the floor. "I'm sorry. I didn't know he would do that."

"Didn't you? You're a smart woman, so I'm sure the thought crossed your mind at least once."

More than once. "I thought it was a crush and he'd get over it." She lifted her eyes to the mother of the man she'd humiliated. "I never expected this. Not a proposal."

"It doesn't make it hurt any less." Mrs. Allyn glanced back at the door and sighed, her eyes closed as if in a prayer. "Go home, Miss Maier. Forget Rick. Let him get over you without having to see you."

She shook her head and held up her clipboard as if that would make things right again. "He still has the reunion show to film. Plus the publicity tour."

"Fine. He'll honor his commitments. But I suggest you find somewhere else to be." She turned, opened the door and disappeared behind it.

Elizabeth heard the decisive click of the bolt sliding into place. What else had she expected? She stared at the door, waiting for it to open again. So she could see Rick. And tell him...

Tell him what? Hadn't she said enough? Maybe Mrs. Allyn was right. She should just stay away, let him get over this. Over her.

She opened her cell phone and dialed Devon's number. "I need to talk to you."

"Good. We need to talk to you, too."

We? That didn't sound good. "Great. Where can we meet?"

"How about the scene of the crime? There's some things we need to take care of."

She stopped walking. "There's nothing to take care of. Because I quit."

ELIZABETH PAUSED OUTSIDE the hospital room. Had she made the right decision? Didn't matter. She was off the show now. Couldn't change that.

And part of her didn't want to. Part of her wanted to see what else was out there besides working all the time.

She walked through the doorway into her mother's hospital room. A month had made a big difference in how she looked. She sat up in the bed, still covered in gauze bandages, but the machines that kept her alive had been removed. "Bethie, you came." Her mom held her arms open.

Elizabeth rushed forward and hugged her. But not too tightly. Still afraid she'd break her mom. "The doctor said they're releasing you tomorrow."

Her mom nodded. "'Bout time, too. Going stir-crazy in here." She turned the volume down on the bedside television with her remote. "Are you doing okay?"

Had everyone seen it? Elizabeth winced. "You watched the show?"

"Never miss it." Her mom patted the side of her bed, so Elizabeth took a seat. "That Rick is something else. Why'd you let him get away like that?"

She couldn't talk about that, not now…

maybe not ever. "Mom, I want you to come home with me."

Her mom looked at her closely. "Why?"

"You have somewhere else to go?" Elizabeth looked around the room. No cards. No flowers. No sign that she had anyone else in the world.

"The last time we talked—"

"I was angry. Upset. Not at you, at least not entirely." She sighed and looked down at her lap. "I'm sorry. I shouldn't have said what I did. Not when you were fighting for your life like that."

"So you're sorry for when you said it, but not for the words you said." Her mom sounded sad, defeated.

Elizabeth stood and walked to the window that overlooked the parking lot. "We can't change our past." She turned back and looked at her mom, who picked at the blanket, not looking at her. "But I'm willing to work on making our relationship better from this point forward."

"Why?"

"Because you're still my mom." She walked back to the bed and took her mom's hand. "And I really need you right now." She started to cry. "I screwed up. And I've lost every-thing."

Her mom gave a soft smile and opened her arms. Elizabeth crumpled into them. "Bethie. Baby." She rubbed Elizabeth's back and rocked back and forth. "I don't think I've seen you cry since you were a tiny thing."

Because she never had, not in front of her mom. Elizabeth sniffled. "What am I going to do, Mom?"

"You'll find another job."

She shook her head. "I meant about Rick."

Her mom continued to rub her back. It felt good. This was the mother she'd wanted. Craved. Elizabeth didn't know if this closeness would survive beyond today, but she would enjoy it while it lasted.

Elizabeth looked up into her mom's eyes. "I want to know what real love is. And I think I let it go."

"So you'll get it back." Her mom wiped her face with a tissue from the box by her bed. "Love always wins." Elizabeth stared at her until her mom shrugged. "At least it does on television. So why can't you find it out here in the real world, too?"

Elizabeth sighed. That was the question.

RICK CHOKED AS DENISE applied more powder to his face. "Am I really looking that bad?"

"Your dark circles have circles." Denise

dotted foundation under Rick's eyes. "You'll have to check those bags before you fly. Aren't you sleeping?"

"Funny." Rick closed his eyes and let Denise work her magic. Truth was, he wasn't sleeping. His mind kept replaying the events of the past couple of days over and over. What could he have done differently? Said differently? Why hadn't she said yes? Didn't she love him?

When would he stop loving her?

"I'll be with you in two secs, hon. I'm just finishing up here," Denise told someone. Then she sighed. "Even a magician can only do so much with what she's given."

Denise removed the cape from Rick's neck, and he opened his eyes. And saw Melissa on the stool in front of the mirror next to him.

He looked at her, but she didn't meet his eyes. He'd been in her situation. He knew what she felt. Thought. He cleared his throat. "Missy."

She glanced at him, then returned her gaze to her own image in the mirror. "Rick."

He wasn't the only one hurting after what he'd done. When was he going to learn? "I'm so sorry. I wish—"

She whirled around and stared at him. "Don't."

He reached out a hand to her, then dropped

it. "If it could have been anyone else, it would have been you."

"Is that supposed to help?" Melissa shook her head and turned her chair, as if she was unable to look at him.

"I didn't mean to hurt you."

She stood and approached him. Rick backed up and felt the stool hit the back of his thighs. He had nowhere else to go. Melissa poked him in the chest. "It still hurts. And you should know that better than anyone."

She stormed off as Rick watched her. She was right. And he couldn't fix things with her any more than Brandy could have fixed things with him.

Great. Now he had regret and guilt.

Rick ran after her. "Wait. Let me explain." She stopped walking but didn't turn around. He paused and closed his eyes. "I wanted it to be you. Hoped I could make it happen." He opened his eyes and stepped closer to her. "You're an amazing woman, Missy."

She turned, her eyes glittering with tears. "But not amazing enough for you."

"I'm an idiot, okay?" He held out his arms so that she could land a punch in his chest if she wanted. "But I didn't want to settle for something that wasn't real." He dropped his voice. "And neither should you."

Melissa turned away, blinking and wiping the corner of one eye with her pinky finger. "They've offered me one of the next seasons on the show. At first I told them no. But I don't know. Maybe."

Rick nodded. "Lizzie will take good care of you."

She narrowed her eyes. "Didn't you hear? Your girlfriend quit."

After dropping that bombshell, she walked back to the makeup department to get ready for their reunion show. Rick staggered back. She'd quit? Since when had Lizzie ever quit anything?

He'd hoped and feared that she'd be at the reunion. He'd wanted to talk to her. To ask her why. Now he wouldn't get that chance.

Rick walked to the wardrobe department and waited for one of the producers to tell him what to wear, what to do. Without Lizzie, he felt lost in more ways than one.

THE LONG SOLITARY drive north from the airport gave Rick time to think. Which could have been a good thing under any other circumstances. In this case, it only made him more anxious. More wary. What would he find when he came home?

He took the exit off the freeway toward

Lake Mildred, and his anxiety level tripled. What was he doing? He couldn't do this. Couldn't face the town that had stood behind him only to watch him mess it all up.

He'd already done what he had to. He'd done the interviews, answered their questions for the past week. Now he wanted only to go home. Lie in bed and lick his wounds. And wonder where he'd gone wrong. Again.

Better yet, he needed to disappear where no one would find him.

And lucky for him, he owned just the place. He checked the road and made a quick U-turn. It would take him a couple of hours to reach the Upper Peninsula, but it would be worth it.

Peace. Quiet.

And completely alone.

RICK TOOK HIS CUP of coffee out on to the covered porch and took a seat in the Adirondack chair that faced the lake. The only sound to break the silence of the woods was the call of a hawk stalking its prey. He sipped his coffee and closed his eyes.

Aah. Peace.

Which was interrupted by the sound of an approaching car engine. He peeked out of one eye and groaned. If he wasn't answering Dan's phone calls, what made him think he wanted to talk in person? He shouldn't have been surprised.

Brandy getting out of the passenger seat made his eyebrows rise. She walked around the car and held hands with Dan as they approached the cottage. Rick scowled. "What are you two doing here?"

"You've been here for a week. That's enough time to sulk alone. Now I'm going to talk some sense into you and get you back home." Dan planted one foot on the lower step of the porch. "And if that doesn't work, Brandy will."

"There's nothing to talk about."

"You're in the middle of nowhere by yourself. The closest neighbor is three miles away." Dan looked around. "I know you, Rick. You need people around you. You thrive on it. That's what makes you a great manager."

People around was exactly what he didn't want at the moment. "I don't feel so great right now. And I definitely don't want to be around anyone. Now please go."

Brandy stepped forward. "No." She walked onto the porch and took a seat in the other Adirondack chair. "Not till you listen."

"And what has that gotten me? Oh, that's

right. A broken heart." He rose from the chair and looked at Dan. "Now leave."

When neither his brother nor Brandy made a move, Rick walked into the cottage and slammed the front door.

Moments later, Dan walked through. "Kind of hard to keep people out when you don't lock the door."

Rick stared at his brother and wished they hadn't been raised to be so stubborn. "Seriously, Dan, I don't want to talk."

"Good. Then you can listen. And maybe read this over and tell me what you want to do."

He handed Rick a small stack of papers. Rick flipped through them. "You got everyone in town to sign a petition? I'm not going back home just because you got people to sign a piece of paper."

"It's not a petition to get you home. They want you to run for mayor."

Rick frowned and reread the papers. "And why would they want that?"

Dan ticked the reasons off on his fingers. "Because you saw an opportunity to help the town and took it. You brought us jobs and a cash flow with the production in town. You saved Allyn Pickles by putting us in the national spotlight again. And you certainly saved Lake Mildred."

"The show's over. The jobs are gone."

Brandy handed him a second sheet of paper with figures and pointed to a colorful graph. "Tourism is up almost 300 percent. And as the new sales agent for Lake Realty, I can tell you that home sales have doubled since the show ended."

Rick glanced through the figures and shrugged. "That's not enough to make me a mayor."

"No, but your love for the community is." Dan leaned in closer. "When everyone else, including me, was giving up, you fought to keep the town alive. To make our town the way you remembered it. No one loves Lake Mildred like you. And that makes you perfect for the job."

"A job I don't want." He closed his eyes. "The first time I did the show because Dad wanted me to save the company. I did it again to save the town. When is it going to be my turn to do what I want?"

"What do you want, Rick?" Brandy sat closer to him and put a hand on his arm. "What is it you really want?"

"I want the woman I love to stand next to me. A partner who can help me conquer the world. Or at least our portion of it. I want to raise my kids like I was raised. To feel safe. Loved." He opened his eyes. "But she turned me down."

Brandy nodded. "There are other women out there."

"None like her."

Rick rose to his feet. "Thanks for coming up here to check up on me. But I'm okay."

Brandy stood and hugged him. "We know you're not, but we'll leave for now. Seems like you have some thinking to do."

Rick hugged her back, then shook hands with Dan, who pulled him closer. "I love you, little brother. The town needs you. But it's your choice. Your decision. It always has been."

ELIZABETH CLOSED her email program and checked her cell phone for messages. She'd sent almost a hundred résumés and portfolios out to production companies in Los Angeles. So far, she hadn't received any responses. No interviews. No requests to see more copies of the shows she'd worked on. Nothing.

Except silence.

She logged in to her bank account and did some quick calculating. She'd already given notice to her landlord and had a lead on an apartment that she could better afford. If she moved to the Valley at the end of the month, she'd cut expenses and could survive the next three months without a job.

She glanced around her apartment and tried to determine what things she could sell. Her cell phone rang, but she didn't recognize the area code. She was about to let it go to voice mail when something told her to answer it. "This is Elizabeth Maier."

"Ms. Maier, this is Ronald Treeman with WPYT. How are you doing today?"

She racked her brain at the station name. It seemed familiar but not local. "I'm sorry, what station?"

"We're northern Michigan's number one station for news and weather." When Elizabeth didn't say anything, he continued talking. "I heard from a friend that you're interested in a producing job. I've seen your work. I've even had a behind-the-scenes look at how you produce. And we're impressed."

"Um...thank you?"

"I'd like to fly you out for an interview."

Elizabeth waited for the joke to be revealed. "Listen, no offense to your friend, but I'm looking for a job here in California."

"I see. And how is that working out?"

More like it wasn't. She didn't respond.

"Then why not give us a shot? We're not Hollywood. And our budget is only a portion of what you're used to. But I think we might be a good fit."

"And how do you figure that?"

"Because unlike Hollywood, we're not interested in your mistakes." He paused. "We love your triumphs. And *True Love,* despite what they said in the tabloids, was your best work."

Finally someone was recognizing her show. Seeing her. "That show was my life."

"Ms. Maier, it was just a show. But you come out and work for me, I guarantee you'll find a life."

Elizabeth paused. Michigan, huh? "Mr. Treeman, what friend recommended me?"

"Rick Allyn, of course."

CHAPTER EIGHTEEN

THE HUNGRY CROWD cheered as Rick brought out the first tray of turkey dinners followed by Dan, Brandy and his mother with equally heavy trays. They moved quickly, placing a heaping plate in front of each man, woman and child. "Don't forget to pick out a new coat before you leave," Rick told them. "And the church ladies made hats, scarves and gloves."

"Bless you, Rick." The thin woman in front of him placed a hand on his. "I didn't know if we'd eat today."

"I know, Shelly." He smiled at her four kids. "And leave room for pie. With extra whipped cream."

Once everyone had been served dinner and dessert, the family helped their less-fortunate guests choose warm winter wear that would hopefully get them through the coming cold months. Rick greeted each one as they left and reminded them about the Thanksgiving parade the next day. It would be his first as grand marshal, but then being the new mayor brought certain privileges.

After dishes were washed and leftovers delivered to the shelter, Rick's family joined him in his apartment for their own Thanksgiving dinner. They held hands around the table as they said grace, then started to eat. "Mom, this stuffing with walnuts is fabulous."

"It was one of my grandmother's recipes I found in an old cookbook." She took a bite and nodded. "It's just like I remember."

Rick nodded at his brother. "You ready for Saturday?"

Dan reached out and took Brandy's hand. "I was ready the day I proposed, but Brandy's the one who's been keeping me waiting."

She slapped Dan on the arm. "I told you I needed time to put a wedding together."

"Well, here's to the happy couple. I wish you an amazing life of love and laughter." Rick raised his water glass. "To Brandy and Dan."

They clinked glasses and returned to their meals.

"And what about you, little brother? I noticed that Tonya's been eating at the diner every day for a month." Dan leaned closer. "When are you going to finally ask her out?"

A knock at the door downstairs saved Rick. He wiped his mouth with a napkin, then stood. "I'll be right back."

He took the stairs two at a time, then paused when he saw Elizabeth peering into the darkened diner. He considered walking upstairs, pretending he hadn't seen her. But his mother had raised him with better manners. Unfortunately for him.

Her face lit up when he opened the door for her. "Did I miss dinner?"

She'd missed a lot more than that. When would she get the hint? "What are you doing here?"

"Ron told me about the dinner you throw for the less fortunate. I came hoping to get a story." She lifted her handheld camera as she looked around the diner. "I missed it."

Rick stared at her, wondering if it was possible to make her disappear by wishing her away. "Elizabeth…"

She frowned. "You always call me Lizzie."

"Elizabeth, I don't want you here." He walked back to the front door and opened it. "I'm spending the evening with my family."

She walked past him toward the kitchen. "Great. I'd love to see them."

He intercepted her before she could head

upstairs. "You don't get it, do you? You're not welcome here. They don't want to see you."

She pawed through her purse and brought out a familiar purple invitation. "This says different." She glanced at it. "Believe me, I was shocked to open my mailbox and find it waiting for me. But I thought if your family could forgive me, then maybe there's a chance with you."

She took a deep breath and smiled at him, knocking the air out of Rick's lungs. Six months since the finale should be long enough to make him forget his feelings for the woman standing in front of him. Six long months to forget her and the way she could turn his life upside down with a simple smile. "I can't, Elizabeth."

A squeal behind him made them both turn. "I knew you'd come." Brandy rushed forward and hugged Elizabeth. "But you missed dinner. I would have saved the dirty dishes for you if I'd known."

"Very funny." The women put their arms around each other and walked upstairs.

Rick cleared his throat. "Don't I get a say in this? It is my place."

"No," they both answered and disappeared up the stairs.

Despite the warm welcome from Brandy, Elizabeth paused before following her into Rick's apartment. His mother's frown might have had something to do with it. But her less-than-warm welcome from Rick made it perfectly clear that she might be wrong for showing up. She shot a furtive look at Mrs. Allyn. "Sorry I'm late."

Rick brushed past her and started to make a plate for her. He brought a desk chair from the living room and pulled it up to the table. Elizabeth took a seat and thanked him as he placed the food and silverware before her. He didn't glance at her once. Not a good sign.

Rick bristled. Kept his gaze on the table rather than on her. "Thank Brandy, not me."

"I invited her, Rick." Dan shrugged at his brother's glare. "No one deserves to be alone at the holidays."

Rick pointed to her. "It was her choice to be alone."

"Maybe I made the wrong choice." She looked down at her hands. "I've made a lot of mistakes."

"Congratulations. Admitting you have a problem is the first step." Rick took his plate to the sink and stood there for several moments before turning back. "I need some air."

After he left the apartment, Elizabeth glanced at his family. "I'm really sorry."

Mrs. Allyn shook her head. "Don't tell us. Tell him."

"He doesn't want to listen."

The older woman touched her hand. "Do you love him?"

That was the question, wasn't it? She'd listened to Ron's job proposal but had calculated the distance from Rick while she agreed. She'd made a mistake letting him go. She wasn't going to do that again. "Yes, I love him."

"Then why are you sitting here? If you want him, go after him."

She got to her feet, hugged them all, then left the apartment without another word. Main Street wasn't that big, so she could see Rick's dark figure at the far end. She ran after him. "Rick, wait."

He turned and saw her. She was half-afraid that he'd turn away and leave her. Instead, he waited. She ran toward him and wondered why she hadn't grabbed her coat. She'd have to get used to the cold weather if she wanted to spend the rest of her life with the man before her. When she reached him, she was out of breath. "Thanks."

"For what?"

"You waited." It encouraged her.

Rick glanced at the ground. "Elizabeth—"

"I told you, it's Lizzie."

He looked up at her. "Why are you here?"

She rubbed her arms, hoping to get feeling back. Tried to think warm thoughts. "For Thanksgiving. For the wedding."

"Is that all?"

"No." She stepped closer to him, but he took a step back. "Rick, I didn't know who I was without that job. I thought I was the job." She shivered and looked down at her shaking hands. "I had to give it all up to find out I'm so much more."

"I'm happy for you." But his tone said something otherwise.

He turned and continued to walk down the street. Elizabeth followed him. "Don't you want to know what else I found out?"

"No." He glanced at her, then took off his jacket and put it around her shoulders. "When am I going to stop having to take care of you?"

"Hopefully never." She looked at him, hope rising in her heart. "I was wrong to turn you down that day. I listened to my head and not my heart. But I won't do that again."

"So you say."

"I mean it. If you give me a chance—"

Rick laughed, but it didn't sound joyful. Bitter instead. "I've been burned twice. What makes you think I would ever let you get a third shot at my heart?"

She reached out and held his hand. "Because I love you. And you love me."

"That was before, Elizabeth." He dropped her hand, crossed his arms over his chest and rubbed his arms. Started walking back to the apartment. She watched him walk back alone. Then she hung her head and prayed she wasn't too late.

RICK TOOK HIS RESPONSIBILITIES as best man seriously. He had insured that his brother showed up on time and in his tux. He'd held on to the ring until it was time to hand it off to Dan. He had signed the marriage license and posed for the pictures that would be perused for years to come.

He'd pretended he was happy.

Not that he wasn't glad to see his brother happily married. But it only made Rick feel lonelier. And more miserable.

He looked around the room of well-wishers, friends and relatives he hadn't seen since the last family function. He clinked his knife against the champagne flute and stood as the room grew silent.

He took a deep breath, then grinned at the crowd. "I'd like to take credit for bringing my brother and his new wife together. After all, I met her first. Dated her first." He leaned forward and said in a mock whisper, "I even kissed her first."

After the laughter died down, he got serious. "But I discovered that while Brandy was an amazing woman, she wasn't the one for me."

He looked out and found Elizabeth watching him. He looked away from her. "Luckily, she is the right woman for Dan. And he's the right man for her." He raised his glass. "To Dan and Brandy. May you have many years ahead of you. May you find in each other the perfect partner and friend."

Everyone raised their glasses and drank to the happy couple.

Elizabeth stood and approached the head table. She took the microphone from Rick.

Whispers started softly and grew as she stood in front of them. "I can tell by your reaction that you know who I am. What I did." She glanced back at Brandy, who nodded. "But there are some things I need to say."

She took a deep breath. "Weddings bring out some of the best in people. Those who are in relationships feel the bond grow stronger.

Those who aren't find themselves looking for the person who might fit into their lives." She paused. "And those who have loved and lost begin to question the mistakes they made. The opportunities they've missed."

Rick leaned forward and tried to take the microphone from her. "Elizabeth, don't do this."

She held on tighter and stepped away from him. "Don't what? Tell the truth?" She glanced at the videographer. "You confessed your feelings in front of an audience of millions. Why can't I share mine with hundreds?"

Rick walked around the table. She moved farther into the room and continued her speech. "I've watched this man walk out of my life twice. The first time, I missed his friendship. The way he made me smile. The second time, I missed him. The way he made me feel. Made me love."

She turned and faced him, and Rick could feel his stomach start to tumble. He looked around the room and found his mom watching him, smiling through her tears. He turned back to Elizabeth.

"Rick…" She got down on one knee and looked up at him. Gasps sprung up around the room. He shook his head and approached

Elizabeth. Tried to get her to stand. When she didn't, he knelt beside her. She looked into his eyes. "I've loved you since the first time you called me Lizzie. You looked past the Elizabeth who could bark orders and make things happen and saw the Lizzie who could be vulnerable and was looking for a man like you to love her."

Rick reached out and moved a wayward wisp of hair off her forehead. "Lizzie..."

"Because that's who I am." She leaned forward and touched her forehead to his. "I'm your Lizzie. Forever. And I want to make my home in your heart."

Rick swallowed around the lump in his throat and pulled her into his arms. Kissed her bare shoulder.

"But before I do, I need to ask you a question." She cleared her throat. "Rick, will you marry me?"

It was as if the entire room leaned forward, waiting for his answer. He hated to disappoint her. He peered into her eyes and warmed at the love shining out of them. But he shook his head. "I can't."

She frowned and tears glistened in her eyes. He brushed his fingertips over her cheek. "Not until I can find you the perfect ring."

Lizzie smiled through tears. "I don't need the perfect ring. Just you."

Rick leaned forward and kissed her soundly amid the applause.

He'd gone on the show to find true love, twice. This time, he was going to hold on to Lizzie forever.

His heart had found a home in hers.

* * * * *

Have Your Say

You've just finished your book.
So what did you think?

We'd love to hear your thoughts on our
'Have your say' online panel
www.millsandboon.co.uk/haveyoursay

- Easy to use
- Short questionnaire
- Chance to win Mills & Boon®
  goodies